PENGUIN CRIME FICTION

THE TWO DUDE DEFENSE

Walter Walker's highly praised first novel, *A Dime
to Dance By,* was published in 1983. Originally from
Quincy, Massachusetts, Walker holds degrees from
the University of Pennsylvania and the University of
California and now practices law in San Francisco.

THE
TWO DUDE
DEFENSE

Walter Walker

PENGUIN BOOKS

To Wendy, to read in the jungle

PENGUIN BOOKS
Viking Penguin Inc., 40 West 23rd Street,
New York, New York 10010, U.S.A.
Penguin Books Ltd, Harmondsworth,
Middlesex, England
Penguin Books Australia Ltd, Ringwood,
Victoria, Australia
Penguin Books Canada Limited, 2801 John Street,
Markham, Ontario, Canada L3R 1B4
Penguin Books (N.Z.) Ltd, 182–190 Wairau Road,
Auckland 10, New Zealand

First published in the United States of America by
Harper & Row, Publishers, Inc., 1985
Published in Penguin Books 1986

Copyright © Walter Walker, 1985
All rights reserved

Reprinted by arrangement with Harper & Row, Publishers, Inc.

LIBRARY OF CONGRESS CATALOGING IN PUBLICATION DATA
Walker, Walter.
The two dude defense.
(Penguin crime fiction)
I. Title.
[PS3573.A425417T8   1986]   813'.54   86-9342
ISBN 0 14 00.8883 0

Printed in the United States of America by
Offset Paperback Mfrs., Inc., Dallas, Pennsylvania
Set in Times Roman

THE TWO DUDE DEFENSE

The Good Luck Motor Hotel had its name spelled out in purple light bulbs inside a neon horseshoe. From where I sat in my Dodge van, I could look past the horseshoe and through the bay window of the office to where a frowzy-haired woman in a pink smock was leaning against a counter reading a magazine. Her smock nearly matched the color of the motel, which was a two-story structure with a black wrought-iron railing running along the upper balcony. A small black horseshoe hung over the door of each of the motel's twenty units.

The building itself was L-shaped. It had a narrow driveway, a parking lot that was crisscrossed with cracks, and a runty, rectangular swimming pool. The pool had no diving board and no deck chairs and its single furnishing was a squat red soda machine that stood out in the sun like a fat metal sentinel.

The only car parked in the motel yard was a battered old Impala and its off-green color clashed badly with the pink stucco. After a while, I grew tired of looking at it and got out of my van on the side away from the motel.

I walked the town's main street until I came to a sad-looking eatery with a distended screen door and a sign that read MILLIE'S LUNCH. I went inside, smiled at the goofy-looking kid behind the counter and sat down on one of the stools. They were the round, backless kind with red leather seats and ornately carved stands. I remarked that I hadn't seen stools like that in many years and the kid put on a puzzled expression that seemed to come naturally to him and leaned over the counter to see what I was talking about.

After a moment or two he straightened up again and cocked his head to one side. "You from out of town, mister?" he said.

"San Francisco."

"Yeah?" The kid's mouth popped like he thought San Francisco was some faraway place.

"Don't people from the City come around here very often?"

The kid shrugged. He was very thin and his dirty white uniform was much too big for him. Sometimes his body would move and his clothes would not. "We ain't too near no highway or nothing. I guess we only see people when they got some reason to be here."

"You got a motel."

"Yeah, old Andy Luck built that," he said, as if that was all the explanation I needed. He saw I was not catching on and added, "My dad said he built it 'cause he heard they was gonna build a freeway from Santa Rosa to Sacramento, only they never did. My dad says it killed old Andy Luck because he sold his ranch and everything he had to get the money to build that place. Then he saw there wasn't going to be no freeway and nobody but a bunch of old truckers staying in his motel and he just up and died." The kid rubbed a bubbly mass of acne on his chin and then inspected his hand to see if he had gotten anything on it. "'Course, I don't really believe that's why old Andy Luck died, but that's what my dad says."

I asked for a menu and the kid brought me a piece of paper encased in plastic. I looked at the selection and grimaced.

"Best thing we got's a hamburger," the kid said, watching me.

I ordered that and a Coke and then went over and stood by the screen door and looked at the motel while I waited for the kid to get the food ready. It wasn't long until I heard the clank of a heavy piece of crockery. I turned around as the kid slid a plastic glass in front of my plate and told me okay.

"Who's the woman working at old Andy's motel now?" I asked as I sat down.

The kid twisted his body without moving his feet in an effort to look through the screen door.

"Well, I can't see," he said, "but it must be old Agnes, his widow."

I took a bite of my burger and found it was just one of those frozen patties that taste like thickened mashed potatoes. "Jesus," I said and pushed the plate away. The kid looked hurt.

"Ain't it done enough?" he said.

"Yeah, it's all right." I pulled the plate back, covered the meat with ketchup and took another bite. "What's old Agnes like?" I asked between chews.

"She's just an old lady, about forty-five or so. Sometimes she comes over here for lunch, but mostly she don't 'cause she lives right there in that motel."

"She from around here?"

"Sure, she's a McCracken. My dad says her and her sister Martha was the prettiest girls around when he was growing up. Martha was Miss Hereford Cattle Association one year and got to go to the state convention and all. My dad says that's how come she went wrong. I guess she met some guy at the convention who said he was gonna put her in the movies, only she ended up working as one of them showgirls in Las Vegas who don't wear no clothes. My dad saw her once down there about fifteen years ago and said she was still real pretty. I don't know, though, she ain't never been back here so I ain't seen her." The kid sighed.

I drained my glass of Coke and reached for my wallet. There was nothing in it but fifties and the kid looked dismayed when I brought one out. "I can't bust that, mister," he said.

"It's all I've got."

The kid chewed on his lip for a long time. "I guess you can pay with a credit card," he said, "although I ain't supposed to do it for nothing under ten bucks."

I used my MasterCard and wrote the kid a fat tip. Then I walked back to my van and resumed my waiting.

It was nearly four o'clock when a chocolate-colored Mercedes rolled slowly down the street and turned into the driveway of the Good Luck Motor Hotel. It stopped across from the door to the office and a large, fortyish-looking man with an impressive head of black curls climbed out of the driver's seat and went into the office. He returned to the car in a little more than a minute and it continued on to the very end of the motel.

When the car stopped again a blond woman in tight white pants got out with the driver and together they walked to the door of the last unit on the downstairs level. I used a telephoto lens to take my first picture.

* * *

When the door clunked shut behind them I started my engine. I drove about a block and a half past Millie's Lunch, U-turned and went back to the motel. But now there was a blue Plymouth blocking the driveway and I had to blast my horn to get it out of the way. The Plymouth's driver accelerated so quickly that the car stalled out. I fidgeted until the Plymouth was able to move on and then I drove up and parked where the Mercedes had been a few minutes before. I took the strobe light out of the camera case, attached it to my Minolta and flicked it on so that it would have plenty of time to warm up. Then I placed the camera on the floor between the front seats and went into the office to see Agnes Luck.

She did not look up from her magazine until she had finished reading the paragraph she was on. "That Richard Burton," she said, shaking her head, "he's so wicked." She had a cracked and throaty voice which I guessed had seen more than its share of lubrication over the years.

I stopped and peered at her. "How you doing today?" I said.

She made an effort to pat her hair into place and smooth out her pink smock. She was a few years beyond the kid's guess of forty-five and she had definitely let herself go to seed, but I could tell that the kid's dad must have been right. Beneath her bleached yellow hair and behind her gray glasses were two bleary but beautiful blue eyes that might have been made of Dresden china. Her bone structure was even and tapered and her hands were long and graceful as they fluttered about, primping here and there.

I shook my head hard. "I'm sorry for staring," I said. "It's just that—oh, never mind. No, I've got to say it. You look an awful lot like somebody I used to know a good many years ago."

Agnes seemed genuinely pleased and moved closer to me until just the width of the counter was saving me from inhaling her breath and suffering almost certain inebriation. "Oh, c'mon now," she said, her fingers fiddling with a revolving postcard rack, "you're not old enough to have known someone like me a good many years ago."

"Let's see," I said, stroking my chin, "it must have been fifteen years since I was in Las Vegas."

"Did you say Vegas?"

"Damn right. I used to work on the light crew for one of the dinner shows."

"I have a sister who was in Vegas about that time. The Dunes."

I held my breath and bent down real close until she blushed and turned her head away. "Wait a minute," I said. "You wouldn't be the sister of Martha McCracken?"

She squealed with delight and her face beamed and shed a thousand degrees of decay. "Do you know Martha?"

"Well, I'll be damned," I said. I reached across the counter and cupped the woman's chin in my hand. "You're the spitting image."

"Oh, c'mon now. Martha was always much prettier. And she's several years younger, too."

I withdrew my hand. "Where is she now?" I asked gently.

She shrugged and a slightly helpless expression crossed her face. "I'm afraid we didn't stay as close as some sisters do. My late husband—I'm a widow now, have been for several years—anyhow, my late husband didn't really approve of Martha going off to Las Vegas and becoming a dancer." She thought about what she had just said and when she spoke again there was bitterness in her voice. "Isn't that

6

a laugh?" She waved her hand in the direction of the units behind her.

"Wait a minute," I said, looking around. "I seem to remember Martha telling me something about this place. Something about her brother-in-law having a real hot tip that a new freeway was going through. Do I have it right or is my memory playing tricks on me?"

Agnes Luck's eyes narrowed for a moment, but then she burst into a head-shaking smile. "Old Andy Luck never had a real hot tip in his whole life and they never did build that damn freeway. But right now I don't care because I'm so flabbergasted that a friend of Martha's is standing smack dab in front of me."

"Well, I tell you, Mrs. Luck—"

"My name is Agnes."

"Agnes? My name is Hector." We shook hands and she giggled and I held on for an extra long time and clucked my tongue and told her I just couldn't believe I was looking at Martha's little sister.

She didn't correct me. Instead she sort of casually swept off her glasses and tucked them into her pocket. "But how did Martha happen to tell you about me and Andy and this old motel?" she said.

Time was wasting and I was getting anxious. I gave Agnes a quick story about how Martha and I used to shoot the breeze between shows and then I said, "And now look at this, I get lost all these years later on my way to St. Helena, stop in a motel to ask directions, and who do I run into but the very sister Martha used to tell me about."

"Well, I'm sure glad you did, Hector, because it won't take me five seconds to tell you how to get on the right road and then I'm hoping that you'll be able to sit down and tell me what was going on with Martha the last time you saw her."

"I'd more than like to do that, Martha—I mean, Agnes, but I think I'm going to need a drink before I can say another word. I've been on the road all day and I'm so dry my throat's like a desert. What do you say you and me go down the street and grab ourselves a bottle of beer at that little tavern I saw when I was coming into town?"

Agnes glanced at her Timex and hesitated. "I really can't leave this place for that long. I'm the only one here."

"You mean to say that you run this big motel all by yourself?"

"Oh, it's not so big."

"Step back there and let me get a look at you. Why, you're no larger than a hummingbird. I bet you can't even carry the keys to all the rooms at the same time."

"Oh, yes, I can, you old flatterer." She laughed delightedly.

"Let me see," I cajoled.

She opened a drawer in the counter and took out a single key on a lanyard which she waved in front of her face. She peeked around it like a little girl playing hide-and-seek. "This is my secret key. It opens everything."

I did some more tongue clucking and gave her ingenuity an admiring wink as she dropped the master key back into the drawer. "I can certainly understand you not wanting to leave, Aggie—mind if I call you Aggie?—so I've got another suggestion. I saw a soda machine down there by the pool and I could just run out and get us a couple of ginger ales if you had a little something to flavor them up with. You strike me as the kind of woman who might have a little bourbon hanging around the house."

A bit of color rose in her cheeks as she pretended to weigh my proposal. "Waaaaa-ll, I might somewhere have a teensy drop of something."

I'll bet you do, I thought, and kept smiling until she

opened a door behind the counter and started back toward her living quarters. "Hey now," she said, pointing at me, "you run and get that soda because I won't be but a minute."

I waved and made for the door and the moment she was out of sight I was back at the counter, easing the drawer open and lifting the master key.

I got the van backed into a position parallel to the Mercedes and facing the street. I put on the emergency brake and got out, leaving the engine running and the door wide open. With the master key poised in my left hand and the camera hanging from my neck and propped in my right, I walked to the door of the last unit on the downstairs level.

I listened for sounds coming from the other side of the door, but I could hear nothing except my own heartbeat. I tried holding my breath and my heartbeat got only louder. "Hell with it," I said and jammed the key into the lock. The door twisted open.

The man's head wrenched around and the first snap of my camera caught a look of sheer terror on his face. Beneath him, the blond woman struggled to sit up. She stared into the camera and I caught that, too. The man let out a roar like a wounded animal and swept the sheet away from him. For the moment they were both exposed and my strobe flashed for a third time. He tried to push himself from the bed but the woman hooked her arm around his neck.

"Jonathan, hide your face!" she screamed, and pointed it right at me. My camera caught their heads together and their naked bodies side by side.

With a swipe of his huge hairy arm, the man flung the blonde away from him and lunged across the room toward me.

"Jonathan, don't," the woman cried. I snapped the

camera without aiming it and was just able to skip out of his reach as he came crashing forward.

I pulled the door open, but he stretched past me and slammed it shut. Before he could recover his position, I buried my left fist in his fleshy side. The man made an *oof* noise as the air rushed from his lungs and I had time to pull the door open once again. He made one last effort to keep it from closing behind me and I slammed his fingers in the doorjamb.

It took me only an instant to throw myself into the van. I had the brake off, the clutch working and the wheels rolling before the motel door even opened again. Everything was going as well as it could until Agnes Luck stepped out of her office and into my path with a fifth of Jim Beam and two glasses held in front of her. The smile on her face did a lightning change to a look of bewilderment as I leaned on my horn and continued bearing down on her. Fortunately, I swerved to the left and she went to the right, or I would have never made it out of the driveway. Things might have been a lot different for a lot of people if I hadn't.

2

Sometimes a little work can be worse than none at all. A little work forces a person to keep going when there is no future in doing so. It forces a person to take jobs he would not otherwise take just to fill the gaps. A man gets a little work, he gets a little overhead, and when the work disappears the overhead doesn't. Then the man might even crash a motel room and spend his Sunday night waiting around his office for a stranger to come and collect his pictures. It was not exactly glamorous, but then again, neither was I.

My office was on lower Market Street in San Francisco, on the second floor of a ten-story building. It was the sort of building in which you could not walk up the stairs, you had to take an elevator. It was the sort of office that was twenty by twenty-five feet, with a closet commode.

The words HECTOR GRONIG—PRIVATE INVESTIGATIONS were painted across the bottom of the opaque glass window that took up the top half of the door. On the inside, the furnishings consisted of whatever I had been able to get my hands on: an oak desk that I bought for two hundred bucks and refinished myself; a used leather swivel chair that I picked up from government surplus for fifty; an imitation leather couch a friend had sold me for seventy. The only new things were two captain's chairs that I had bought for clients. They were still pretty much in virgin condition on the day the man who wanted the pictures from the Good Luck Motor Hotel first appeared in my office.

I had been alone and working at my typewriter. I knew someone was standing in the doorway, but I did not look up immediately because I was trying to get my last thought down on paper. Besides, prospective clients do not usually stand holding the door open, half in and half out of the office. People who want directions do that. But then this man came and stood by my desk and that distracted me. I ended up ripping the paper out of the carriage and firing it into the wastebasket.

He was a rakish fellow of about thirty years, with thick, curly brown hair that floated about like seaweed on the surface of the ocean when he moved his head. He had a slightly hooked nose, a small mustache and pink-and-white skin that looked as though it did not see too much sun. He was fairly tall and might have been considered good-looking by some, except that he carried his belly before him like a nightclub girl carrying a cigarette tray. His eyes were small and very blue and they looked at me curiously.

"Are you the detective?" he asked.

I nodded and kept my seat. I knew from experience that it is best not to appear too anxious in front of a client. People don't trust detectives to begin with and they don't want them leaping all over the place like real estate agents.

"My name is Nicholas Glenn and I need something done."

I motioned him into one of the captain's chairs and

asked who had referred him to me. He said he had seen my name on the directory downstairs.

I asked how he happened to be in the building and a little smile stretched the corners of his mouth. "I was looking for a private detective," he said.

I told him I was flattered at being so highly recommended.

He shifted his position and toyed with his mustache. "Do you follow people?"

"Sometimes," I said. "If there's a reason."

"I want you to follow my wife."

I sat forward with my arms on the desk and studied him closer. He held my gaze confidently and kept an almost imperceptible smile on his lips. "You don't look the type," I said.

"I think she's cheating on me."

"You don't need that for divorce in this state, you know."

"There are children involved and I want custody."

"Are you presently living together? All of you, I mean."

The man's eyes shifted away from me and took in the rest of my office. He glanced at the wall behind me where my license was framed. He looked over at the army-green file cabinets and then above them to the picture of Abraham Lincoln that had been left on the wall by the previous tenant.

"There's also a great deal of money involved," the man said, and I knew what he was thinking about my office. "She'll fight me for the divorce and she'll gouge me for every cent of alimony she can get unless I make it clear to her that I've got so much evidence it won't be worth her while to attract the attention." His blue eyes came back and fastened on me again.

"Exactly what is it you want done, Mr.—ah . . . ?" I tend to be bad with names and he didn't help me.

"I want pictures, Mr. Gronig."

"Of what, Mr.—?"

"Of my wife and her lover. In the act. *In flagrante delicto,* isn't that what they say? I know the motel where they are going to be."

"Then you don't really want her followed."

"I know what time they're going to be there."

"You want me to bust into the motel room with my little Instamatic and catch them playing horsey."

We had been talking almost simultaneously, but now he stopped. He looked down and distastefully cleaned the lint from his pants and then he carefully crossed his legs. "Do you want the job?" he asked quietly.

I shook my head. "I don't do that kind of thing. Try someone else." I dismissed him by pretending to turn back to my work at the typewriter, but there was no paper in the carriage and I had to thrash about my desk looking for some. The man remained sitting as he had before.

"Two thousand dollars," he said.

"Jesus," I said, the word escaping before I had a chance to check it.

"It will involve about two hours' drive in each direction. How you get inside the motel is your business, but I'll need as many pictures as you can get. I'll want the whole roll of film, fresh from the camera and undeveloped. When you hand me that, I'll hand you your two thousand dollars."

"That's not the way I work."

"That's not the amount you usually get paid for working, either, is it?" He had a nice way of saying things like that. He left you insulted without feeling bad.

He waited until he was sure I wasn't going to answer and then he sighed and took out his wallet. Holding it away from me so that I couldn't see what was inside, he took out a group of fifties and dropped them on my desk. "Here's three hundred bucks. I'll come back Sunday for the film and then I'll give you the rest. Agreed?"

I eyed the money and the man eyed me. "You keep the money whether you get the pictures or not," he said. "If that's what you're worried about."

A man who works by himself tends to be a little egocentric, and there are limits to what an egocentric man will take. "I'll tell you what I'm worried about. I'm worried because people don't just walk in and throw money on my desk every day." I could feel my voice growing taut. "I'm not some schmuck who's going to start salivating just because you've got a little cash you want to get rid of. If that's who you're looking for you can go right downstairs to Market Street with your money in your hand and I'll guarantee you that within five minutes you'll have a dozen people asking who you want killed and with what weapon.

"I may not look like I've got much of an operation here, Mr. Whatever-you-said-your-name-was, but I like to pretend I'm a professional because it keeps me going, see? It keeps me thinking I've got some reason for sitting up here high atop the World Trade Center instead of being out on the curb with the rest of the bums. Now if you're willing to tell me why it is you need a private investigator and why you came looking for me in particular, we may be able to work out some arrangement. Otherwise you can take your money and get the hell out of here and I won't really care."

It was a lie. I would have cared very much if that three hundred dollars had gone walking out the door.

The man's curly hair moved up and down as he looked intently at his wristwatch. It was dime-thin and had a leather band. From where I was sitting I could see the long hand pointing straight up and I knew it was five o'clock. "There are a couple of other operatives named Dickenson and Upson with an office on the fifth floor," I said softly. "If you hurry you can probably catch 'em before they leave."

The man dropped his hand back into his lap and shook his head. A feeling of relief surged through me. "I want a single investigator and I think you'll do just fine," he said.

"Why?"

"Because now that you've said your piece I'm convinced you're exactly the man I've been looking for. I need a private detective because I have a delicate job that has to be done and I don't want any mixups. That means I need a professional—like you. I need someone I can depend on, who's not going to disappear overnight. That's why I came downtown. I need someone who is going to be impressed with earning a lot of money and who is going to be completely loyal to the person who pays him. I need someone who is not going to be too careful keeping his books, who's not going to ask me to put anything in writing and who's not going to be selling his memoirs to the *National Enquirer*. That's why I came to Market Street. Lastly, I want someone who doesn't have to talk things over with anybody. Not even his partner or his secretary. You fit the bill, Mr. Gronig."

The man's mouth twisted into a semi-smile again.

"Besides, now that I've told you what I want, I hope not to have to tell anybody else." He stood up and held out his hand. "I'm sorry if I've been presumptuous. To ease any pain I've caused I'm willing to pay another five hundred dollars if you're able to get clear pictures."

"What did you say your name was?"

"I said my name was Nicholas Glenn, but it's not."

"Let me think the whole thing over."

He shrugged. "Sure, take a minute."

The bizarreness of the man's attitude attracted me almost as much as his money did and after taking the full measure of my alloted time I found myself shaking his hand.

He told me where his wife would be, how to get there, and what to look for.

"I'll return Sunday night at ten o'clock," he said, and when I asked him why it had to be so late he told me that if he had wanted to come earlier he wouldn't have paid as much.

So at ten o'clock Sunday night I was waiting; and at ten thirty I was still waiting. At eleven I was about to leave when I got a call from the security guard in the front lobby telling me that a man who claimed he had an appointment with me was waiting downstairs. I told him to have the man come up and a minute or two later my door opened and the man whose real name was not Nicholas Glenn came in wearing a tan raincoat and his usual twisted semi-smile. He was carrying a cardboard briefcase in front of him by gripping the handle with both hands. I wondered about the cheap briefcase. It seemed out of character. Like the perspiration on his forehead.

"Here are your family portraits," I said and tossed a roll of undeveloped film across the desk.

He watched the film bounce to a halt and then he cocked an eye in my direction. "Did it go all right?"

I gave him a quick rundown on what had happened inside the motel room and watched his face for signs of shock. There were none. He stepped forward, picked up the roll of film and studied the canister as if it were showing him the things I had been saying.

"And the man with my wife, he was big? With black bushy hair? In his forties?"

I nodded and his teeth flashed in the first full smile I had seen him give. He dropped the film into the side pocket of his coat. "I'll deliver the rest of your money as soon as I have this developed, if you don't mind."

I had been leaning back in my chair and now I thumped forward as briskly and loudly as I could. "I damn well do mind," I snapped. "You expect me to give two thousand bucks' worth of credit to some joker who doesn't want anything in writing and won't even tell me his real name?"

The man made a face and nodded. "I understand, Mr. Gronig. I understand completely." He flopped his briefcase on my desk so that the locks and snaps were facing him. "So I brought along what you need." He opened the case and reached inside. "This," he said, and with a flourish he jerked out a small-caliber revolver.

I thought it was a joke. At first.

"I fully intend to pay you, Mr. Gronig. I meant it the other day when I said I wanted a man who was going to respect making a good deal of money and I'm going to pay you to maintain that respect. I just can't do it now. Maybe in a couple of days, maybe a week, but I'll get the money to you."

"As soon as you've reaped your profits, huh?"

He looked startled and then his eyes went hard and cold. "What do you mean by that?" he said.

"That woman at the motel wasn't your wife. You're going to do a little blackmail with those pictures. Then you figure to keep me quiet by paying me off."

He hesitated. "I have the alternative of killing you."

I looked into the barrel of his gun and looked away.

"It doesn't appeal to me either," he said, but he kept the gun pointed at my face.

"Ah, what's a little credit between friends?" I tried a grin, but it wouldn't hold.

"Then you'll agree to a deferred payment?"

"It's better than none at all."

"In that case, I'm sure you won't mind accompanying

me outside. Just so we'll both be sure that I'll be able to get you your money."

I asked if I could get my coat and he picked up his briefcase and followed me across the room to where the closet was. As soon as I had slipped my arms into my corduroy sport coat he stepped up close and pressed the revolver to the back of my head. I became acutely, almost singularly conscious of that whole area of my scalp. I wouldn't have moved for a week in Tahiti.

"Where's your gun?" he asked, and before I could answer he pulled my stubby out of the pocket of my corduroy coat. "God, fella," he said, "you've got to do better than that."

"I forgot it was there."

"Right," he said and awkwardly tapped under my arms and around my belt. When he was done he stepped back and picked his briefcase off the floor. He told me he was going to keep his gun in his pocket, that it would be trained on my back and that if I made any disturbance he would, as he put it, let me have it. Once we got down to Market Street, he said, I was to turn right and walk until I reached the Bay. Not until then was I to look back.

I told him I understood and we headed out the door and down the hallway to the bank of elevator doors. At his order, I pressed the down button and we stood in silence while an elevator clanked and wheezed its way toward us. At this time of night I did not have much hope that anyone was going to be on it, so I tried to concentrate my thoughts on the lobby, where the armed guard would be sitting just to the right of the door we would have to use to exit the building.

The elevator slid open and I was nudged inside. "Press *L*," my guide said and we jockeyed for position until he was behind me and the door was closed. When it opened again we walked out into the narrow marble lobby. Our shoes made noisy, reverberating sounds, but the guard was listening to a talk show on his electric radio and didn't appear to notice us until we had halved the distance between the elevators and his desk.

"How do, Mr. Gronig?" he called out cheerfully. He was a short, rotund black man, somewhere near middle age, who seemed to take an inordinate amount of pride in the cleaning and pressing of his dark blue uniform.

I fixed a teeth-gritting smile on my face and tried to motion behind me with my eyebrows. The guard, whose name for some inexplicable reason was Franz-Josef, hunched his shoulders and peered closer at me. "Somepin' wrong with your face, Mr. Gronig?"

I kept my eyes wide and tried to gesture with my mouth.

"Your face just sailin' all over the place tonight, Mr. Gronig." Franz-Josef chuckled. "You better go home and get you some Jack Daniel. He know what to do 'bout that."

The man behind me muttered something and stepped closer so that we were almost touching as we walked. I stopped suddenly in front of the door and he banged into me. "Keep going," he said.

"It's locked," I told him. "Isn't it, Franz-Josef?"

"Just give it a good push, Mr. Gronig. It'll go." The guard made no move to get up, not even when I was shoved and went stumbling out to the street.

My captor was beside me in an instant. "You're some kind of fool, Gronig," he said angrily, pointing me in the right direction. "Next time you try talking to anybody I'm just going to pull this trigger and run. So much as look around and I'll put a bullet in your spine."

I began walking east on Market, past rows of porno shops and third-run movie houses, past an army surplus store and clothing stores that had chain screens lowered in front of their entrances, past the lighted stairs leading up to the Crystal Pool Hall, past an all-night eatery that advertised itself as being a favorite of tourists since 1968, past a pensioners' hotel and a Jack-in-the-Box. I passed two males with their arms around each other's waists, a gang of Filipino youths who cooed and heckled at the lovers from a darkened entranceway, a surly-looking kid with a tinny-sounding ghetto blaster that was playing loudly enough to drown out the occasional trolley car that rattled down the middle of the street, a religious pervert who clung to a lamppost and shouted scripture at the top of his lungs and a scattering of derelicts in various positions on and about the sidewalks. I went five blocks before it was quiet enough for me to be able to tune my ears to the sound of footsteps behind me. They were still there and I kept walking.

I reached the foot of Market Street and stopped at the corner of Embarcadero. "Keep going," a voice growled.

"Which way?" I asked and when there was no answer I turned around. A destitute-looking bum with pants that stopped two inches above his ankles stared helplessly into my face.

"How long have you been following me?" I demanded.

He shrugged and looked behind himself.

"What happened to the guy in the raincoat?"

The bum shrugged again. "Gave me a buck," he said and then stood there waiting for me to kick him in the tail.

"Beat it," I told him and he turned around and wandered back in the direction we had come from. I had to go that way myself, but I was in no hurry. I wanted to give my Nicholas Glenn friend plenty of time to get away from me. I wanted him to get wherever he was going and develop his film. I wanted him to reap the full benefit of twenty color snapshots of the Bay Area Touring Side playing rugby in Golden Gate Park.

3

Franz-Josef was obviously surprised to see me when I came back into the lobby. His open face was glistening with sweat when he said, "How doin', Mr. Gronig? I thought you gone tonight."

I stopped in front of his desk and planted my hands on my hips. "Franz-Josef, what the hell are you getting paid for?"

He folded his hands and looked solemn. "I getting paid to guard," he said as if he were reciting a catechism.

"Didn't you have any idea that something might be wrong when I left here half an hour ago?"

"You mean with that other fella walkin' right close to you and looking real skittish and you tryin' to walk slow as you can and doin' crazy things with your eyebrows and all?"

"Yes, by God, that's exactly what I mean."

Franz-Josef nodded. "What would you liked for me to do, Mr. Gronig? Call the po-lice and tell them two guys gone walkin' funny out of my building?"

"You're a security guard. You have a goddamn gun, don't you? You're not supposed to need the police. If something's wrong in the building you're supposed to put a stop to it. That's what you're getting paid for."

A curtain seemed to drop over Franz-Josef's fat-cheeked face. In an instant he lost all traces of his normal good humor. Slowly he got to his feet and very carefully leaned his two fists on the desk between us. The meekness he had always shown was gone and I found myself tensing as his eyes bored balefully into mine.

"You mean that's what I getting paid a hundred and sixty bucks a fuckin' week before my fuckin' taxes for?" Franz-Josef's voice was soft and had a dangerous quality to it. "You mean I supposed to shoot it out with some gangster for a lousy four bucks an hour so that some honky Dick Tracy can earn hisself a fortune messing where he don't belong? You plannin' on slippin' me part of your fee for protectin' you or you just figure on throwin' this worthless nigger's life away because he gettin' paid as much as you spend on a shoeshine?"

I said nothing as Franz-Josef snorted.

"I tell you what I getting paid for. I getting paid for to be a scarecrow, that's what. I sit here in the door and keep the streetbirds from flyin' in here, because they say, 'Oh, oh, this buildin' got some pro-tection,' but if they come in here anyway then I ain't about to waste my children a daddy tryin' to stop them. So if you think I wasn't doin' my job while you was down here paradin' by, well, I be happy not to collect the semmin cents I got paid for that minute."

I began to feel guilt well up inside me as I stood withering in front of his increasingly impenetrable stare. I knew that if I continued to eyeball with him for much longer

I would be overwhelmed with illogical compulsions to apologize for anything and everything I had ever said or done to the man.

"Fuck you," I said impotently. But the obscenity seemed to loosen me up. "You keep the seven cents, Franz-Josef, and return the rest, because that's about what you're worth sitting here like a cigar-store Indian. We could get ourselves a decal and plaster it on the window if all we wanted was to pretend that the place was guarded."

I made about three stomps toward the elevator before the electric radio hit me in the back of the head. Pain exploded between my ears and I stumbled forward. I spun around to see what had happened and caught a fist flush on the jaw. It numbed me for a moment and I started to sag, but Franz-Josef held me up as he drove his fists one after the other into my stomach. I tried to cover myself and he shoved me over backward.

"Okay, chump," he panted as I struggled into a sitting position and stared at him incredulously. "Long as you gonna get my ass fired, I guess I'll make it worth my while." He backed up to his desk, grabbed his lunch pail and left.

I sat on the edge of the guard desk and dialed the number of the building manager. It took me a dozen rings to get him to answer.

"I'm asleep," he screamed into the phone.

I told him who I was and what had happened. He was not impressed.

"Goddammit, Gronig, Franz-Josef Moore is one of the finest guards I've ever had. What the hell did you do to him?"

I was stunned. "What did I do to him? I'm the tenant— the guy you make your living off, remember? One of your employees just beat me up and you're asking me what I did to him?"

"Franz-Josef's been a guard for nearly five years and except when he doesn't show up we've never had a bit of trouble with him. You move in for a month and drive him to quit in the middle of the night. It's twelve o'clock, you know. How the hell am I going to get somebody to replace him? And what are you doing there at this time, anyhow? You rented an office, not an apartment."

"Hey," I said. "Who the hell do you think you're talking to? If I've rented an office, I'll do whatever I damn well please with it. I'll turn it into a bowling alley or a home for wild ponies if I want and you'll get someone to guard it because I've paid for that security. Now tonight I need a guard, a new guard because your guard is gone and I have something that needs guarding and I don't want to guard it myself. So either you get someone out here to replace Franz-Josef or I'll do it and send you the bill."

"What the hell do I care?" he said and hung up.

I fired the phone back into its cradle. It missed and flew the length of the extension cord before it smacked back against the side of the desk. The sound echoed around the empty lobby like a gunshot. I tensed and ducked my head, but the only other thing I heard was the now soft bumping of the telephone as it swung back and forth.

I went to the front door and tried to make it lock, but it required a key which I obviously did not have. I searched the drawers of the guard desk and found nothing. I let out a string of curses and gave Franz-Josef's desk a vicious kick in the ribs.

As it turned out, I could have spared myself the anxiety. Even as the elevator gasped open on the second floor I could see that my office door was standing ajar. I walked slowly forward, expecting the worst and getting it. In the time I had been gone somebody had forced the lock and had torn the place apart. I passed by the overturned drawers and the scattered papers and went straight to the bathroom where the mirrored door to the medicine cabinet was standing wide open. Whoever had ransacked the place had been thorough enough. The plastic vial in which I had placed the actual film from the motel lay empty in the sink.

From what I could tell, my visitor had left as soon as he found what he wanted. I could even see his path of progress as he had gone from my desk to my file cabinets to the floor beneath my rug, to the bathroom. He hadn't gotten to the couch or the closet on the other side of the room and I was grateful for that. I took an unopened bottle of Wild Turkey down from the closet shelf and brought it over to the couch for consultation.

Over a glass of bourbon and water stirred with an index finger, I pondered the mystery of who might have wanted the film badly enough to steal it. Nicholas Glenn was the most likely suspect, but there was no way he could have known so quickly that I had given him the wrong film.

Nothing I thought of made sense, and yet as I traced and retraced the events of the day the one thing that kept standing out like an open wound was the peculiar conduct of Franz-Josef. Certainly if he were in league with Nicholas Glenn he would not have come to my aid when Glenn was taking me out of the building. Certainly he would have allowed Glenn to come right back to search my office. And certainly, if he knew Glenn was inside, he would have done everything he could to keep me from catching him when I returned.

I liked that theory and drank myself into oblivion working it into all manner of illogical conclusions.

4

The voice startled me and I came awake. For several seconds I could not remember where I was. I reached out with one hand and felt something soft and very tall. I reached out with the other and felt nothing but air. I fixed my eyes on a point on the ceiling and tried to keep the room from spinning.

"Hey, Gronig, wake up."

I realized I was in my office and that I was flat on my back on the couch. I turned my head just enough to see that sunlight was streaming in my alleyway window. I turned it again and saw the bottle of Wild Turkey and gagged. Retching and holding my hand over my mouth, I sat up. I still had on all my clothes, even my shoes.

"Jesus, Gronig, this is a hell of a way to inspire confidence in your clients. You throw all your shit in the middle of the floor and even leave the goddamn door open so people will be sure to see what kind of slob you are."

I looked at the scowling, olive-skinned man who was

speaking to me and said nothing. He was a cop. His name was Artie Palmieri and he was an inspector out of homicide. He usually worked with a black guy named Shepard, but this time he had with him a little round-shouldered man in a fedora hat with a tiny red feather in the brim.

Palmieri shook his head and looked disgusted. "I heard you hit some bad times, Gronig, splitting from the old lady and all, but, Jesus, I didn't expect to find you living in the goddamn office."

"What time is it?" I said, talking through my hand.

"After noon. If I'd known you were keeping banker's hours I would have come later. Got somebody here who wants to meet you."

"Give me a minute, will you?" I forced myself to my feet and stumbled into the bathroom, where I just managed to get the door shut before I collapsed on my knees in front of the toilet.

It took me a while to get rid of everything I had so injudiciously poured down my throat the night before and when I was finished I slumped back against the tiled wall and closed my eyes. I felt narcotically calm and seventy percent healthy.

"Hey, Gronig, you still in there?" Palmieri called.

I grunted something and Palmieri told me he didn't want me going out the window or anything like that. I had no idea why he should say such a thing, but the remark made me mad enough to get to my feet and wash myself clean in the sink. With a lot of care and a lot of slow deliberate movement, I brushed my teeth and combed my hair and went out and joined the other two men.

Palmieri had picked up my two captain's chairs and with characteristic sensitivity had arranged them for himself and his buddy without bothering to move the files that were on the floor. I did not feel strong enough to complain so I eased myself into my soft leather chair behind my drawerless desk without saying anything.

"Little bit of heaven here." Palmieri snickered as he swiveled his head this way and that to inspect each of my four walls.

"Better than sitting in some huge room with a couple of plastic partitions and thirty guys pumping away at their typewriters." It took me two or three breaths to get the whole sentence out, but Palmieri did not seem to notice.

"You got any coffee?" he said, loosening his tie.

I told him I didn't and he frowned. "I remember when you were working out of your garage and your old lady would bring out the coffee from the kitchen. I liked that. Hey, what happened to you guys, anyhow? I heard she was getting it on with Jerry Seales or something like that."

The little man in the hat looked embarrassed.

"Jesus Christ," I said. "Is that what you came here to ask me?" I kicked myself away from the desk and stared out the window. The motion made my empty stomach turn over, but I didn't care.

"Ah, I didn't mean nothing, Hector. I was just trying to make some small talk."

"That so? Well, you're about as glib as a professional wrestler, Artie."

"Hey, don't call me Artie no more. Call me Ed."

"Huh?"

"Ed. You know, short for Edmund. It's my middle name. I don't go by Artie no more."

"Huh?"

"Yeah. It got real confusing now that my kid's growing up. We had Big Artie and Little Artie and I didn't like that. Somebody calls up the house and you gotta say, 'You want Big Artie or Little Artie?' Christ, Little Artie's six feet two, and something my wife was reading said it does weird things to a kid's head if he always thinks of himself as being a mini-version of someone else. Besides, I like Ed better. I sign everything Arthur Edmund anyhow."

"What do you mean . . . Ed?"

"Hey, it's not me, Hector. It's Cornell here who wants to talk with you." Palmieri looked at the little man expectantly and then realized he had not yet introduced us. "Sorry," he said. "Cornell Pruitt . . . Hector Gronig."

The little man got halfway out of his chair and extended his hand. He studied me with soft brown eyes that reminded me of melted chocolate. The thought made me sick.

"Tell Hector how you got your name," Palmieri chortled.

"I was named after my father's college," the little man said simply. He spoke from beneath a thick, neatly clipped mustache that gave his harmlessly sober face an almost comical look.

"I told him it was a good thing his father didn't go to West Point." Palmieri slapped his leg and exploded with laughter. "Or U.C.L.A. How about that? U.C.L.A. Pruitt."

The little man looked sideways, as if he had already heard that joke two or three times.

"We could have fun like this all day long, Artie," I said wearily. "But what is it you want?"

"Cornell's a police chief," Palmieri said. "Tell him how big your department is, Cornell."

"We have four officers."

Palmieri grinned again. "Cornell's from up north. Sonoma County."

Something clanged in my mind like a barbell on a gymnasium floor. I looked at Pruitt expectantly.

"Do you know anything about the Good Luck Motor Hotel, Mr. Gronig?" Pruitt asked gently.

"Should I?"

Pruitt spread his hands. "Somebody firebombed it last night."

"Nobody hurt, I hope."

"The owner was killed." I had the feeling Pruitt was waiting for my reaction.

"That's too bad," I said.

"As far as that goes, I think it was a mistake." Pruitt took out a briar pipe and a yellow package of tobacco. "Mind if I smoke? I've been up most of the night and I need the nicotine to keep going." He packed the pipe and lit it while Palmieri watched him as if he was a magician.

"Near as we can tell," Pruitt went on, "Agnes Luck had drunk herself cold and was passed out in the office when some type of homemade gasoline bomb came through the window. Doesn't look like she made any effort to try to get out. We had the volunteer fire department there in fifteen minutes, but by then it was too late to save anything in the office, although the boys managed to keep the fire from the rest of the motel."

Pruitt didn't like the way his pipe was going and he stirred it up with a wooden match.

"Not much happens in my town, Mr. Gronig. So if a place gets blown up everybody for miles around comes out in their pajamas to see what's going on—see if they can lend a hand, maybe. Naturally, everybody's talking. Naturally, anybody's got anything important to say, it gets to me. Like the kid from the lunchroom comes over to me and says there was a fella from San Francisco in his place yesterday afternoon asking a lot of questions about the motel. Kid says the fella was real nice to him, so he remembered him, noticed him when he drove up and down the street, noticed him when he turned into the motel yard. Noticed him when he raced out. I said to him, that's fine, but who is this guy?"

Pruitt reached into his coat pocket with one hand and drew out a credit card slip. He let it flutter onto my desk. I didn't bother looking at it, but Palmieri snatched it up like it was a message from Garcia.

"I was up there on an assignment," I said.

Pruitt nodded. "I figured as much when I found out you were a private investigator. You want to tell me what it was about?"

I shrugged. "I'm not sure I know myself. A guy came in here last week and said his wife was cheating on him. Said he wanted pictures for child custody purposes and told me where to go and when to be there. I was waiting outside the Good Luck yesterday, like he told me to do, when the wife and lover pulled up. I needed some way of getting inside their room, so I sweet-talked the old lady and got the key out of her. Then I got my pictures and took off."

"And who was your client, or won't you reveal that?"

"Hell, I'd tell you if I knew his real name. The son-ofabitch pulled a gun on me and refused to pay what he owed."

Palmieri had been rocking back on the hind legs of his chair, crunching my files into dust. Now he slammed forward onto all four legs again. "You don't even know who you were working for?"

"He told me his name was Nicholas Glenn. Then he told me it wasn't."

"Nicholas Glenn? Nicholas Glenn is a psychotic little punk who works for a hoodlum named Jimmy the Dog."

Pruitt looked interested until I described the Nicholas Glenn I knew.

"That ain't him," Palmieri said. "Who was it you got the pictures of?"

"A good-looking blonde and a hairy beast she called

Jonathan." I described them both and got blank looks in return.

"You're a lot of help, Gronig," Palmieri said and we all sat glumly for a while.

Finally Pruitt broke the silence. "You'll have to excuse my skepticism, Mr. Gronig, but I find it hard to believe that a businessman like yourself would accept as a client someone who just walked in off the street with no name, no address and no references and that you would then allow this same person to come back and steal your—ah, how should I put it? Your product."

Pruitt's comments would have been more of a cause for embarrassment if my senses had not been so dulled by hangover. As it was, I simply stared at him. "It wasn't quite like that," I said. "First of all, the guy gave me some money up front. Secondly, the film I let him steal from me was not the one he wanted. I had the real one hidden away and I wasn't going to give it to him until he paid me what he had promised."

"Ah, good. Then you've still got it."

I waved my hand at the mess in the office. "That's what this is all about. When my client pulled the gun on me he made me leave the building with him and walk all the way down Market to the Bay. Someplace between here and there he cut out. I was gone from the office for about forty minutes and by the time I got back the place had been ripped off and the real film was gone."

Palmieri let out his breath. "That's a dumb story, Hector," he said.

"It's true, Artie."

"Ed."

"Ed."

"I get better stories than that all the time, Hector. Better stories from street punks. 'It weren't me, man. It was some dude, not too tall, not too short, not too light, not too dark, not too young, not too old. Some dude.' You know how many times I hear that in the course of the day? I'll tell you, that Dude family is just wreaking havoc in this city, and us stupid cops, we're constantly missing them and picking up the wrong people by mistake. If it wasn't for the fact that the people we pick up seen the Dudes do it, we'd be putting a lot of innocent folks in jail." Palmieri shook his head and loosened his collar another inch. "Jesus, I expected a little more meat from you, Hector. I mean, I know you a little better than Cornell here. I can see you climbing in a motel window and getting ripped off by your client and all, but I didn't really expect you to come up with the 'some dude' defense."

"All right, Palmieri, there's one more thing I can do for you. There was this guard here last night who seemed to know the guy who called himself Nicholas Glenn. I don't know what his connection to this whole mess might be, but when I confronted him last night he took a poke at me and stormed off in the middle of his shift. Let me try talking to him again and I'll get back to you. Will that do you? Good. Now take your insults and beat it. I'm sick as a dog and I don't have anything more to tell you."

Palmieri looked at Pruitt and the little man looked at his watch and nodded. They stood up together and at least Pruitt moved his chair off my files.

"I'll be in touch, Hector," Palmieri said. "Try to have some coffee ready next time, will you?"

5

It was getting dark in Hunter's Point, San Francisco's invisible ghetto; home to thousands of descendants of those who had come up from the South to work the shipyard during World War II and then had been left adrift when the war ended; home to Franz-Josef Moore. I had gotten Franz-Josef's address by telling the building manager I was going out to his house to apologize.

I had barely hit the sidewalk in front of a green barracks-type building that figured to be the street number the manager had given me when a nine- or ten-year-old kid came and told me that he would watch my car for a dollar. I told him I would be looking out the window and watching the car myself and he smiled and drifted away. I walked up a flight of stairs and beat loudly on the door to the unit marked with a number 5. There was a radio roaring inside and so I stepped forward again and beat extra hard so that the people would be sure to hear me.

It took time, but the door was finally pulled open against

two burglar chain locks and a young girl with bows of red yarn in her hair stared at me in surprise. "Hi," I said. "Is your daddy home?"

The girl just looked at me without speaking. I repeated what I had said and this time a girl of about ten or twelve joined the first girl and poked her face into the crack of space. "What you want?" she demanded.

"I'm looking for Franz-Josef Moore. Does he live here?"

There was no answer.

"Is your father here?"

"No."

"Is your mother?"

"Momma!" the older girl screamed over her shoulder without taking her eyes off me. "There a white man at the door who wanna see you."

The radio was silenced. A woman's husky voice shouted back from deep inside the apartment, "You tell him to get outta here."

"Tell your mother I'll just take a minute of her time."

"He say you come here," the girl relayed.

There was a tremendous bustling, as though a gale wind was tearing through the inside of the apartment, and the two girls scattered as if they were rag dolls knocked off the stand at a carnival. The door closed, the locks popped off and the door flew open again to reveal a solid-shouldered, big-breasted, middle-aged black woman whose smoldering brown eyes were level with my own.

"You didn't believe me on the telephone. You had to come here, see for yourself, didn't you?" she said accusingly.

"I don't think we've met," I said, holding out my hand. "I'm looking for Franz-Josef Moore. Are you his wife?"

"Well, you should know," she said, planting her hands on her hips. "You been calling for two days."

"I'm afraid you've got me mistaken for somebody else. My name's Hector Gronig." I looked behind her to where five children, ranging in age from very young to about fifteen, were gathered at a respectful distance. "I used to . . . I used to work with your husband."

"That so? On which job?"

"You mean he has more than one?"

Her eyes swept me from head to foot indignantly. "He got three jobs. And when Patsy was going junior college, Franz-Josef work four jobs. Right now he work as a doorman during the day, a guard at night and a janitor on weekends. Now which one you work with him at?"

"He was a guard in my building. He walked off last night and I'd like to talk to him about it."

"Why he walk off?"

"I don't know. I kind of feel responsible, though, and I'd like to apologize."

"Well, he ain't here, so you don't have to do no 'pologizing and you can just leave."

"I'd be glad to pay you for your trouble."

"Oh, you would, would you?" she said, her head rising and falling slowly. "Now that's real nice. My man don't come home, people call me up in the middle of the night axing for him and then a private detective come to my door and tell me he gonna pay me for my trouble. Mister, where you get off at?"

"How did you know I was a private detective?"

"Oh, you surprised I know who you are? You thought maybe you come out here and fool this dumb old colored girl?"

I smiled at her. "It's my shoes, isn't it?"

"What you talkin' about?"

"It's the rubber shoes that gave me away, isn't it? I knew that would happen, I knew it when I bought them, but I figured it would be easier to sneak up and down hallways if I had shoes that didn't make any noise. Now everybody who sees me thinks I'm either a cop or a private detective. I mean, otherwise I look just like a regular person, don't I?"

"Otherwise you look like a fool . . . and now you acting like one, too."

"Hey, c'mon, Mrs. Moore. I didn't come here to get nasty with anyone. Franz-Josef may be in a good deal of trouble and whether he is or whether he isn't, he's going to be a lot better off if he talks with me before the police find him."

Heavy lids dropped over the woman's eyes until she was staring at me from mere slits in her flesh. "What kind of trouble Franz-Josef in?" she said softly.

I looked back at her children and even the oldest was watching me wild-eyed. I tried to speak so they did not hear. "He may be an accessory to a murder."

I expected her to challenge me, to call me a liar, even to slam the door in my face. Instead, she let out an unearthly moan of pain and collapsed into a heap at my feet. It took me a second to react and then I bent down and struggled to get her into a standing position again. But she was dead weight and two or three of her children had to come and help me. Pushing and pulling, we got her back inside the apartment. I wanted to drop her in the first chair we came to, but the children insisted that I guide her into the kitchen.

"Oh, Lord, I know somepin' wrong when he don't come home last night," she cried as we got her into her seat. She buried her head in her arms and made the whole room shake with her sobs.

I looked on fearfully while she called for her man, called for Jesus, begged for forgiveness. The children watched silently and occasionally one would glance up at me. We all waited and gradually she stopped.

"I gonna need your help," she said to me through tearful eyes. "The Lord just told me that's why he sent you here. Now you sit down at this table with me and tell me what Franz-Josef do and why he do it." She wiped her face with the back of her hand. "You want somepin' to drink? Tyrone, you get this man a bottle of strawberry soda and get me one, too."

"I only need a little bit," I said, sitting down cautiously. I was somewhat worried now that the Lord had been brought into the picture and I was a good deal uncertain as to what was going to happen next.

The boy, Tyrone, handed me a bottle from the refrigerator. "You don't finish it you just put the top back on and give it here when you done," he said.

"You get the man a glass," his mother barked and in two seconds there was a glass in front of me. She appeared not to need one herself.

I thanked Tyrone, thanked his mother and then spent a long time sipping my soda and wondering how best to phrase whatever it was I was going to say. Mrs. Moore took me off the hook.

"I knew he in trouble when he don't come home, but I never figured no murder." She heaved a tremendous sigh. "Still, I should have knowed. Nothing ever make Franz-Josef leave his job before, 'cept when he get the crazies and then anything can happen. It usually do, too. He be good for months and he work and work and I don't have no problem with him and he bring all his money home and me and him makes our plans for all our children and he don't do no drinkin' and he don't do no dopin' and then one day, *bam,* somepin' set him off and he gone for a week. Then he come shameassing hisself home and not rememberin' nothin' about where he been or what he been doin'.

I know, I seen it before. Just somepin' happen to set him off, that's all, and then he gone. One time he win some big money on the Super Bowl and we didn't see him for days. Lost two jobs and had to go stand in line for a month 'fore he got another. One time his sister die, she got hit by a car, you know? and the next thing I hear, he in jail in Texas. Now, how he get to Texas? I had to take money out of the children's bank for to get him home."

I shook my head in sympathy. "Think he might have come into some unexpected money this time?"

"Now how he do that when you say he at work?" The look on Mrs. Moore's face suddenly changed. "I know what you sayin'. You talkin' about that murder."

I did not like the way she was beginning to glower at me and I quickly held up my hand. "It could have been for something as innocent as not paying attention. Tell me, did Franz-Josef ever mention a guy named Nicholas Glenn to you?"

"Never. Now I gonna ask you a question. Who got killed and how come you think Franz-Josef involved?"

"It was a woman who owned a motel up in Sonoma County. The police want to question a man who hired me to go up there and take some pictures at her place." I got that far and I stopped. Mrs. Moore looked at me expectantly. She was waiting for the big explosion and I had none to deliver. I looked at my hands and wondered if I should try to explain to her how I was sure Franz-Josef knew I was being held up and yet refused to come to my aid. It sounded unconscionably weak, even to me, so I just told her how the pictures had been stolen last night while Franz-Josef had been on duty, and how he had run out before the theft was discovered.

"You think Franz-Josef just gived up his job to let somebody steal somepin' from you?" was all she said. Of course, it was the way she said it.

"Mrs. Moore, can you think of any reason why Franz-Josef needs money right now? Why he might be willing to give up a job to get some money in his hands immediately?"

She twisted her head slowly from side to side.

"There's Patsy," Tyrone said and his mother turned and looked at him angrily.

The kitchen went so quiet we could hear a conversation going on in the apartment next door.

"Patsy's your daughter, the one who was going to junior college?" I said.

Mrs. Moore thought about her answer, and then said, "Mister, how much was you offerin' to pay me for my trouble?"

I opened my wallet, a bit too eagerly, drew out a twenty and pushed it across the table. The bill seemed to shrivel into waste paper before her eyes and she made no move to pick it up. I took out another bill, another twenty, and laid it on top of the first.

"How much you get paid for to find someone?" she demanded.

"It depends."

"Forty dollar?"

Since I had nothing other than fifties to give her I said yes.

"Then I accepts this money for my trouble, like you said." She straightened the two bills and patted them together. She held them out to me. "And I hire you to find Franz-Josef before the police do."

I laughed. She didn't. I stopped. "Mrs. Moore," I said, "that's what I'm already trying to do."

"'Cept if you work for me I can tell you what little bit I know and you can't tell no police. My children needs their father without him going off to no prison. And me, I needs you to find him so me and him can talk and decide what we gonna do. But 'less you work for me, I don't tell you nothing. I ain't no Judas."

The woman's simple cleverness touched me, and her forceful presence kept me from showing it. I took the money and put it back in my wallet. "Agreed," I said.

"Where my receipt?" she said.

I took my pen and notebook from my inside jacket pocket and wrote a receipt for my own forty dollars. She gave it to one of her daughters and told her to put it in the Bible. "Put it in Revelations," she said, eyeing me significantly.

"Now tell me about Patsy," I said.

"She joined the Revelations Temple," she said, as if that disclosed everything I needed to know. She must have noticed the blank look on my face because after a moment she went on to explain. "The temple out there in the Richmond district that's run by that devil Reverend Franklin. I know he a devil because he took my baby, who is the most beautiful girl who ever walked, beautiful both inside and outside, and he made her leave her family and the church of her mother and father and go join that crazy church he just made up. It not a Baptist church, it not even a Methodist church. He say it a Christian church and he talk about Jesus all the time, but he try to make people believe that he the Messiah come again. I saw him and he ain't no Messiah. He just a big white man with a pretty voice and a good idea.

"My girl Patsy, she going to City College and she meet this boy who talk to her all about his new religion, which he says is ordained by the Book of Revelations. He take her to this church of his, which, like I say, is called the Temple of Revelations. She meet some people there and they invite her to go up north somewheres on a retreat. I didn't want her to go because I knowed that boy was gonna be there, but Patsy say, 'Oh, Momma, it's all right.' Only it wasn't no all right and when she come back she move right out of this house and into that temple. She even quit the school her father work so hard to pay for." Mrs. Moore paused long enough to take a pull on her soda and glare at the children in the kitchen as if to say that none of them better have any ideas of doing what Patsy had done.

"Then Patsy don't see us for weeks," she went on. "Finally, when she don't answer our phone calls, her father, he go up to that temple and he try to talk to her, only she wouldn't come out. She just send a message saying she love us, but she can't see us because she still in training. So then Franz-Josef, he try to go inside and the men there, they grab him and gets him into a fight, only Franz-Josef won't give up until finally this man come out and say his name Tom Blodgett."

"Tom Blodgett."

"That's right. He the second in charge of that whole temple. He standing there talking nice and soft to Franz-Josef about how Patsy not just our daughter no more, but also a woman of her own and a child of God. And while Franz-Josef listening the police comes up behind him and arrests him for trespassing. They take him all the way to the police station before they lets him go and tells him not to try to see his own daughter again.

"So what we s'pose to do then? Even the police working with this devil Franklin and his made-up church. Then Franz-Josef hear about this man Henry Willis, who a famous deprogrammer. You know what that is? They say this man the best for getting children away from the Temple of Revelations. Only when Franz-Josef go to him he ask for three thousand dollars before he even start. We don't have no three thousand dollars and Franz-Josef tell Mr. Willis that.

He tell him he only a night watchman, but Mr. Willis he just say, come back when you get it." She drained her bottle of red soda and slapped it on the table. It took me a moment or two to realize that she had finished her story.

"That's it?" I said. "That's all you have to tell me?"

Mrs. Moore looked surprised. "What else you want? You axed me if there any reason why Franz-Josef need big money right now and I told you."

"So where do I find this Henry Willis?"

She shrugged. "Franz-Josef know."

I sighed and stood up. "If he comes home, Mrs. Moore, give me a call and let me know, will you?"

She lowered her eyes to her hands, which were folded on the table in front of her. "You s'pose to be out looking for him," she said.

"I will be, but you don't want me doing that if he's not missing."

She did not look up as I made my way to the door.

"Don't worry, Mrs. Moore, if he's out there I'll find him."

She still did not look up and I stopped, waiting for some kind of sendoff and not sure why I needed it. "I still haven't figured out how you knew I was a private detective," I said.

"When Franz-Josef don't come home I call the building manager and he tell me how Franz-Josef been in a fistfight with a private detective who have an office in the building. The building manager say he don't know what the fight about, but he sure it wasn't Franz-Josef's fault. He tell me not to worry." Her eyes lifted to meet mine and they were the saddest eyes I have ever seen. "How I s'pose not to worry when I know Franz-Josef out there doin' somepin' crazy?"

6

Even in the dark the Dodge van was easy enough to find. It was the only vehicle on the street with four slashed tires.

I thought about the kid who had offered to watch my car for a dollar and at that moment I would have happily killed him. I settled for smashing my foot into one of the deflated tires and sagging against the side of the van.

The situation was, to say the least, rather bleak. Not only were there no friendly faces around to lend me assistance, there were no faces period. There was not much chance of finding a taxi or much sense in trying to hitchhike. There were buses, I knew, but I did not know where or when they would run. Taking everything together, I seemed to have no choice but to return to the Moore household and use their telephone to call for a tow truck and a ride back downtown.

Just then a red Datsun pickup truck came gliding slowly down the street. It passed me, stopped and backed up again. A homely, sandy-haired man stared out at me for a moment before rolling down his window.

"You need some he'p there, buddy?" he said. Both the accent and the face were pure country.

"Some asshole slashed my tires," I said.

"Waal"—he looked the tires over—"don't think there's much we kin do about it tonight, but if you kin he'p me find my way out of this godforsaken pisshole I'll be glad to take you wherever you going. Maybe tomorrow you kin git out here and put on a new set or something. Maybe call the Triple A and they'll do it for you." I lost some of what he was saying because I was hurrying around to get in the passenger's side of his truck.

The man looked me over as I settled into the seat. I gave him a few seconds of free time and then I looked back. He had a pair of beady brown eyes that watched me from beneath the foliage of two thick gray eyebrows. His skin was creased and crevassed. His nose and his ears were long and his chin looked like the blade of a small shovel. The man had not gotten his new Datsun pickup on account of his beauty. "Name's Jarmon," he said, "and you're the first white man I see'd in half a hour."

"Name's Gronig and is that a fact."

The man cackled. His eyes were gleaming, and for a moment a feeling of trepidation passed through me. "It's a fact," he said, turning his eyes to the road and moving the car into gear. "What was you doing out here in colored town?"

"Visiting a friend."

"Yeah? Well, not me. I was just lost. Just plain lost."

We made our way out to Third Street, took Third to Army, and then crossed over to the Bayshore and followed that into downtown. I told Jarmon he could let me off anywhere that I could catch a streetcar, but he claimed he was in no hurry, having just come to the city on business, and he insisted on driving me to my door. When we got there he put the pickup in neutral and glanced up at my building.

"You live very far up there, Gronig?"

"One flight of stairs," I said as I opened my door and started to get out.

"You'll forgive my saying this, I know, old buddy, but it just don't look like a real good place to raise a family. Why, out where I am, near Ukiah, we kin let our children run just as far as they want and they can't never git out of sight of our windows. Now I know you must have some good advantages living in a big building like this one, but tell me, where do your children play?"

"I live alone."

"Well, then I don't feel quite so outta line in asking my next question. Would you let a feller use your bathroom for a quick pit stop? I been knocking back the Budweiser all day and if I don't do something about it quick I'm gonna end up like a high school kid pissing in the alley. I mean, if you got a lady friend or something up there I don't want to intrude or nothing, but if I could just make a quick pit stop I'd surely appreciate it."

I had a twinge of apprehension at the thought of an unwanted guest settling in for the night, but I could not very well deny the use of my bathroom to the man who had just saved me from a rather difficult situation. "Sure," I said and waved for him to follow me.

Jarmon unloaded nearly six and a half feet of himself from behind the steering wheel and followed me up the stairs, panting apologies in my ear while I concentrated on how I was going to get rid of this nice but boring old cowboy once he got inside my apartment.

"This is it," I said, stopping in front of my door and

searching around in my pocket for the key.

"Say, this really isn't such a bad place, Gronig. I bet you git to know your neighbors real well. 'Course, my wife and me, we know'd most of our neighbors all our lives. . . ." He went on and on while I bent over and fit the key into the door handle.

I pushed the door open and started to straighten up to tell Jarmon where the bathroom was when the whole world shot silver and black. I felt as though the top of my head had been picked up and slammed down again. Pain shot the length of my body like a train roaring through a tunnel. I was on my hands and knees and a foot was planted in my butt, shoving me flat on my stomach.

"Goddammit, tough guy, get the hell inside," a voice said. There was another loud sound and my body jerked spasmodically, but it was only the door being slammed shut. I struggled to get to my knees and was pushed flat again. I knew where the pain was coming from now and I grabbed for the back of my head and screamed because my hand came away covered with blood.

Somebody was down close to my ear now. "Shut up," he hissed. I opened my eyes and it was Jarmon. "Shut up, you squealing bastard." He was shaking something in my face, but all I could focus on was his mouth as it worked, ripping and chewing out words and spitting them at me from inches away.

"You busted my sap, boy. Now I'm gonna have to strangle you. You ever see a man get strangled? It ain't a pretty sight. Face turns purple and then goes gray and the shit comes flying out both ends. You feel the man's energy coming right into your hands. Gets almost like electricity. Comes into your hands, goes up your arms. 'Course, it takes a while, but I think you gonna go sooner than most 'cause you just lying there with your goddamn brain oozing out the back of your head picking up the fuzz off the carpet. So you better start talking fast before you lose your remembering power altogether. You ready, Gronig? Where's that goddamn film?"

7

I could hear her voice above the sounds of everything else that was going on. I could not make out her words, just her voice, and then suddenly I realized she was talking to me. I snapped my mind into attention, fearful that I was too late to catch the message. "What?" I said. "What?" Something more was said to me, but I could not understand it and then I knew for the first time that I was sleeping. I forced my eyes open and found myself staring at the square toes of two baby-blue boots a few inches away from my face. The boots were where they were because my face was pressed into the wall-to-wall, indoor-outdoor carpet of my apartment.

"My head," I said, half feeling and half remembering that something had happened to it.

Fingers moved roughly through my hair. "You got a big goose egg and some dried blood. What did you do, fall off your skateboard?"

I pushed myself up to my knees and waited to see what

would happen. Nothing did. The pain was a good deal less than when I had my hangover. Encouraged, I turned to see who was taunting me and nearly fainted dead away.

The woman standing just inside the door of my apartment was beautiful, there was absolutely no doubt about that. She was dressed entirely in blue and white. She had a rope belt and silver studs running down one leg of her jeans. Above that she wore a long-sleeved striped jersey and a white linen jacket. Her blue leather purse was slung over her shoulder and held close to her waist with one hand while her other hand hooked itself in the corner of her jeans pocket. She wore no jewelry other than a gold chain at her throat, but the chain looked expensive and it was set off nicely by the tanned brown of her skin. Her hair was blond and hung naturally to the shoulders. She had a wide, full mouth and high cheekbones and her teeth would have shamed Katharine Hepburn. And yet, even with this near perfection of features, there was something almost coarse about her, as if she had seen many things in many places and wasn't impressed by any of them. The coarseness came through in the set of her face. It seemed to say, I know who I am and I don't care who you are. Except in my case she cared. I was the one who had taken pictures of her in the Good Luck Motor Hotel.

"What are you doing here?" I said, turning myself around so that I was sitting on the floor with my back to the wall. The woman appeared to be alone, but I wasn't inclined to take any chances.

"Looking for you," she said. "I guess you recognize me."

"I do, but I was in such a hurry that I didn't get a real good look at you when we last met." Heroically, I attempted to smile. "It was my loss."

"Don't try to hustle me, Jack," she snapped. "I'm here on business."

"Business, right. I should have known. This hasn't exactly been my lucky day." I looked around at the mess of my plundered apartment. I was getting used to finding my places torn apart, but Jarmon had been ridiculous. He had gone so far as to empty all my boxes of foodstuffs on the kitchen table. Even now some of it was dropping on-to the floor. Everything I owned seemed to be someplace on the floor.

The woman was looking around with me. "You should get a housecleaner," she said.

"This isn't the way it normally is," I told her.

"Yeah? Well, you wouldn't know it by me, Jack. I've spent most of the afternoon sitting in your office and it's almost as big a pit as this place. Don't you ever go to work? Don't you ever call your answering service, or check in or anything?"

"What were you doing in my office? How did you know who I was and how did you find me here?"

"What's this, twenty questions?" She looked around for a place to sit down. It was just a studio apartment and from where she stood the whole place was visible.

"The plastic cushions on the floor go to that armchair," I said. "You might want to make sure they haven't been slashed."

She arranged the armchair and eased herself into it as if she thought it might break. "I managed to get your license plate number. I put in a call to a friend of mine on the Highway Patrol and he told me who you are and where to find you."

"That's a good story," I said, sucking in a new breath of fresh air, "but it's a lie. The car's registered in my wife's name at my wife's house."

The woman's eyes flashed. "All right, smart guy. Figure out for yourself how I found you."

"I'd say you knew who I was ahead of time."

The woman drew back in surprise. "Is that what he told you?"

"Who?"

"Ferrell Dumont, of course."

"Who's Ferrell Dumont?"

"We're not getting anywhere, are we, Jack? Why don't you just tell me everything you know?"

"Because I don't know anything. Of course, that hasn't prevented me from spending the last twenty-four hours getting punched out, yelled at, accused, and blackjacked, but that's beside the point. Look, a man came to me last week and said he wanted pictures of his wife going at it with some guy in a motel. Said he needed the pictures for child custody purposes. He was a good actor and I almost believed him."

"But you didn't."

"No."

"Then why did you do it?"

"He paid me."

She nodded; a bit too knowingly, I thought. "He also promised me a lot more than he actually paid," I said.

"He's going to blackmail me, you know."

"I figured he was blackmailing someone. Why you?"

"Ferrell Dumont is my brother."

"How do you know he's the one who hired me?"

"Because that slimy little bastard is the only person in the world who would."

She closed her blue eyes as if to compose herself.

"All right," she said, "I wasn't going to tell you all this, but I'm here and so I will. Several years ago I married an older man. He's wealthy, he's good to me and I love him. But he has a—well, it's a physical problem and he's very jealous." I looked at her hands. There was a plain gold band on her left ring finger.

She took a deep breath. "The point is, I've had some affairs from time to time and my brother knew about them. Ferrell's into a little bit of junk and he's the sort who's always looking for an angle that's going to help him support his habit. I thought it was just one of those things that we ended up at that motel until you came busting in. When the man I was with saw how upset I got, he broke down and told me how Ferrell had arranged the whole thing and had hired you to take the pictures so I wouldn't know who was responsible. He told me the plan was to send me anonymous notes demanding money in exchange for the pictures. Meanwhile, Ferrell's going to go on about his business, pretending he's my loving little brother."

"And Jonathan?"

She looked startled.

"You called him Jonathan in the motel room," I explained. "What's happened to him?"

"Nothing. He drove me home and then he just disappeared. He said he wanted to get away before Ferrell found out that he had told me. Anyhow, he's not important. The important thing is the pictures. I stayed up all last night trying to figure out what I should do. Then today I tracked you down. I found your office, only there was nobody there."

"I left around one."

"I must have just missed you. Anyhow, the door was unlocked and I went inside and sat around in your mess waiting for you to come back. When you didn't, I called the building manager and he told me where you lived."

"Thank God for the building manager. I don't know what I'd do without him."

"I want those pictures, Gronig, and I'm willing to pay plenty for them."

"How much is plenty?"

She hesitated and looked at me as though she were trying the words in her mind before she said them out loud. "Five thousand dollars."

"You're kidding."

"I am dead serious." She made a big deal about pronouncing the word "dead."

I got up from the floor and began to pace back and forth, pretending to think about the offer. I wanted to give her every opportunity to raise the ante, but after a while I stopped pacing because she showed no interest and it was making my head throb.

"There's one tiny little problem," I said, sitting down on one of the pullout couches near her. "I don't have the film anymore."

She caught her breath. "Then I want you to get it back."

I spread my hands. "But I don't know who has it."

The woman's eyes, which were none too warm to begin with, developed an etherlike frost. "Don't play games with me, Jack. If my brother came by and picked the film up, all you have to do is go get it back from him."

"I can do that, all right. But even if I find your brother, it doesn't mean I'll find the film. There seem to be some other people involved."

The woman obviously had not expected this. "Like who?" she demanded.

"Your brother came into my office last night, pulled a gun and stole what he thought was the film with the pictures of you and Jonathan. But the film he took wasn't the one he wanted. That one was hidden in the medicine cabinet in my bathroom. Your brother made me leave the building with him and by the time I got back somebody had broken into the medicine cabinet and stolen your pictures. And that's not all that happened last night. Up in Sonoma, somebody firebombed the motel you were at and killed the old floozy who ran the place."

The woman's implacable face seemed to shatter before my eyes. Her hand went to her throat. "My God," she said, half to herself, "this can't be happening."

"Do you know a tall cowboy named Jarmon?"

She shook her head.

"He found me just before you did. Followed me up here and bashed me over the head. He was looking for the film too. This is his artwork you're sitting in the midst of."

"I've got to go," she said and started to get up.

I was on my feet in an instant, forcing her back into her chair by the sheer suddenness of my action. "Don't you move, lady," I said. "I've got a few more questions to ask you. Like, did your friend Jonathan ever mention anything about a building guard named Franz-Josef?"

"I don't know any of these people," she cried, and for a moment she was almost vulnerable. But the moment passed and suddenly she was as hard as ever. "Look," she said, reaching into her pocketbook and pulling out a bill, "this is for your time. But I want you to forget everything I've said. Forget I was here. The deal is off."

I slapped the bill out of her hand. "The hell it is. I'd be glad to forget about this whole sordid little affair, but nobody will let me. Every time I turn around it seems somebody is attacking me because he figures I know more than I do. So I've given up forgetting about it." I leaned over and grabbed the arms of her chair so that I was speaking directly into her face. "Now I'm involved, just like you, and I want to know more about what's going on so the next time somebody threatens me I can tell him something."

"Get out of my way," she said.

"Not until you answer some questions. You can start by telling me who this guy Jonathan is."

"He's no one, now get the hell out of my way." Her foot lashed out and connected with my shin, sending burning pain shooting up my leg. I grinned and didn't back off.

"All right, then tell me who your husband is, or better yet, tell me who you really are."

She pivoted on her haunches just enough to get some leverage and smashed her open hand into my face. Lights danced in front of my eyes and I began to be convinced that there was not much hope in pursuing the discussion. I straightened up slowly and shook my head to relieve the stinging, but I still did not move away from her. I should have. She came up out of her chair and drove her knee into my testicles. For a moment the world was without air as I grabbed myself reflexively and fell, gasping, onto the carpet.

She left me more or less as she had found me.

8

The Delphi Apartments were located in one of those large, brick-faced buildings that had once been fairly luxurious and were now clinging to the last vestiges of respectability. The brick was a bit chipped in places and the upstairs windows were encased in dirt, but the marble steps were still wet from a recent hosing when I arrived shortly after ten o'clock Tuesday morning.

I paused on the sidewalk for a moment and tried to imagine the man who had come into my office living in this building. The white columns that stood outside the entrance gave the place a scholarly air I knew it did not deserve. My experience with this neighborhood told me that the inhabitants were likely to be old people with little dogs, stoop-shouldered women who wore tennis shoes and raincoats, and single men who liked to stare at each other for long periods of time. Maybe people like Ferrell Dumont, if indeed that was his name, really did live in the Delphi and the dozen places like it that lined Ellis and its neighboring streets, but I had never seen them.

I mounted the marble steps and began inspecting the mailboxes for Dumont's name. I had not been there more than a few seconds when a woman's voice came over the squawk box: "Who is it you want?"

"I'm looking for the manager," I said, speaking loudly because I was not sure where the intercom was.

A buzzer sounded and I pushed open the heavy, wood-framed door with its glass center and its iron filigree covering and walked into the tile-floored lobby. The long narrow room was claustrophobic with age. Its only concessions to the present were two heavy-leafed rubber plants which stood, one in each, in the corners closest to the street. Even they seemed so overcome by the musty atmosphere that I at first thought they were not real.

The walls of the lobby were covered with faded yellow wallpaper bearing brown watermarks which were eerily illuminated by the electric candlelight wall fixtures. A gold carpet ran like a trolley track down the center of the floor past a yellow-and-white striped couch, a marble-topped stand, and a love seat that matched nothing and looked as if it had been temporarily placed for the past twenty years. The carpet ended at an ornately banistered staircase, which casually wound its way out of sight.

There was a door in one wall marked MANAGER and it stood ajar. I went over to it and tentatively pushed it open.

"C'mon in," a voice beckoned from somewhere among a million pieces of clutter. The room was literally filled with bric-a-brac. There was barely an inch of wall space, floor or shelves that was not covered with some figurine, vase, statuette, painting, hanging or obscure piece of Depression glass. The windowsills were covered. So was the mantel above the bricked-in fireplace. So were the rows upon rows of bookcases, none of which held a single book. Three coffee tables stood in the middle of the floor and each was nearly buried beneath all manner of candy dishes—filled and unfilled. Most jarring of all were the paintings that lined the walls in irregular columns from floor to ceiling. All were pastoral scenes done in gaudy colors with lump strokes of paint that made them three-dimensional. Each showed itself from the depths of a garish golden frame.

Faced with this kaleidoscope of objects, it took me a second or two to focus on the woman who sat like a bespectacled ball of wool behind an English writing desk at the end of a trail of plastic runners that wended its way between the coffee tables. The woman was old and gray-haired, but her color was most definitely pink. It radiated from the shawl she had wrapped around her shoulders and it spurted flamelike from the rouge she had apparently slapped on her wrinkled old cheeks with a spatula.

"If you've come about the apartment, I'm afraid you're going to be disappointed," she said, regarding me sourly, as if she expected an argument.

"Oh, no," I said. Then, trying to be pleasing, but still somewhat unglued by my surroundings, I added, "I think it looks just fine."

She sucked in her breath and gummed soundlessly at me for a moment. "But this is my apartment," she croaked indignantly. "The one I had for rent is on the fourth floor." She went through a great deal of physical exertion, shifting her seat and pulling her shawl tighter around her shoulders. "Anyhow, it's not available. It's already rented."

"I'm not here about an apartment," I said. I gave her my card and she held it out at arm's length to get a good look at it. I noticed that the lenses of her eyeglasses were thick and frosted with fingerprints.

"What's this say?" she demanded. "The printing's awful small."

"It says my name is Hector Gronig and that I'm a private detective."

She kept looking at my card. "Like those fellas on television, I suppose."

"Yes, ma'am. I'm looking for a man named Ferrell Dumont. I heard he might be a tenant of yours."

"Oh, him." She sniffed. "He's gone. It's his apartment I thought you were here about." She put the card down and squinted at me. "What's that man done, killed somebody?"

I tried to keep my jaw from hitting the floor. "Why do you ask that?"

"Well I wouldn't be surprised if he did, the way he acted all the time. Wasn't here one month and left without giving me any notice. Didn't want his name on the mailbox, didn't have a telephone, didn't even have any visitors—that is, until now. Since he's moved out he's had more people looking for him than you could shake a stick at."

"Oh? Who else was here?"

She rested her chin on her hand so that one finger was pointing up along her cheek. "Well, first there was that blond woman with the foul mouth. She was here yesterday about ten o'clock. Watched her march right up those stairs like she lived here, and then watched her come right back down again and drop her carcass on that couch in the lobby. Now pretty young woman like that don't go sitting around the lobbies of nice apartment buildings like this without a reason, so naturally I went out and asked her what she wanted. Said she was waiting for Dumont. I said you're waiting in the wrong place, he moved out already. Well, she didn't believe me at first, but when she did it was Katie bar the door. Never heard such language. I had to ask her to leave."

"Did she identify herself?"

"She did not. Simply turned her vile tongue on me

until I threatened to call the police. That got rid of her in a hurry."

"You say this happened yesterday? When did Dumont move out?"

"The night before. Sunday night. Left nearly all his belongings, too. Came down here about nine o'clock and stood right where you're standing now with a suitcase in one hand and a briefcase in the other and said, 'I'm moving out.' Just like that. Well, I was never so thunderstruck in all my life. I told him he couldn't leave without giving me two weeks' notice and he just laughed and told me to keep his security deposit, as if that was all there was to it." She stopped and peered at me. "What's that you're doing? You're smoking a cigarette, aren't you? You put that out. I don't allow smoking in my apartment—and don't use that ashtray, either. Can't you see it's got a picture of the President and his wife on it?"

I ground the cigarette out on the sole of my shoe, caught the ashes in my hand and put them in my pocket. All that got was a sniff from the manager.

"Where was I?" she said. "Oh, yes, the security deposit. That security deposit wouldn't even pay me to throw all his stuff away and I told him that, too. But he didn't care. I would have been in a fine kettle of pickles if Mr. Harris hadn't come along and rented the place as is."

"You mean with all Ferrell Dumont's stuff still in it?"

"I said, 'as is,' didn't I?"

"Was Mr. Harris looking for Ferrell Dumont when he rented the apartment?"

"That's right. He was a friend of his from out of town. Oklahoma, I'd say by the accent. Let me see, he came just after lunch. Said Dumont didn't know he was coming, but that he was hoping to be able to stay with him for a night or two until he found a place of his own. Told him just what

I told you and right away he said he'd rent the place. Said he'd solve both our problems at once and that he was glad Dumont's things were still there because he didn't have any sheets or dishes of his own."

"This Harris, what did he look like?"

"Look like? God knows what he looks like. There's something wrong with these eyeglasses of mine and I haven't had a chance to get out of here and get them fixed. Mr. Harris is a big man, though. I can tell you that for a fact. Taller than you. And he's got kind of a long face, too."

I was on my feet. "What number apartment is he in?"

"It's four-ten, but no sense in you going up there now. Mr. Harris isn't at home."

"Is he coming back?"

"Well, of course he's coming back." She hesitated. "Least I expect he is. He hasn't even signed his renter's agreement yet. Just gave me a week's rent and went upstairs. Said he'd be back in a little while to sign the agreement, but he came down in less than an hour and passed me by like an old shirt." She saw me watching her and rather lamely added, "I figured he was just going to get his belongings."

I turned and ran for the stairs.

"Where are you going?" she called after me. "Don't you close that door; I have to know what's going on out there."

I was only half surprised to find the door to apartment 410 unlocked. It was a small place. The door opened on the kitchen, behind which was a main room where a pullout couch was stretched into a bed. Off that was a narrow bathroom painted a morbid brown, the color of rotten fruit. I didn't bother going any farther than the kitchen. The boxes of food that had been opened and dumped on the counters in that room bore a distinctly Jarmonlike touch that told me all I needed to know.

The sound of an old Superman television show was coming from apartment 409 across the hall. I went over and knocked on the door.

A hulking, soft-bellied man with a swarthy complexion beneath at least two days of beard jerked the door open immediately as if he were expecting someone. He seemed disappointed with what he got.

"I'm looking for the guy across the hall," I said. "You know him?"

"He split," the man mumbled hoarsely, and started to close the door.

"How about the guy who just moved in?" I said, pushing it back open. "Did you meet him?"

"What's his name?"

"Harris."

"Never heard of him. Ask the old fart downstairs."

"Did you know Ferrell?" I said, pushing the door again.

The guy looked as if he wanted to slam the door in my face but was not sure if he dared try. He slumped back against the wall and glanced over his shoulder for help. Superman stayed in the tube. "Say, who are you, anyway?" he said.

"Friend of Ferrell."

"Yeah?" The man's dark eyes narrowed. "He owe you money?"

"I used to date his sister."

There was a rustling in the back of the apartment and a blue-eyed woman with a round face and graying, waist-length blond hair padded forward in an orange bathrobe and fuzzy slippers. "I hear the man say he was a friend of Ferrell's, Bob?" she said with her eyes fixed on me.

Bob looked resigned to something he wanted no part of and made a half gesture toward me. "Guy says he knows him."

The woman came up close to me. She was prettier up close and I smiled at her. "I'll talk with the gentleman, Bob," she said.

Bob bit his lip and didn't move.

"I'm Grace," the woman said. "Did Ferrell give you a message for me?"

"I was hoping you could tell me where to find him."

Bob grunted. "If I knew I'd go after him myself and get my damn money back."

"Shut up," Grace snapped. "It's not your money." She tried to turn back to me, but Bob interrupted her.

"What's yours is mine," he said petulantly. "That's the law." He looked at me for help. "Guy borrowed ten bucks from Grace the day before yesterday and then snuck out of here for good."

"He didn't have any money, Bob," she said like she was explaining something to a child. "He didn't have one cent to eat with."

"Well, we only had fifteen bucks and you gave him ten of it. What was we supposed to do after that? Go eat at the Colonel's until I get my check on the first of the month?" Bob turned to me again. "She gave the bum money on Thursday, too, but she thinks I don't know it."

"He's not a bum and don't call him that," Grace said, her voice rising. "You're the bum."

Bob jabbed himself with his thumb. "I got a veteran's disability. What's he got? No job, nothing. Just some stupid religion, that's all."

"You don't know anything about it, Bob."

"Well, he must have told you all about it, all that time you spent over there."

Grace's eyes flashed. "What's that mean, big mouth?"

"I suppose he was filling you full of Jesus, huh, Grace?"

Grace stared at him. I stared at him. He laughed nervously and shifted his eyes from her to me and back again. "Lady in church has hope in her soul, lady in the bathtub has soap in her hole," he said and she let him have it, hitting him flush on the mouth with her fist.

I pulled her away and jumped in front of Bob, ready to hold him off, but he made no effort to get at her. Grace ducked around me, threw back her head and spit in her husband's face. Bob stumbled back into the other room, wiping his face with the sleeve of his shirt.

Grace looked up at me with tears in her eyes and tugged her bathrobe tighter. "Let's go out in the hallway for a minute," she said.

I took her arm and guided her out, pulling the door shut behind us. From the other room we could hear Bob scream, "I suppose you're gonna do it with him, too."

Grace turned furiously as if she was going to go back inside, but then she stopped and leaned her head against the wall as big tears rolled down her face. "He's crazy, you know. He can't help it and I have to keep reminding myself of that." She wiped at her tears. "Look, that was a mistake back there, what I did. I mean, I don't want Ferrell's friends to think I go around spitting on people all the time."

"Just on Bob."

She shook her head. "The truth is, I'd be leaving him anyhow, even if I hadn't met Ferrell."

"You and Ferrell were..." I was not quite sure how to phrase it.

She was. "We were lovers." She smiled at their accomplishment. "Oh, I know, he probably never mentioned me to you, but that's because it all happened so quickly. Just two weeks ago was the first time we ever... you know.

But there was something magical that happened between us." She looked to see if I understood what she meant. I found it hard to imagine, but I nodded anyway.

"He was going to take me away from all this," she said. "He told me he was coming into some money and he thought it would be this week. That's why I can't understand why he just disappeared like he did."

Grace searched my face and then stared at her fingernails, which were bitten short and uneven. "I know what you're thinking, but I don't believe it. Ferrell would never have done that to me. He was in some kind of trouble and I'm afraid it caught up with him."

"Police?"

"I don't think so. I think it had something to do with the money he was supposed to get, only he wouldn't talk about it, so I don't know."

"Did he ever mention anything to you about his sister?"

"His sister? No. I didn't know he had one. He told me about his father, though."

"What about him?"

"Well, Ferrell hates him, you must know that. His father just got remarried a little while ago and threw Ferrell out of the house, even though he knew Ferrell had no money and no job. That was the whole reason he was living in this dump. Didn't he tell you?"

"Yeah, well, I haven't seen Ferrell in a while. Still, he was kind of an old boy to be living at home."

"Well, what else was he supposed to do? He hasn't even been out of prison a year and he's not allowed to go near any known drug users or drug hangouts."

I can jump to conclusions as quickly as the next person. I said, "The reason I'm looking for him is his sister's worried. She seems to think Ferrell's shooting junk again."

"What are you talking about? Ferrell never shot anything in his life." She searched my eyes. "He never did, did he?"

I shrugged.

"He told me that was just part of his plea bargain when he was busted for dealing. He said if they thought he was a junkie they'd parole him as soon as they figured he was cured. He said it worked, too, even though when they paroled him they made him go join that church group."

"What church group?"

Grace stepped back, eyeing me suspiciously. "Say, are you sure you're a friend of Ferrell's."

"I'm damn sure. I just haven't seen him in a while, that's all."

"Well, he was supposed to go to Synanon or one of them places, but then he heard about this church group that didn't make you shave your head or go live with them or anything, so he managed to talk the parole board into letting him go with them."

"With whom?"

"I think it's called the Revelation Temple."

There it was. For the second time in twenty-four hours that name had come up. I said, "Ferrell ever talk to you about a friend of his named Franz-Josef Moore?"

Grace's round face contracted as if she were trying to remember the name, but I could see right away that it meant nothing to her. "No," she said, giving me a tight little smile. "It's kind of funny, but Ferrell never really talked much about his friends. Mostly we talked about the future—what we'd do when he came into his money—or we'd talk about me and Bob. I don't know, though, looking back we never really had that much time together. I mean, Bob's always around and the only way I could get to see Ferrell was to pretend I was going to the store and then sneak back up the stairs."

Her eyes got dreamy. "I always had to do a special little knock so Ferrell would know it was me, because otherwise he wouldn't open the door. At first I thought he was afraid of Bob, but I told him he didn't have anything to worry about there."

Suddenly the door to Grace's apartment was flung open and Bob came out with his shoulders hunched, panting like a dog. "How come, Grace? Did you tell him I wasn't a man, was that it? You must think I'm a real dumbbell, Grace, you think I didn't know where you was going and what you was doing. Anyone stupid enough to take some fat little tub of lard like you can have you, as far as I'm concerned." He thrust a finger at me. "You want to fuck my wife? Go ahead, everybody else does."

Grace stepped forward and the back of her hand came across her body in a blurring motion. She smacked Bob in the side of the face and he dropped to his knees as if shot. I made a brief attempt to pull Grace away, but she twisted out of my grasp and drove her foot into Bob's chest so that he fell backward into a sitting position.

"Whore," he cried, grabbing her legs and tackling her so that she came down on top of him. "Goddamn whore."

Grace was straddling him, punching away with her balled fists, when I left. The bathrobe that she had been so conscientiously holding closed had billowed open and she was exposed from the waist up. Bob lay on his back, whimpering and trying to protect his face from her blows, but not making any real effort to get away. I figured what they were doing was no longer any of my business and I headed for the stairs.

9

A chunky little man was sitting in the hallway when I got off the elevator on my floor. He wore a brown double-knit suit and was sitting in a wooden chair with a newspaper folded in his lap. The chair was tipped back against the wall so that its front legs were off the floor. He didn't try to hide the fact that he was studying me.

I paused in front of my door and looked back at him.

"You got business in that office?" he said.

"From time to time," I answered.

The man threw his newspaper to the floor and got out of his chair. "You Gronig?" he said.

I lost my head for a moment and admitted I was.

"Mellon, S.F.P.D.," he said, pushing his badge toward me. "Get up against the wall."

"What the hell for?"

Mellon, who was a good four inches shorter than I, tried to twist me around, but I wouldn't twist. He pushed me and I pushed him back. In a flurry of motion he yanked his gun from inside his coat and jammed it into my stomach. After that I started doing what I was told.

"Where's your piece?" he said, spread-eagling me against the wall and patting me down with his free hand.

"The last guy who pulled a gun on me took it away and he hasn't seen fit to give it back yet."

"Get inside and kiss the floor." He grabbed a fistful of my jacket and shoved me into my office.

"You oughta get a lock on that door," he said. Then, surveying the carnage, he added, "This place is a pigsty."

"You like it?" I said. "I got your mother to decorate it for me."

"Lie down, punk," he said, forcing me to my knees and then shoving me over with his foot.

I listened while he dialed my phone. I heard him tell someone his name was Mellon. I heard him say he had me in my office. Then came the part I liked best. "Don't worry, he's pushing dust with his nose."

When he hung up I said, "Who taught you to talk, Mellon, George Raft?"

Mellon hawked phlegm from deep in his throat and spit on my floor and that pretty much ended our conversation until my door burst open some fifteen minutes later and Artie Palmieri and two uniformed cops came charging in like the Dallas Cowboys football team. They stomped around my office for a while and then Palmieri came to rest on one knee next to my floor-level vantage point.

"You want to talk about it, Hector?" he said, breathing the stale smell of coffee and cigarettes into my face.

"Do I want to talk about what?" I said, lifting my face off the boards.

"Murder."

"Oh, of course, how silly of me. I mean, you did give me twenty-four hours." I rolled my eyes in disgust. "Well, the fact is, Palmieri, I did find out something and if you tell this bag of shit to let me up I'll spell it out for you."

Palmieri put a hand under my arm and hoisted me to my feet. He guided me over to the couch and dragged me down into a sitting position next to him. "Talk," he said.

It was awkward, sitting that close. I had to clasp my hands between my legs and lean away from him. "I found the woman who was in the motel room. I don't know what she's going by now, but her maiden name was Dumont. She's married to some rich old man and has an ex-con for a brother named Ferrell Dumont. He's a junkie and apparently did time for heroin. The sister says he's been living in an apartment house on Ellis, but when I chased him there he had already moved out."

"That's great, Hector. So what?"

"So Ferrell's the one who hired me. Seems he knew his sister liked to get involved in some extracurricular activities from time to time, so he got some guy he knew to meet her in a bar and take her up to this motel in Sonoma. He used me to get the pictures and then he was going to blackmail her. Problem was, the guy she was with got to like her and told her everything. Even told her who I was so that last night she came and found me. We were having a nice time until I told her what happened to Agnes Luck, and she bolted."

Palmieri listened to what I had to say and studied the knuckles on his hand. "And the guy she was with—I believe you called him Jonathan when you were talking to Cornell and me yesterday—what happened to him?"

I shrugged. "She said he took off before Ferrell found out what he had done."

Palmieri slipped his big hand inside his coat and came out with a photograph that he dropped in my lap. "Look familiar?" he said as I stared into the face of the man I had fought with in the motel.

"That's him," I said, nodding and trying to hand the picture back. But Palmieri would not take it.

"We found him last night," he said. "Did you see this morning's newspaper?"

I had a feeling like I was going down the Niagara River in a barrel. I shook my head.

"Do you ever read the papers, Hector?"

"Yeah, I do," I said defensively, "but this morning I had to make arrangements to get my car towed out of Hunter's Point and then I had to try and get a rent-a-car and—"

"Shut up, Hector, I don't give a good goddamn. You know who this guy is?"

Again I shook my head.

"He's the Reverend Jonathan Franklin of the Revelation Temple."

And now the river dropped out from underneath me.

". . . you know the Revelation Temple?" Palmieri was saying. "It's out there in the Avenues. One of them religious-type places the kids run away and join, causing the parents to go crazy. Any parents ever hire you to get their kids back from there, Hector?"

"It's not quite my line of work."

"Yeah, well, we found the Reverend stuffed in a trash can in the Tenderloin. Not more than a couple of blocks from here."

Every eye in the room was watching me. I'm a bright boy; it doesn't take me long to catch on. "Well, it was just so damn convenient," I said. "I mean, it was such a perfect place. I could hide him and walk back to my office without having to get in my car again and look for another parking space."

Palmieri lit a cigarette and watched me from behind a screen of smoke. His eyes were small and narrow. "That a joke, Hector?"

"Boy, have you got my number, Palmieri. You knew all this affluence didn't come from some crummy little trench-coat gig. You knew this was all a front for a secret assassination bureau."

Palmieri watched my hand sweep around the room and then his eyes came back and fixed on mine again. "We found a brown-handled thirty-eight Smith and Wesson revolver with a two-and-a-half-inch barrel in one of the other trash cans. If it sounds familiar, it should. It was registered to you. It had been fired and showed traces of blood and hair around the aperture." He paused. "The Reverend was killed by a thirty-eight from point-blank."

"And you figured an experienced old hit man like me thought you would never look in any of the other trash cans."

"Seemed kind of obvious," Palmieri admitted.

"That's how come we know it's you," Mellon jeered from out of nowhere, and immediately Palmieri signaled him to shut up.

"It seemed obvious enough that I thought I'd give you a chance to explain before I picked you up."

"All right, Palmieri, one step at a time. You know already that Ferrell Dumont held me up when he came to get the pictures. Now when somebody does that to a private detective, the chances are that he's going to know the private detective has a license to carry a gun and he's going to frisk him and take that gun away. Right? Well, that's exactly what happened to me. Dumont took my stubby out of my coat pocket and that's the last I've seen of either him or the gun."

Palmieri looked around for an ashtray, saw none within reaching distance, and tapped his cigarette on the floor.

"Where were you last night, Hector?"

"Passed out on the floor of my apartment."

"Been drinking again?"

"A guy named Jarmon came looking for the film. He hit me over the head in his enthusiasm." I bent forward and showed Palmieri the damage.

Palmieri grunted. "Who's Jarmon?" he said, and I told him the whole story about going out to Franz-Josef's home, finding my tires slashed, meeting Jarmon, and waking up to find Ferrell's sister.

"Everything else she told you was bullshit, but you still think she's his sister, huh?"

"Fair enough. I'll tell you what I know instead, and that's not much. One: the building guard did some mighty strange things the night I was held up and burglarized, he hasn't been seen since that night, and he's got a daughter he's been trying to get out of the Revelation Temple; two: I talked with some of Dumont's neighbors and learned that he attends meetings at the Revelation Temple as part of his parole program; three: Dumont was trying to use me as part of a blackmail scheme that involves the head of the Temple; four: that same head of the Temple has just been found murdered. Now mix that up with factor A: some unknown party has the film; and fact B: at least one other party is still looking for the film—and you've got a nice little cake for Mother."

Mellon made a farting noise with his mouth, but Palmieri ignored him and called over one of the uniformed cops, who had been rapidly writing down everything I said. He told him to find out what they had on a parolee named Ferrell Dumont. Then he stood up and motioned me to come with him. "I think it's time you and me paid our own little visit to the Revelation Temple," he said.

10

The Revelation Temple was buried deep in the City's Richmond district. I had known it when it had been a Catholic girls' school named St. Brigid's. Some cosmetics had been imposed on the old building, but even with a rainbow painted over the door it still looked like an old Catholic girls' school to me.

Thirty-fourth Avenue, where the Temple was located, was lined with vehicles when we arrived. People were clumped together on both sidewalks, talking with their arms folded across their chests and facing the general direction of the Temple entrance. When we slammed to a halt in a fire hydrant zone two people broke loose from a crowd standing around a television van and came scurrying toward us. The front scurrier was an earnest-looking young man wearing a blue sport coat and holding a microphone in his hand. Behind him came an older, curly-haired man with a television camera fitted over his shoulder.

"Inspector," the newsman said to Palmieri as we started

across the street, "any leads in the death of the Reverend?"

Palmieri would not stop walking and the newsman wheeled in front of me. "Officer, are you working with Inspector Palmieri on this case?"

I stopped and looked into the eye of the camera. The newsman snapped his fingers at his partner and jammed the microphone to within a few inches of my mouth. "My name is Hector Gronig," I said, "and I'm a private investigator located at seven-oh-three Market Street, San Francisco. I've been asked to assist the police in the investigation of this tragic—"

A big hand covered the microphone and shoved it away from me. Palmieri grabbed me by the arm and half dragged me toward the door of the Temple. "You ever tell another person you're assisting me again and I'll bust your goddamn head open," he hissed. "And then I'll sue your ass for slander."

Together we banged in through a door that bore some biblical inscription I did not have time to read, and then we were standing on the freshly washed tile floor of the main corridor. Palmieri's partner, Shepard, was there, looking distinctly out of place in a bright madras sport coat and talking to a long-haired Asian girl whose face was either temporarily distorted in grief or permanently ugly. Shepard knew me and pretended he didn't.

He greeted Palmieri, though, and said, "Ed, this here's Barbara Toy, she's the Temple's Minister of Information. I got that right?"

She nodded her head and looked from Palmieri to me. I smiled gently and she started to cry. Shepard gave me a very quick, very annoyed look and addressed himself to Palmieri again.

"Miss Toy says the Reverend left here last Friday to spend the weekend at the Temple's retreat in Sonoma. He drove back here on Sunday morning to perform services and then left immediately after they were over to return to the retreat. Apparently, he never arrived. The people at the retreat thought he had stayed down here. The people here thought he had gone back there." Shepard turned to Miss Toy. "I got that right?"

Miss Toy's head jerked erratically. She seemed unable to catch her breath and we all had to wait. Palmieri took the occasion to glance at his watch.

At last, Miss Toy said, "The first I learn that the Reverend is not at the retreat was when the police call me at seven o'clock this morning looking for Mrs. Franklin."

"Miss Toy's the liaison person," Shepard explained in his own inimitable fashion. "She lives here at the Temple and is in charge of handling all outside inquiries except unless somebody's asking about joining the Temple or going to one of their meetings or something."

"He got that right?" I said for no reason other than I was miffed at having been slighted by Shepard. Miss Toy nodded anyhow.

"Where is Mrs. Franklin now?" Palmieri asked.

Miss Toy said she was in her own quarters and could not be seen by anyone.

"She been sedated?" Palmieri said and Shepard answered that she had not. "Then I want to see her," Palmieri declared. After a second he inclined his head toward Miss Toy. "Please," he added.

We followed the Temple's liaison person into an office off the corridor which had probably once been the administration office for St. Brigid's. Miss Toy picked up a telephone and tapped out two numbers on the phone's pushbutton plate. She told someone at the other end of the connection that some police officers insisted on seeing Mrs. Franklin. There was a brief exchange in which she said that she had no choice and then she hung up, looking extremely worried, and told us to come with her.

We went from one corridor to another, passing a series of closed-door rooms and meeting not another soul until we stepped out into an open-air courtyard, off which was a small churchlike structure that was fairly ringing with the sounds of chanting voices.

"You are hearing the Temple members in prayer for the Reverend," Miss Toy said and I thought she was going to break down again, but she recovered and led us into another building, which appeared to have been the convent for teachers at St. Brigid's.

This building, like the one we had been in before, was spotlessly clean. But here carpets covered some of the tile floors and plants were stationed wherever daylight shined. We went up a flight of stairs and caught a brief glimpse of the second floor, where the rooms seemed to be more like apartments than the cells I imagined were behind the closely spaced doors on the first-floor level. We continued up to the third floor, where we entered a corridor covered with a thick red Persian carpet. Just two doors were visible here, one directly in front of us as we came off the stairs and one at the end of the hallway to our left. Both doors were of a heavy dark wood I did not recognize. Miss Toy knocked at the door in front of us and then looked at her knuckles. The door had been recently oiled.

A young man, his hair short on the sides and tufted on top, pulled the door open and gaped at us. His neck was too long, his ears were too large, his eyes were a dull green and he looked altogether dismissable. Miss Toy addressed him as Mr. Riordon.

"These are the police officers," she said, inclining her head toward the three of us. But Mr. Riordon only had eyes for me.

"Are you a police officer?" he said to me.

Remembering Palmieri's admonition, I shrugged non-committally.

"Peter!" Miss Toy implored.

He mumbled something apologetic and stepped back to allow us to enter the Franklins' private quarters, but I know he kept his eyes fixed on me. The quarters themselves were sparingly but ornately furnished. A white carpet was spongy beneath our feet. A walnut side table held two large, delicately painted Chinese vases. On the wall opposite hung a large silk rug with intricately woven panels and borders.

We passed these apparent treasures and moved into a spacious sitting room where a pinch-faced, nervous-looking man stood before a marble fireplace with his hands clasped behind his back. He was wearing rimless eyeglasses and a white robelike garment that he had belted over his fleshy stomach.

"Gentlemen," he said, almost springing forward to meet us, "I am Thomas Blodgett, First Assistant Reverend of the Revelation Temple."

Palmieri caught the hand Blodgett waved toward him and shook it for all of us. "Fine," he said. "Where's Mrs. Franklin?"

Blodgett turned to Shepard. "Inspector, isn't there any way we can avoid this? She really cannot be expected to submit to interviews until she has had some time to recover. I can answer almost any questions you have, so can't you just leave her alone for now?"

"Right," Palmieri said before Shepard had a chance to answer. "We'll get to you later. But for the moment we'd like to speak with Mrs. Franklin about some personal matters. So if you please . . . ?" He held out his hand palm up.

Blodgett sighed and turned to the big-eared kid. "Peter, would you get Mrs. Franklin. Again. Please."

Peter Riordon left the room and was gone for some time. I passed the minutes yearning for a cigarette while Palmieri watched the hands go around on his watch, Shepard scribbled in his notebook and Blodgett nervously moved up and down on his tiptoes. And then at last the door opened and a short, dark-skinned woman wearing a very simple burgundy-colored dress appeared on the arm of Peter Riordon.

I was surprised by Mrs. Franklin's age. She must have had a good ten years on the man I had seen in the motel. She was no longer beautiful, if indeed she ever was, but she had a certain handsomeness to her features. Her jaw was strong, perhaps too strong for a woman; her cheekbones were high and well defined; and her eyes were deep and infinitely dark. She wore her brown hair braided and wrapped tightly on top of her head in a way that was particularly becoming to a woman of her age and stature. It occurred to me as she seated herself on one of the low-slung couches that she may not have had the beauty of the woman in the motel, but she had twenty-five years of character on her husband's steel-eyed lover.

Palmieri stepped up and introduced himself. She nodded. He offered his condolences and she nodded again.

"I have some very personal questions I'd like to ask you, Mrs. Franklin, and you may prefer to answer them in private."

"These people are my family," she said and Palmieri, who didn't give a rat's ass anyhow, said all right.

"Mrs. Franklin, did you know where your husband was on Sunday, the day before yesterday?"

Thomas Blodgett went over and got in a position behind the couch where he could rest his hand on her shoulder. She did not seem to notice.

"I saw him at the services and then he left to go back

to the retreat around twelve or one o'clock."

"Was that the last you saw of him?"

"That's right."

"Mrs. Franklin"—Palmieri started off slowly and then hit her like a cannonball—"were you aware that your husband was having an affair with another woman?"

"Now just a minute," Blodgett yelped.

"Shut up," Palmieri told him softly, pointing a finger in his direction without actually looking at him.

Mrs. Franklin's eyes were on the floor. She raised them only as far as Palmieri's knee. "I don't believe you."

Palmieri moved his pointing finger to me. "Do you know this man?"

She looked at my face. "No."

"His name is Gronig and he's a private detective. He was hired to go to a motel in Sonoma on Sunday and take pictures of your husband and another woman."

"Is that true?" she said.

I told her it was.

"Let me see the pictures."

"I don't have them. The film was stolen from me that night."

"Then I think you're a liar and I'll continue to think so until I see the pictures for myself."

I cleared my throat, started to speak and then had to clear it again. "Mrs. Franklin, do you know a man named Ferrell Dumont?"

"You mean the parolee in my husband's consciousness class? Yes, I know who he is." She glanced up at Blodgett, who stared stoically straight ahead. "But I believe Thomas knows him better than I do."

"Well, I don't really know him all that well," Blodgett protested.

"I didn't mean to say that you did, Thomas. I just

remembered that I saw you talking to him after that meeting you covered for Jonathan a few weeks back. I sat in on that meeting and you asked him to stay after, don't you remember?"

"Well, yes, I suppose I did."

"What was it you were talking to him about, Mr. Blodgett?" I asked.

He waved his hand and then jerked it back as if it might be fluttering away from him. "Oh, it was just Temple-related matters," he said. We all continued looking at him until he went on. "As I recall, I was afraid I wasn't getting through to him with the weekly lesson and I just wanted to see if there was something he didn't understand." Blodgett glanced around the room. "I don't think Mr. Dumont comes to our meetings of his own volition," he added after a spell. "I didn't want him to be a disrupting force because of his inattention."

Mrs. Franklin stared up at him curiously, but she said nothing.

"So which was it, Mr. Blodgett?" I said. "Were you helping him or reprimanding him?"

"A little of both," Blodgett declared with a tight smile. He saw that Mrs. Franklin's eyes were still on him and he gave her a little pat of reassurance on the shoulder. When she kept watching him he said, "I suggested he might benefit from one of the Reverend's retreats."

"Oh? Did he go?"

"I don't believe he ever did. Did he, Mary?"

Mrs. Franklin turned to me. "He was supposed to go on this last one. But then he canceled out. He got sick at the last minute, I think."

"What was the relationship between him and your husband?"

"I know that Jonathan was trying to build a relationship

with him, but I think their contact was rather limited." She paused and twisted her fingers together. "Most of our members come here because they want to, because they are seeking the truth. But, as Thomas indicated, Ferrell comes because he has to. This whole thing of being responsible for parolees is a recent development for us. It was Jonathan's idea and he went down to the state Community Release Board and offered the services of the Temple to any prospective parolee. Ferrell Dumont was the first one we took and so I know Jonathan was very concerned about his progress. He was hoping to establish some sort of common ground with him so he would talk to him about things other than the Temple. Jonathan and he would talk football, or—or—"

"Or women?"

Mrs. Franklin looked at me sharply. "Knowledge of the opposite sex is an integral part of religious training."

"But you weren't talking about religious training, you were talking about—"

"I was talking about Jonathan's efforts to establish contact with a troubled young man so that we could lead him upon the true path of revelation as to the meaning of life and man's purpose here on earth." Her face suddenly got very brittle as she looked at me. "And despite your cynicism, my friend, Jonathan's approach was working. He told me that in recent weeks Ferrell has shown increasing interest in the Temple and its teachings and he's even introduced new innocents."

"Innocence?"

"Innocents, Mr. Gronig," Blodgett interjected, "is what we who are members of the Temple call those who are not."

"Can you tell me who it was that Ferrell introduced?"

"It is our right and policy not to discuss Temple business," Blodgett said.

"Do innocents ever get taken up to the Temple's retreat?"

"It's common."

"Was one of these innocents that Ferrell introduced a blond woman of about thirty years of age?" I asked.

"I do not know."

"Mrs. Franklin?"

"It may have been. I don't know."

"Was one of them a young woman named Patsy Moore?"

Blodgett started. "Why do you ask about Patsy?"

"I understand you had a run-in with her father not too long ago."

"Aha, now I see. That's your real purpose in being here, isn't it?" Blodgett turned to Shepard. "Really, officer, don't you think this has gone on long enough? It's only been a matter of hours since Mary learned of the death of her husband and now you let this charlatan come in here and badger us with a series of inane, irrelevant questions about our members. I think"—and here he stepped around the couch and took up a position with his weasel face just a few inches away from me—"that the only reason you're here is to try to get Patsy Moore away from the Temple."

Mrs. Franklin spoke up behind him. "If that is so, Mr. Gronig, you're too late."

"Too late?"

"Patsy Moore disappeared yesterday."

"Now, Mary," Blodgett said, turning to her, "she's only been missing for a short time."

"Since when?" I demanded.

"That's none of your concern, Mr. Gronig."

I ignored him and went directly to the figure on the couch. "Mrs. Franklin, Patsy Moore's disappearance is just one more in a series of unexplained events, all having to do with your Temple, that have been taking place since Sunday."

"See if you can explain yourself without slandering my husband."

"Last week Ferrell Dumont came into my office and hired me to take pictures of his wife cheating on him. I've since found out that the people I photographed did not include his wife but did include the head of a church who, I'm sure you will agree, is extremely susceptible to blackmail. I've also found out certain things which lead me to believe that Patsy Moore's father is very much involved in some way or another."

"And have you confronted Miss Moore's father?"

"I would if I could find him."

"And Ferrell Dumont?"

"I was hoping you'd help me out there."

"You mean he, too, has disappeared?"

"I'm afraid so."

"And I'm afraid you're very low on proof for a man who's spreading such slanderous lies."

"You don't know the half of it, Mrs. Franklin. Since Sunday, the motel where your husband was has been fire-bombed and its owner killed. The film I took has been stolen. Your husband's dead and we don't know who the woman was that he was with."

"The only thing we have to go on that tells us Jonathan was in that motel with another woman is your word, is that correct?"

"I'm afraid so."

Mrs. Franklin shook her head slowly from side to side. "You and your ilk are rotten and ungodly, Mr. Gronig. I've seen the kinds of things you do to my people, but I never thought that your fear and hatred of my husband were so great that they would carry over after his death. Was he such a threat that you have to disparage him even now?"

Mary Franklin's body began to quiver and suddenly she broke down and sobbed into her hands. Blodgett pushed past me and went to the couch, where he gathered her into his arms and began to speak soothingly to her.

"All right, Hector," Palmieri said after a minute, "that's enough."

Out on the street the big cop looked at me. "What am I supposed to do with you, Hector?"

"Why don't you try giving me a little support? After all, I'm busting my ass to help you solve the biggest murder case in the city."

"Always a wise guy, aren't you, Hector? I should take you down to the Hall just to put the bright light on you and let some of the guys beat the shit out of you."

"All you'd get would be bruises on your rubber hose."

"You wouldn't enjoy it, Hector. You can count your friends in the Department on your middle finger." He stuck his hands in his pockets and regarded the dozen or so people who were still milling around the outside of the Temple buildings. "She's right, you know. Inside, I mean. The only proof I got that this Reverend Franklin was involved in any hanky-panky is your word, and that ain't much when you figure what I got tying you in with two murders. I'll let you in on one thing, though. I don't think you killed nobody. I known you for a couple of years now and I checked around with the guys at the Hall and there's nothing in any report about you even firing a gun, much less hitting anyone."

"I appreciate it, Ed."

He shrugged. "All in all, I give you enough credit to realize you're not gonna fool us by stuffing no murder weapon in no trash can. Still, I gotta answer to some people, too, you know. I mean, there's a lot of guys who don't know your credit's so good. They think you got some client, maybe even this Moore guy you were talking about, wants to get his kid out of this wacko religious thing, and you go about doing it by blowing the head man away. These guys, they think I should haul you in. But me, I act like a good Joe and I bring you up here and let you run roughshod over all these people, grieving people, you know? I do it because I believe you're all right even though everywhere I look the only signs I see say Hector on 'em." Palmieri turned around and stared at the Revelation Temple. "Jesus," he said, shaking his head, "what kind of religion you think this thing is, anyway?"

"Artie, I don't know a damned thing about it. I never even heard of it until yesterday and I didn't know where it was until an hour ago."

Palmieri looked sad for a minute and said "Jesus" again. "This used to be a nice Catholic school. We used to have dances with the girls that went here when I was at Sacred Heart. They used to come to our football games when we played at Kezar Stadium. You ever play at Kezar when you were in high school? Boy, that was something. Specially the Sacred Heart–St. Ignatius game." He nodded toward the building. "These girls would all be there. I remember, 'cause one time there was a real bloodbath in the stands and some nun from here tried to break it up and she caught one right on the kisser. I'm sure the kid who did it didn't mean it, I mean he was probably just swinging away and that nun probably figured God gave her some kind of magic shield that was gonna stop the fists before they spread her nose from here to San Jose. But anyhow, that's what happened, and then we had a big school assembly the next Monday and we got bawled out like we all popped the nun. They canceled the next dance, I remember that. Jesus, I wonder what they would have thought if they could have seen their precious school now."

Palmieri stopped his reminiscing because Shepard was beginning to make little impatient noises from a few feet away.

"So here we are, Hector," Palmieri went on. "We came out to get some answers and all we got is more questions. Maybe that's a good thing, I don't know. But I do know that me and Shepard ain't gonna follow you all around the city while you tie a bigger and bigger knot that we can't never get undone. We start off, I say, 'Hector, you were in Sonoma, a lady was killed there, what were you doing there?' You say, 'Taking pictures for some dude. But some other dude stole the pictures, so I can't prove it.' I say, 'Hector, the guy you tell me you were taking pictures of just got killed with your gun.' You say, 'Hey, the first dude stole my gun.'"

"They're not just dudes, Artie, I've given you their names."

"Ed. The name is Ed. You give me some names, I'll admit that. With that and a pot I can take a piss. The names are for you to follow up, Hector, not me. I don't have to go running around giving you an alibi. I got you by the short hairs already."

"And if you book me that's all you've got."

"Hector, as far as I'm concerned, that's all I need. You're the main suspect in this case. For that matter, you're the only suspect. It just don't smack right, that's all. I mean, a private detective can't pull that trick in more than one or two cases or somebody's gonna put two and two together.

"So I've made a decision, Hector. I'm not gonna chase down your leads for you, but I am gonna leave you on the street to do it yourself. I want you to find that Ferrell for me. I want the lady friend and I want the security guard.

And most important, Hector, I want you to stay close, because any sign of wandering feet and I'm gonna change my mind about private detectives."

"Hey, Palmieri," I said as he started to walk away. "Who's going to pay me for my time while I'm doing all this?"

"Write it off to professional enhancement," he said and he and Shepard got in his car and laid rubber halfway up the street, leaving me to find my own way home.

11

Taxicabs, as a general rule, do not prowl the streets of the Richmond district looking for forlorn private investigators in need of a ride downtown. So when Palmieri and Shepard screeched off without me, I set out in search of a bus stop. I had to go to Balboa Street to find one and then I pitched camp waiting for the public transportation to find me.

To my surprise, a bus arrived within minutes. I boarded it with my hand in my pocket, and discovered for the first time that I did not have one cent in change. I was willing to overpay with a bill until I checked my wallet and found nothing but four of the fifties Ferrell Dumont had dropped on my desk an eternity ago. I had put too much effort into earning those fifties to waste one on a bus ride and so I mumbled something inane and backed my way down the steps to the street. The driver ripped the door shut, just missing the end of my nose by a sixteenth of an inch, and I let him know what I thought of his manners by banging my fist into the side of the bus as it roared by.

I was still cursing to myself when a blue Plymouth sedan pulled up next to the curb. I glanced at the driver and then did a double take. It was Thomas Blodgett and he was waving me into the car. I opened the door and slid in next to him.

"Can I give you a lift somewhere?" he said.

"Obviously," I said.

"It looks like it's about to rain."

In fact, the sky had begun to look rather threatening, but I knew that was not the reason Thomas Blodgett was offering me a ride. He had taken off his ridiculous-looking robe and was now wearing a rather limp brown suit that may or may not have survived World War II.

"Did you have something you wanted to tell me, Mr. Blodgett?"

"Why do you ask that?"

"For one thing, you started driving without asking me where I'm going."

Blodgett hit the brakes suddenly and we both were lifted forward out of our seats. "I'm sorry," he said. "Where do you want to go?"

"My office is on lower Market Street. That should give you more than enough time to clear up some of these matters you're afraid I may not understand."

Blodgett gave me a sidelong glance. Then he pursed his lips. "You're a perfectly dreadful human being, Mr. Gronig."

"I should probably join your church. By the way, will it be yours, now, or Mrs. Franklin's?"

"It's God's church, Mr. Gronig."

"Right," I said.

Blodgett looked at me sharply. He nearly hit a UPS truck when he did so and had to swing into the oncoming lane to avoid it. "I'm beginning to change my mind about you," he said, regaining control of the car.

"I'm not surprised. You were dead wrong before when you implied that I had come to steal your kiddies away from the Temple."

"I'm almost beginning to think you're a part of this whole scheme."

"Ah, what scheme is that, Mr. Blodgett?"

We sailed through a red light. "Well, there is quite obviously a scheme afoot to discredit Reverend Franklin, wouldn't you say?"

"Why bother discrediting him when he's already dead?"

"Because he cannot defend himself, of course."

"But you forget, Mr. Blodgett, I was there in the motel room with Franklin. There is no defense."

Blodgett cleared his throat. It sounded like two freight cars coupling. "How well did you know the Reverend, Mr. Gronig?"

"I didn't know him at all."

"But surely you had heard of him. Seen his picture, perhaps?"

"Look, Mr. Blodgett, I hate to knock your life's work and all that, but San Francisco is a mecca for true religions like yours. You could fill a convention hall with saviors in this city."

"Yes, but the Revelation movement is different."

"I'm sure it's uniquely divinely inspired."

"Among other things. We also have more money than most."

"You're about to tell me something, aren't you, Mr. Blodgett?"

"Nothing that isn't already well known. If you read the article in the *Chronicle* this morning on the death of the Reverend, you will have noted that we have in our Temple several hundred members, each of whom has turned over all his worldly assets to the Temple and each of whom continues to contribute to our community through the area of his or her expertise. Consequently, for example, our members with backgrounds in real estate have helped us to invest wisely in that area. We have made no secret of our success, Mr. Gronig. Rather, we consider it to be yet another manifestation of the propriety of our movement. God has looked down upon us and has smiled, and to each who has true faith there will come riches on earth as well as in heaven."

"Is that in the Book of Revelation?"

Blodgett looked puzzled. "Do you mean the Revelation of St. John the Divine?" he said, taking his eyes off the road again. "I don't think so."

"Hey, Blodgett, watch where you're driving, will you? And what's the point you're getting to?"

"The point is this: Did you get a good look at the man in the motel?"

I started to tell him that you get to see a man pretty well when you're punching him in the stomach, but I stopped. "No," I said, "the truth is that I saw him very close and very quickly. Things were happening awfully fast and he was not just standing there posing."

"The Reverend was a big man, Mr. Gronig, but he was by no means remarkable looking. I, myself, on more than one occasion have mistaken someone else for the Reverend from a distance."

"Look, Blodgett, the man I saw was the man the police identified to me as being Jonathan Franklin."

"The mistake is understandable, my friend. It was designed to fool you."

"Now hold on a sec—"

"Hear me out. You saw a man under the most arduous of circumstances. You saw him quickly and, I would suspect, through the viewfinder of a camera. Please don't take this personally, Mr. Gronig. I'm sure you are an excellent investigator, but you have said yourself, or at least you intimated, that you had never seen or heard of the Reverend before you had this encounter."

"That's true."

"Now the Reverend is dead and if we are not very, very careful we can expect every tabloid in the country to start carrying lurid headlines about the sex-and-death mystery of the San Francisco messiah. Are you following me? A young man gets out of prison. He is forced to join a temple group he has no real interest in joining as a condition to his parole. He discovers the temple is fairly affluent and has a devotion to its leader. He can't get the leader to do anything wrong, so he fakes a little scene in a motel and hires an innocent private investigator to substantiate it. He kills the leader and then he leaves the investigator—who thinks he's just reporting what he saw—to set us up for the big blackmail because he knows as well as we do that if those pictures get out and the Reverend is not alive to rebut them our whole movement could come tumbling down around us."

We slammed to a halt, jumped forward, braked hard again. Except for my wife, Blodgett was the worst driver I had ever seen.

With my feet pressed hard to the floorboards, my eyes straight ahead and my seat belt gripped with both hands, I said, "So let's assume you're right. Where does that leave us?"

"It leaves us, Mr. Gronig, with the likelihood that Mr. Dumont arranged everything so that he could steal your pictures from you and leave you with nothing but the memory of what you saw. It leaves him in a position to blackmail us."

"You have a suggestion where I might start looking for him?"

"Have you tried his father?"

The road ahead was clear and Blodgett's driving was improving to the point where I felt I could let one hand go free. "His father?"

Blodgett sniffed. "Mr. Gronig, if you're going to smoke I'm going to have to roll down all these windows and neither one of us is going to like that since it's now raining quite heavily."

"Shit," I said, cramming the as yet unlit cigarette back into its pack, and returning to my two-handed grip. "What were you telling me about Dumont's father?"

"Well, as I understand it, Ferrell's father is something of a minor fixture over in the North Beach area. A nightclub owner, I believe."

"Do you know the name of his place?"

"I'm afraid not. I was hoping you could—" He did not finish what he was saying.

Private detective work is not for the faint of heart. I saw my chance to get paid for the work I was doing and I leaped at it. "Mr. Blodgett, I make my living by finding people."

My living nearly ended as Blodgett snapped his head around to see if I was serious. "But you're looking for him anyway. Besides, Mr. Gronig, I have no money. Everything I have belongs to the Temple."

"Then the Temple should pay me. A hundred bucks a day plus expenses."

"You're unconscionable," he said.

"Think it over," I told him. "I can get out at the next corner."

Blodgett, being the Christian soul that he was, made an illegal left turn onto Market Street and stopped right in front of my building. I handed him my card as I got out; told him to call me when he had the money.

12

North Beach has two distinct personalities. They exist side by side in an unlikely marriage of old Italian culture and tourist exploitation. There is Washington Square with its family restaurants, its twin-spired Catholic church of St. Peter and St. Paul and its narrow little bars where old men still drink burgundy out of shot glasses; and then there is Broadway, electric monument to the female breast, where a score of nightclubs line a five-block stretch of road that fronts Chinatown like a neon wall.

At ten o'clock I was in an old Broadway restaurant called Verdi's. I had been there almost two hours, drinking cold Budweisers with an occasional shot of Wild Turkey. I was waiting for a man named Martinelli, the unofficial mayor of North Beach. Martinelli was what was known as a fixer. Everyone knew Martinelli.

The bartender, a knobby-boned cretin who seemed to move in slow motion, had worked out a pretty good routine with me. Every fifteen minutes he would stagger by and I would ask him if he was sure Martinelli would be coming in. He would lapse into deep thought that invariably terminated with him shrugging his pointy shoulders and saying Martinelli should be coming in any time now. Then I would flip him another quarter tip for the beer I had just bought.

By the time Martinelli did show up I was half bombed. I knew he had arrived because Knobby-bones came by and made a furtive little flip-flopping motion with his hand.

"He just took the table by the door," he whispered as he pretended to mop the bar in front of me.

I glanced at the mirror which hung along the molding and watched a middle-aged, three-hundred-pound man in shirt sleeves and stretch slacks slide into a semicircular booth that gave him a view of the entire room. He saw me looking at him in the mirror and I nodded, but he did not acknowledge me. He spoke briefly with the tuxedoed waiter and then the waiter nodded and stepped away.

"Right," I told Knobby-bones and threw him a buck. I went over and stood in front of Martinelli's table.

"Mr. Martinelli," I said, "you may not remember me—"

He squinted up at me. "That's right."

"—but I'm Hector Gronig."

He pushed his curly black hair out of his eyes so that he could see me better. "Who?"

"I used to work for Jerry Seales." I gave him my card. It was the third one I had handed out that day, a record.

Martinelli looked the card over and a flash of recognition lit up his eyes. "Jesus," he said, "you the one with the wife?"

I shifted uncomfortably. "I used to work for him when he did you a couple of favors."

"Sure, I remember you. You used to be a young kid,

right? Jesus, what happened to you? You don't look so good anymore."

I spread my hands and told him I had been in a hanggliding accident.

"Huh," he said thoughtfully. "You want to sit down?"

I took the seat across from Martinelli and the waiter came back and replaced the setting he had removed a minute before.

"What do you want?" Martinelli said.

"I need some information about—"

"Nah, I mean to eat."

The waiter was standing with his pencil and paper poised. He had a look on his face like I was about to explain to him the theory of relativity.

"I'll have fettucine with clam sauce," I said. "Side order of sausage. Tomato salad. Marinated mushrooms, you got any of those? Little garlic bread. Some pasta al brodo. Bottle of valpolicella, Bolla, if you have it."

Martinelli looked at me in surprise. "You hungry?"

"No. Just a little drunk."

Martinelli shrugged. "Change my order," he said. "I'll have the same thing as this guy. But none of them mushrooms."

The waiter left and I started to tell Martinelli what I wanted, but again he cut me off. "I like to make small talk first and then talk business later. That way it don't spoil the dinner if we can't get together. Okay?"

I nodded.

"Good," he said. "So tell me what happened with your wife and Jerry."

"Nothing happened. There was a little misunderstanding among the three of us, that was all."

"I heard he gave you a case that took you out of the state and when you got back you caught the two of them in the sack together. That right?"

"I told you, it was just a misunderstanding."

"That why you quit working for him?"

"Look, Mr. Martinelli, I haven't worked for Jerry Seales for a number of years and the little misunderstanding we had came a long time after I'd gone out on my own. So if you don't mind—"

"They together now? Jerry and your wife, I mean."

"Jerry lives with his family. My wife lives alone with our kids."

Martinelli finally picked up the curtness in my voice and opened his hands as if he was hurt by it. "Okay, you don't want to talk about it, fine. We'll talk about something else." And then all during the soup, the salad and the bread he told me anecdotes showing what a funny guy Jerry Seales really was. We were well into the sausage and the fettucine before Martinelli grew tired of the subject.

"So, you're out on your own now," he said, pouring off the last of the wine and signaling for another bottle. "You're probably having a tough go of it, by the looks of you, but you got a case and you done the right thing, come talk to Vito. I'm a good friend to have. Maybe I send some business your way."

Martinelli was quiet long enough to stuff his face with noodles.

"Only problem is," he said, "I got all these friends already. So you want something from me, there's not much room to work. Maybe a girl. You need a girl?"

"I want to know something about a guy named Dumont."

"Mmm," Martinelli said, shaking his head and rubbing his mouth with a napkin. "Carl Dumont, nice fella. Owns the Dirty Dawg."

I knew the Dirty Dawg. It was a medium-sized place

a couple of blocks up the street. "Does he have a son named Ferrell?"

Martinelli smirked and when he did so some of his noodles came slithering out of the sides of his mouth. He poked them back in with his fingers. "The lover boy," he said. "He in trouble?"

"Not much. Blackmail, arson, murder."

"You don't say?" Martinelli was interested. "He's into that much good stuff, maybe he can pay some of his bills."

"Come again?"

"Word's out on him, I heard. Somebody's after Ferrell and if he ain't got him already he will soon." The new bottle of wine came and Martinelli waited until the waiter was gone before he continued. "Seems Ferrell bought a losing piece of a heavyweight fight with borrowed money, and it wasn't the first time he did something like that, either."

"Wouldn't his father help him out?"

"Sure, but how many times he gonna do it? The damn kid's thirty-something now, ain't he? Look, I see you don't got the first notion of what I'm talking about." He went through an exaggerated charade of making sure nobody was listening as he leaned across his dinner with his fork in one hand and his knife in the other. "The kid's full of plans. He's always got some way of getting rich in a minute. Couple of years back he was gonna do it with cocaine, only he got torn a new asshole by some slant-eye down the street here in Chinktown. Couple of people lost some money on that deal. People you might know. People who were friends of his father and should have known better. So the way I heard it, the kid goes up a step and starts dealing a little junk and he's making some money, but he's not paying back the guys who got burned in the Chinktown deal. At least he's not paying them back fast enough for what they hear he's making. The reason, it turns out, he's taking the chickies up to Tahoe and losing it all there on the dice tables. Finally somebody got tired of waiting around and let it be known that Ferrell was gonna get hit. At this point, so I heard, the old man came into the picture and saved Ferrell's life by making some timely payouts. So instead of getting killed, Ferrell only got busted."

"Set up?"

Martinelli cocked one eye at me and for the first time said nothing. He spied the rest of his sausage and began to carve it. "Up to this point, Hector, everything I been telling you is common knowledge. Maybe it ain't the stuff you read in the papers, but it's stuff everybody who cares already knows. I figure you should know it if you're working this street. But beyond that I got nothing much to tell you except that somebody's out there again looking for Ferrell on gambling debts big enough to keep that boy on the endangered species list."

"You mind telling me who it is?"

Martinelli looked at my plate. "Jeez, they never did bring you your mushrooms."

"Mr. Martinelli, this is a real big case for me. The person I represent needs Ferrell Dumont for his alibi and I really could use some help."

"Why don't you go talk to Carl? He's a nice fella." He finished his meal and threw down his napkin. "He never should have married that dancer, though," he said, shaking his head until the loose flesh rippled all over his body. "She thought he had lots of bucks, he thought she had lots of sense. That's no way to begin a marriage. You scooping this check?"

"That's right."

"Sure. Bill it to your client." Martinelli gave me his hand and squeezed his great bulk around the semicircular table.

He was no sooner out the door than the waiter dropped a bill for $57.50 in front of me. I left him sixty bucks and figured I would never go back.

The Dirty Dawg Saloon did not occupy one of the better spots on Broadway. It was located west of Columbus between an occult shop and an all-night fast food stand with a sign that read UGI'S TACOS, CHINESE FOOD, SLICE PIZZA, FRENCH FRIES—BEST IN THE WEST.

The Dirty Dawg's own marquee featured a poodle raised up on its hind legs with its tongue lolling suggestively out of the corner of its mouth and a blinking eye made lecherous by a single yellow bulb. It was a smaller marquee than most of the others on the street and its message was simpler: THE DANCE OF LOVE . . . IN THE FLESH . . . RATED XXX.

Along the street I could hear the barkers chanting at the rubes who paraded by their doors with half-embarrassed little grins and half-disguised little side glances. The barkers called out, "Hey, don't be timid, folks. This show's got something for everyone. Bring the lady. Ladies love our show. Everyone loves our show. Best girls on the street." Then they would gesture with big arm-sweeping motions toward their doors.

In front of the Dirty Dawg the barker was a youngish man with pale hair, a wispy mustache and a hat that made him look like the Artful Dodger. He saw me coming toward him and, like one of those old-fashioned desk fans that pivot from one direction to another, he bowed away from a group of Japanese tourists bedecked in cameras and redirected his incessant banter at me. "Yes sir, you're gonna love it. Naked stewardesses cavorting right before your very eyes."

I stopped directly in front of him just as he was leaning to get the door for me. He straightened up. "The show's right this way."

"How long you been here?" I asked him.

"For eternity, man."

"How long's that?"

He shrugged. "I don't know. Two or three weeks. Why?"

"You know Ferrell Dumont very well?"

"Don't know him at all. Should I?"

"He's the boss's son, isn't he?"

"Wouldn't know if he was. Check with Gil behind the bar." He turned away from me with a tip of his oversized hat and went back to the Japanese tourists.

I pulled the door open without his aid and went inside to a room that was so dark I could barely see. What lighting there was came from little candles that sat in red glass bowls on tables arranged in a semicircle to face a darkened stage that ran along one entire wall. The wall opposite the stage was taken up by a bar that was also lit only by red candles. Badly taped rock music roared from the four corners of the room and drowned out the words of the miniskirted hostess who materialized in front of me.

"I'm looking for Mr. Dumont," I shouted, and with the words half out of my mouth the music was abruptly cut and every one of the dozen or so customers who sat waiting for the floor show turned to see what I was yelling about.

Suddenly the stage was flooded in garish, unscreened white light and a disc-jockey-type voice came over the speaker system and announced, "Ladies and gentlemen, the Dirty Dawg is proud to present the sweetest little piece of candy ever unwrapped, Miss Tootsie Popper!" The music picked up again, not quite as loud as before. There was a rustling of curtains at the back of the stage and out stepped a chunky but determined-looking brunette in a turquoise-trimmed cowgirl's costume. She did a fast turn or two and then began whipping her hat round and round her head.

I watched, fascinated, as she twirled the hat until it became a blur and then flung it behind her and began parading up and down the stage, kicking her left leg at one end and her right leg at the other. This went on for half a minute or so and then she threw herself into a couple of more spins and began easing her way out of her shirt. Once it was off she was very careful to throw it behind the curtain before she continued to dance in her skirt, boots and red tasseled bra.

"You'll have to sit down, sir," the hostess said and I told her again what I wanted. She told me to ask Gil at the bar.

I went over and sat on a low-backed, high-legged, plastic-covered bar chair and took another look at the dancer. She had wasted no time in getting rid of her skirt and now had her hands clasped over her head and was thrusting her body in and out like a wounded dolphin. Her eyes were fixed dead ahead, her mouth was formed into a little O and her body was whipping up hurricane breezes. I found the whole effect kind of appealing.

"What'll it be, bub?" a voice asked and I turned to greet a meaty-faced bartender with slicked-back hair and a massive body. His stomach hung considerably far over his belt, but it appeared to be hard as a rock. His white shirt sleeves were rolled back at the cuffs to reveal two immense forearms.

"A little information," I said.

"Dial four-one-one," he answered, without much humor.

"Where can I find Mr. Dumont?"

"He ain't here."

I took my card out and laid it on the bar. "Then be a good fellow, Gil, and run along and find him. Tell him it's about his son."

Gil did not like being talked to that way and he told me as much by staring at me for a long time before he picked up my card. It took him an even longer time to read it. I was sure I saw his lips move.

"Wait here," he said and lumbered off. I saw him grab a pony-tailed girl in a red satin mini-jumpsuit and point to the bar area and then he disappeared in the darkness. The girl angled by me and smiled. She was young and attractive, despite a mouthful of crowded teeth. I was just about to try my charm and wit on her when a customer thundered an order from the other end of the bar. She flashed what I took to be a smile of regret and moved on.

I looked over my shoulder at the stage, where the cowgirl was now bare-breasted and clawing at the sides of her turquoise panties. She was not taking them off, just dipping them down—first one side, then the other, as though they were stuck somehow in the middle. The blackness down and to the left of the stage suddenly and briefly opened up and Gil reappeared. He came lumbering toward me and threw my card down on the bar, where it immediately began soaking up water.

"Boss says he's busy and doesn't know anything about his son," he said and stomped away.

I slid off the stool, picked up the card, wiped it on my pantleg and put it back in my pocket. It was the last one I had with me. Gil was standing with his back to me, talking to the jumpsuited girl with the ponytail. Up on the stage the song had ended and the cowgirl, now clad only in a sequined patch, was busily scooping up her discarded clothing.

A new song, "Life in the Fast Lane," came ripping over the speakers and a behemothic redhead came scooting out from behind the curtains, fully clothed but thrusting her hips this way and that while the handful of customers hooted in appreciation at her apparent enthusiasm. In the meantime, I was making my way down the aisle to the black-curtained area from which I had seen Gil reenter the room. I slid the curtain aside as unobtrusively as I could and entered a tiny, well-lighted hallway which led to four separate doors.

I found what I was looking for on my second try. The door opened onto a small, crowded office. A lean-looking, oily-haired man was sitting behind a cluttered and messy desk, surrounded by cases of liquor. He was wearing a red-and-white checkered sport coat, a solid red shirt, and a white tie. Despite what Martinelli had said, I had no delusions that Carl Dumont was really a nice guy.

He was writing something when he looked up and saw me. He tensed in his chair and his pen dropped on the paper in front of him. "What do you want?" he said, speaking from a slit beneath a serpentine nose that started high up between his eyebrows and hooked and slithered the length of his face.

"You Dumont?"

"No," he said, but I knew he was lying.

"I'd like to talk with you about your son, if you've got a minute."

"Well, I don't." The nostrils on Dumont's snake of a nose flared just a little bit. The man had a dangerous quality to him and I was very conscious of it as I watched his small gray eyes searching me, looking for something I might not be showing.

"Then you better find time," I told him.

Dumont's eyes flicked and I responded automatically, shifting just enough so that I probably saved my life. What felt like a two-hundred-pound sack of cement tried to sever my head from my shoulders and drove me to my knees. I didn't black out, but for one second my mind left the room. Then my arm was wrenched up behind my back and I was jerked onto my feet again, not enough so that I could stand but in a bent sort of way so that I was groping for the floor with my toes while an oak branch of an arm clamped itself across my throat. Gil had arrived.

Dumont kicked himself out of his chair and came around his desk, planting himself in front of me. "Where the fuck they come up with an amateur like you?" he said. He was a tall man, two or three inches taller than I would have been had I been standing up straight, which I wasn't, being somehow balanced on Gil's big ball of a stomach so that I was half floating in the air and half hanging by my neck. Dumont leaned into my face. "What makes you think you can just walk into my place and strong-arm me for something my boy did?"

"I didn't think that," I protested in a high, squeaking voice as Gil winched his arm tighter around my neck. I tried to tell Dumont I was a private detective and was just there to help the kid, but he was not listening—or else I was not making sense.

He jammed a ramrod-straight finger into my chest. "Maybe you didn't notice in all your hotshot dealings, Ferrell's a grown man now. He's got his own brain, his own mouth, his own arms and legs. He's even got his own diddly, I heard. So you got a problem with him, you go find him. He owe you some money? You get it out of him, not me. You go back and tell Jimmy the Dog I said that. You tell him I assume he forgot this time." Once again Dumont jammed his finger into my chest and I went through an almost totally irrational vision of internal bleeding. "Now carry your ass out of here before I put my foot in it," he added and jerked his head at Gil.

The big man did the carrying for me. Like some absurdly coupling beasts, we crashed through the black curtain into the nightclub and bumped our way up the aisle. Somebody laughed and it affected me just enough to put up a futile struggle. Suddenly Gil jackknifed me over a table until my nose was two or three short inches from the rim of a thin-sided beer glass.

"If I ever see your faggot face around here again I'm gonna tear off your head and shit down your neck," he hissed in my ear. Then, with one hand sunk into the back of my shirt and one on the seat of my pants, Gil threw me toward the door.

I just had time to put up my arm to cover my face, but the only thing I hit was the sidewalk, where I landed with a painful, skin-scraping slide that took me all the way to the gutter. I looked up and the Artful Dodger was standing there with the door wide open, grinning down at me.

"No luck, huh?"

Anger swept over me as I got back on my feet. I put my head down and started to charge back in, but the Artful Dodger let the door slam shut and held his arm out straight. "I wouldn't if I were you," he said. "Gil will be standing right inside and he'll level you with his nightstick. No shit. Saw him do it to a marine last night."

"You tell him I'll get him," I blustered.

"I'll tell him," he said.

Blind with rage, my pants torn, my skinned hands and knees singing with pain, I backed off down the street. There was a lot of happy chirping going on around me and I turned to see some of the ubiquitous Japanese tourists busily snapping my picture. I shook my fist at them and they took pictures of that, too.

13

At two A.M. I was standing in the doorway of a Chinese grocery store at the corner of Broadway and Stockton, watching the entrance to the Dirty Dawg Saloon. The plan I had formulated in my liquor-besotted brain was simple enough; I was going to wait for Carl Dumont to emerge and then follow him home. Perhaps by bearding the lion in his den I could pick up a clue or two as to his son's whereabouts. Of course, I knew that Carl Dumont might just as easily exit by the nightclub's back door, but I was only one drunken investigator and I couldn't be both places at once.

I had been standing there about ten minutes when a little Chinese kid came by and offered to sell me hashish. I thanked him and said no and he offered to sell me benzedrine. "Beans," was the term he used. I told him to beat it. About five minutes after that a nondescript-looking Ford stopped at the curb and a cherubic-faced man asked me if I was "available." I told him he was in the wrong neighborhood and he drove off. A few minutes later he was back again, slowing down to a crawl and smiling at me, just in case I might have changed my mind. I told him the next time he came by I was going to throw a brick through his windshield and that made him speed up. And then something else happened and I lost all interest in circling perverts.

A woman came out of the Dirty Dawg. She had a ponytail and beneath her short jacket I could see that her legs were bare to within inches of her hip. It was the woman who had smiled at me in the bar.

I watched her as she headed up Broadway, waited at the light and then crossed the street in my direction. She did not come down Stockton where I was, but continued up the hill on my side of Broadway.

"Hey," I called impulsively, but she did not stop.

I ran after her, my feet slapping on the sidewalk, sending off little sprays of water from the day's rain. I was within a few feet of her when she suddenly whirled around. A blade flashed in her hand and I stopped cold. Seconds passed as I stood with my arms and upper body thrust forward, my stomach sucked in, my eyes fixed on that deadly piece of metal. A car horn honked and somebody shouted off in the distance and still we stood frozen.

"Say, don't I know you?" the woman said, and I relaxed.

"I was in the bar tonight," I said.

"Aren't you the guy Gil bounced around?"

I nodded.

"I was wondering about you. What was that all about?"

"Damned if I know. I was just trying to find a buddy of mine named Ferrell Dumont and his father got real upset with me."

She laughed, not a real laugh, but one which was meant to be friendly. "You just asked the wrong question, brother.

Ferrell and his old man aren't getting along so well these days."

"Well, I heard. . . . Look, will you put that knife away? My name's Hector and I just wanted to meet you. I'm not a mugger or anything."

She thought it over for a moment and then slipped the knife into her coat pocket. "A girl can't be too careful in this neighborhood at this time of night," she said. "A lot of my friends been mugged going home. Sometimes it's niggers, sometimes it's druggies, sometimes it's just weirdos who been to the show. You aren't none of them, are you?"

"I'm just a guy who thought you looked real good inside."

"How would you know?" she said and laughed. I laughed, too, but I was not sure why.

"I had a girlfriend," she went on, "and she had an admirer waiting outside for her. Offered to walk her home and after they'd gone about four blocks he grabbed her by the hair and dragged her into a back street. Beat her up and then pissed all over her. You don't want to do that to me, do you? You don't want to piss on me, do you?"

"Jesus, no. I just wanted to talk with you."

She laughed again. "That's good. But you'll have to try another time. I've got an old man at home who'll do more than piss on me if I'm not there by three o'clock."

"Meet me tomorrow then."

She spit neatly and cleanly between her teeth: a single squirt of saliva that hit off the curb and went into the street. "Sure. Maybe we'll ride the cable car and go to the Top of the Mark for lunch, huh? Look, why don't you just walk me to my car and I'll decide what we'll do from there."

So I walked her to her car, which was on Powell Street, and she told me what good luck she had had in parking in a particular lot that only cost three bucks and stayed lit all night. We talked about where she was from, which she claimed was Sacramento, and where she had been, which she claimed was Alaska, and what her lover did, which she claimed was nothing. Finally I got the conversation around to Carl.

"He's all right to work for if you stay on the right side of him," she said.

"Yeah, well, I guess I didn't."

"Like I told you, you asked him the wrong question."

"I must have." We walked in silence for a while. I asked her if she knew Ferrell.

"Not as well as I'd like to. He's some hunk."

The answer surprised me. I had not thought of Ferrell in those terms. "He's got a potbelly," I said.

Once again the woman laughed. This time it was genuine. "You men," she said, "you never have any idea what guys are good-looking and what aren't. I bet, I betcha it never even occurred to Carl that he had this dreamboat of a son when he brought Helen home to live with them."

"Helen?"

"Oh, you probably know her as Danielle."

"I do?"

"You know, Dancing Danielle, the Devil's Debutante. She used to be the headliner at the Dawg until Carl married her, which, believe me, was the biggest mistake of his life."

"Somebody else told me the same thing."

"Yeah? Well, it's true. Once she got married Helen refused to dance anymore and she was the only reason the place ever got any business. Carl came up with that stupid Dance of Love with one of the other girls and that faggot Gary who likes to twitch his little buns at all the men in the audience. That's gone over like a lead balloon, so he's looking for somebody else right now. He'll never find another Helen, though. She was the best-looking piece on the street. Not as famous as Carol Doda, maybe, but better looking."

Little synapses of excitement began taking place all over my body. I was stumbling onto a lucky break, and I knew it. "Did you like Helen?" I asked.

"Hell, no. She was a king-size jerk. But she made us all money, so I can't complain too much even if she did always think she was better than anyone else. Had to have her own dressing room, you know. But Carl fell head over heels in love with her and kept trying to get her to move in with him. She must have been counting on a meal ticket or something because she held out until he offered to marry her."

We reached the parking lot and found her car, a little yellow Pinto. She took out her keys and leaned back against the door, smiling at me. "Well, here we are," she said. "You're not going to get weird with me now, are you?"

I was somewhat surprised. "Hey, I just want to keep talking with you."

"You can talk from in closer," she said. She put her hands on my waist and guided me in so that we were touching along the length of our legs.

"Hasn't Dumont's marriage worked out?" I said.

The woman looked disappointed in my choice of subjects, but she answered, and as she did she began slowly easing her thighs apart. "Well, they're still married, if that's what you're asking. But after Helen quit her job we all knew what was going to happen next. I mean, big dumb Carl is probably the only guy in the world who didn't realize that it was not smart to leave a piece like Helen home all day with a hunk like Ferrell."

Her fingers were gently moving through my hair, softly massaging my scalp. "Be careful," I told her. "I got banged up back there."

She touched the scab wound Jarmon had left me. "I know," she whispered.

"So what happened between Helen and Ferrell?" I asked.

Her fingertips were flirting with the edges of my cut and I could hear her breathing intensify as she moved her lips close to my ear. "All I know," she said, "is that Ferrell came into the Dawg one afternoon about a month ago and him and his father got in a tremendous fight. They were back in Carl's office and some of us accidentally on purpose were working down in that area. Ferrell was yelling and I heard him swear that he had never touched her—and I figured *her* was Helen because I mean, like, who else? And then Carl was yelling back that he knew what had been going on and that he wanted Ferrell out of his house that night. He said if Ferrell ever went near her again he'd break his neck. Then Ferrell went storming out making all kinds of threats about what he was going to do to Carl. We just pretended like we were working and weren't paying any attention."

She made direct contact with the wound and I flinched. "Hey, what are you doing?" I said.

"Oh, let Mama make it better," she cooed. Bending my head forward, she kissed the sore and open area. Then she kissed it again and I knew her lips were spread wide apart. I jerked my head away and looked down at her, but her eyes were closed and she smiled as she rotated her hips into mine.

"Were Helen and Ferrell having an affair?" I said coldly.

"Now don't be like that, sugar. You got to give me a little something if you want something from me."

I pressed in closer. "Like this?" I said.

"Mmmmm." She arched her head prettily. She lifted her feet off the ground and I was pressing so hard against her that she was hanging suspended, bolted through her

116

pelvis to the side of the automobile. Somehow her fingers got inside the ripped leg of my pants and were groping about.

"This Helen," I said breathlessly, trying to keep her dangling off the ground and yet at the same time keep my bloody knee out of her reach, "she wouldn't happen to be blond and blue-eyed, would she? About five feet six?"

Our rubbing came to an immediate halt and our little structure of human limbs collapsed. "Who you interested in, brother? Ferrell or Helen or me?"

I chuckled. I laughed. I knew who Helen was. "Where can I find her?" I said.

I got a shove for an answer. "Well, fuck you," my friend with the ponytail and the weird predilections said.

"Hey, nothing personal," I told her, moving in close again. I put my hands on either side of her jaw so that even in the dim light of the parking lot she could see the torn flesh of my palms. "I've got to find Ferrell on some business and the only way I think I can get to him is through his stepmother. The way you talk, they must have been close enough for her to know where he is, don't you think?"

She lifted her shoulders begrudgingly. "I suppose," she said.

"Doesn't mean I don't like you," I said. "Fine little piece of ass like you." I put my hands inside her coat and she melted into my arms. "So where do you think I can find Helen?" I said after a moment.

"They live in Marin someplace, but I don't know where."

"Damn," I said and we both pulled away from each other. "Do you think Carl's still at the club?"

She shook her head. "He was leaving the same time I was, but he wasn't going right home. He was going to Marvella's for breakfast."

I looked at my wristwatch. Apparently it was the wrong thing to do.

"What, are you looking to see how many strokes you can get in before you gotta run and catch Carl?"

"No," I protested, "it's just that you said you had to get home before three."

"That gives us time to get in the back seat," she said.

I looked at my watch again. It was nearly half past two. It would take fifteen minutes to get across town to Marvella's, if Carl Dumont had left the Dirty Dawg around ten after two—

"You scumbag," the woman suddenly spit at me.

"What?" I said.

"You're just like everyone else in this city, you're a fucking queer, aren't you?" She began fumbling with her car keys.

"Hey, no, I was just trying to figure out if I had time."

She flung the door open hard enough to make the whole car shudder. She turned back to me with eyes that were red with rage. "Oh, that's just great," she said. "My God almighty, I can wake up my old man at home if all I want is a wham-bammer."

"I'm really sorry," I said.

A look of contempt exploded across her face. "I guess," she said. "Sorry excuse for a man." And then she roared off with her left hand out the window and her longest finger thrust upward in a farewell salute.

I didn't care. I didn't want a woman who was into scabs anyhow.

14

Marvella's was an all-night eatery known for serving large portions of not particularly good food at not particularly expensive prices. It was a thirties café that had managed to survive the decades without changing much beside the songs in its jukebox. It had a hook-shaped counter and a row of red plastic upholstered booths along one wall. I had never been in there when there had been any waitress other than a four-hundred-year-old woman named Peaches. Not only was she not much to look at, but she was quite possibly the slowest waitress in all San Francisco. Her normal gait consisted of a series of shuffling steps followed by a pause to catch her breath and then another brief flurry of shuffles.

Rumor had it that she was the mother of the cook, a thick-armed, bald-headed man named Harvey who had been a boxer of no repute, but who had served time for beating the living daylights out of a San Francisco cop. Harvey had once been knocked out in Madison Square Garden by Isaac Logart, but now he spent his life in front of a fry stove glaring at customers through a rectangular slit in the wall. He was supposed to have a speed bag set up in the kitchen, but I had never heard or seen it. Then again, I did not hang around Marvella's that often.

But at a few minutes before three o'clock on a Wednesday morning I stood happily on the sidewalk, my hands thrust deep in my coat pockets to ward off the night chill, looking through Marvella's plate glass windows at my friend Carl Dumont. He was sitting at the long side of the counter, sideways to the door, his back to the red plastic booths. He had a plate full of fried eggs and sausage and a huge mound of toast in front of him. In one hand he gripped a half-empty glass of milk and every now and then he would throw some into his mouth along with the eggs and sausage and toast. He fit in real well at Marvella's.

What I now understood was that Carl was as much a victim of this situation as I was. His obvious ignorance of my identity told me he had no idea what his wife and son had been doing, whether it involved conspiring against the Temple or plotting against each other. My knowledge, limited as it was, gave me an advantage I fully intended to exploit. All I needed was to set the situation, and Peaches helped me do that.

She meandered over in front of Dumont, waving the coffeepot in his face. He shook her off and she looked crestfallen. They exchanged a few words and I walked in.

A little bell tingled, but nobody looked up. The grizzled old man in the porkpie hat, plaid shirt and plaid hunting jacket, sitting two seats down from Dumont, ignored me. So did the person seated next to him, a round-headed dwarf-sized woman who was eating a doughnut with a knife and fork. Behind them, in a booth in the far back, a junkie remained motionless with his legs crossed and his face resting on his uppermost knee. Drool was running down his chin and dripping into a puddle on the café floor. A cigarette burned between his fingers, running an ash at least two inches long. Across the booth from him sat a skinny, ratty-haired woman and a pomaded black man in a green topcoat. They were laughing together and casually picking food off the junkie's plate. He obviously didn't care and, from what I could see, their own plates were already licked clean. These five and Dumont were the only customers in the restaurant except for a young kid who sat alone in the front booth with a Coke and a piece of lemon meringue pie. Compared to the rest of the assemblage, the kid was a veritable prince.

I took a counter seat directly opposite Dumont. Between us were two countertops and four or five feet of space, some of which Peaches was taking up as she chatted with Dumont. She heard me behind her and lurched around with her coffeepot held high. I nodded and she poured me a cup three quarters full. I told her I needed a spoon and she wandered off, presumably to find me one. When she moved Dumont's eyes locked on mine.

"You got milk all over your upper lip, Carl," I said. "You look like a five-year-old."

He put his glass down and wiped his mouth.

"That's better," I told him. "Tough guy like you drinking milk, I'm surprised to see it. You must have an ulcer or something. You get that worrying about your boy or your old lady?"

Dumont hunched his shoulders and rested both his forearms on the counter. "Didn't I tell you what would happen if you bothered me again?"

"Yeah, but the simple truth is, I didn't believe you, Carl. Besides, I got some things I thought you might want to hear."

"I doubt it," Dumont said smugly, glancing from side

to side but looking at no one in particular. I grinned at him maliciously. I was remembering the ignominy of being dragged out of his bar and I was feeling spiteful. After a moment Dumont wiped his mouth again, even though he did not need to do it.

"Don't you want to hear the story of the Reverend Jonathan Franklin, Carl? Great story. All about those good old American pastimes: sex and death."

"Why don't you beat it, chump, before you get hurt?" Dumont picked up a piece of toast and began swabbing furiously at the yolk on his plate, but he never stopped watching me. "Chump," he repeated, and I just smiled at him.

"Seems there was this young man, fresh out of prison and living with his daddy and his daddy's new wife. The young man ran into some trouble over gambling debts. That wouldn't have been so bad, his daddy might have bailed him out just like he always did, except that Daddy found the young man fooling around with his wife and threw him out of the house."

Heads were popping up all around the restaurant. The dwarf woman had almost crawled onto the counter to get a better look at Dumont.

"We don't have to talk here, you know, Carl," I said. "I've got my car outside and we could go for a little ride."

Dumont tapped his fork on his plate and said nothing.

"Suit yourself." I shrugged. "You don't mind everybody knowing you're a cuckold."

"Keep it up, pal," Dumont said, threatening me with his fork, "and I'm gonna come over there and cram your ass into your coffee cup."

"Now, boys..." Peaches moaned.

"But just think about that poor young man, Carl; living alone in a sleazy apartment, no job, no money, Jimmy the

Dog looking all over town for him. The poor guy couldn't hide out forever. He had to get some money someplace to get Jimmy off his back. So what was he to do?"

Carl Dumont was back to tapping his fork on his plate. He was so tense I could see the muscles throbbing in his face.

"Right you are, Carl," I said cheerily. "He went to see good old Stepmon and asked her to give him a helping hand . . . or whatever. Seems the young man was attending meetings at one of these local cult churches and he'd managed to get pretty tight with the head man. Found out the Reverend had an eye for the ladies, he did, and of course the young man had just the perfect lady for him. After all, Helen's certainly good-looking and God knows she's willing enough."

Dumont's fork bounced off his plate and went clanging to the floor. In the silence of the restaurant its ringing seemed very loud. When it stopped, Carl Dumont hunched forward. "Bullshit," he said.

"Don't say bullshit to me, Carl. I was there. I'm the one Ferrell hired to take the pictures."

It was as though Carl Dumont had just been slapped. He sat up ramrod straight and repeated what he had said before. "Bullshit."

I shook my head. "I saw her, Carl, the bait in Ferrell's blackmail scheme, up there in that motel room in Sonoma, flopping around underneath that big old bareass minister—"

Maybe it was my tone of voice that brought Dumont bounding off his chair. His quickness surprised me and I reacted with what I had. I threw my coffee in his face.

His hands flew to his eyes and he backed up, roaring. I could hear shouts of surprise from the rest of the people in the restaurant as I got up from my seat and slammed my fist into his stomach.

Dumont was soft where he should not have been. He staggered and dropped to his knees the way a horse will when shot. I brought my own knee up and cracked him in the mouth.

"Boys, boys, you stop that now," Peaches pleaded.

"Bash the bastard!" a female voice screamed and I guessed it was coming from the ratty-haired woman in the booth at the back.

Blood was dripping from Carl Dumont's mouth and hitting the floor with popping sounds as he crawled forward and made a grab for my leg. I stepped back, faked a second step and kicked him. He sagged and I grabbed him by the hair. I pulled his head so far back that his mouth sprang open and gargling noises came out of his throat.

"I want to see that kid of yours, greaseball, and if I can't see him then I want to see your wife. Understand?"

But Carl Dumont didn't answer. His eyes were rolling uncontrollably around in his head.

I felt something sharp stick into my back and I turned to find Harvey glowering at me. Between the two of us was a carving knife held as flat and steady as if it were lying on a tabletop.

"Leave him be, Harvey," the ratty-haired woman called out. She was chorused by an incoherent series of approving noises from her pomaded companion. Even the junkie got into the act. In the general excitement his body inclined a little too far forward and went crashing to the floor, where he lay in a semifetal position with the butt of his now ashless cigarette still clutched between his fingers.

Harvey, the ex-pug, surveyed the scene with equanimity. Silently he jerked his head toward the door.

I hoisted Dumont to his feet and removed his wallet

from his back pocket. I got out a five-dollar bill and threw it on the counter, then I stuffed the wallet back into his pants and shoved Dumont out to the street. I heard someone follow me through the door and when I spun around the ratty-haired woman was standing there.

"Hey, you do nice work, buckeroo," she said.

"He and I are even tonight. He had me beat on once already."

"You're quick," she said. "I like that. I get off on guys like you." She danced around and mimicked the way I had kicked Dumont. "Pow," she said.

"Jesus," I said. I looked closely at her. She was grinning and it was a nice grin. It made her look vibrant, if you did not notice how dirty and disheveled her hair was. Her smile made her fine blue eyes light up, but it was not enough to make her an attractive woman. She was, in fact, barely a woman at all, being only about nineteen or twenty years old and weighing no more than one hundred pounds. She was wearing boots with skin-tight blue jeans tucked into them, a turtleneck shirt and a crocheted cape. She looked cold from the night air.

"What the hell are you doing out this late?" I asked her.

"Getting by, getting high . . . whatever it takes."

"You want to earn some money?"

"Always."

"Can you drive?"

"Like a Beach Boy," she said. Whatever the hell that meant.

I pointed to my rented Chevrolet and handed her the keys. "Help me get this bozo in the back seat and then head for the Golden Gate Bridge. Keep away from any place where there might be people."

"At this time of night?"

"There are a lot of weirdos in San Francisco. You're out, aren't you?"

Together we dragged Dumont across the sidewalk and threw him on the back seat of the car as if he were a pile of dirty laundry. He hit and rolled onto the floor, where he lay without moving while our ratty-haired driver, who said her name was Joyce, raced from red light to red light. As she tore over the hills of Pacific Heights she kept up a constant barrage of chatter, complaining that there was no FM radio in the car, singing along with whatever music she happened to find on the AM band, complimenting me on what a bad dude I was.

We went hurtling down toward Lombard Street, took the corner onto that brightly lighted strip, and went roaring past the Palace of Fine Arts. If this was Beach Boy driving, I wanted less of it and I told Joyce to slow down as we approached the Golden Gate Bridge. She cruised through the no-toll booths at fifty miles per hour.

As we drove into the fog that enshrouded the bridge, Dumont stirred. I reached down, grabbed him by the back of the red-and-white checked sport coat and tugged him into a sitting postion next to me. "You want to tell me where Ferrell is now?"

"My face," he moaned. "My goddamn face is on fire."

"Take your hands away and let me see." I flicked on the overhead light and then shut it off again. "You're in for some blisters, but I'd say you have an even chance of living. You want to tell me where your son is?"

"I don't know," he said. "He's been gone about a month."

"Then we'll go see your wife. I can guarantee you she's seen him more recently than that."

"Yeah, well, I don't know where she is, either." Carl Dumont was fast becoming his old nasty self again.

"You wouldn't want to tell me where you live, would you?"

"Daly City," he snarled. Daly City was in the opposite direction.

I cuffed him right beneath the cheekbone with the heel of my hand and he pitched forward into the well behind the front passenger's seat. He thrashed around and tried to come back at me, but I planted my foot on his spine while his head was still down on the floorboards and told him I was going to blow him apart if he tried to move. He did not ask me what I was going to use to blow him apart and I didn't tell him, but I kept my hand bunched in my coat pocket in case he could somehow see from the position he was in.

My driver was delighted. I ordered her to keep her eyes on the road, but she kept looking back over her shoulder while I busied myself maneuvering Dumont so as to get his wallet out of his pocket. I read his address off his driver's license and told Joyce to take the Larkspur turnoff.

Dumont groaned.

"What's that you say, Carl?"

"I'm getting sick," he muttered.

"Be my guest. We'll just roll down the windows."

"You bastard," he said. "You never would have taken me if I wasn't drunk."

"It's a poor workman who blames his tools," I said and laughed at him. "I'm downright shitfaced myself."

15

Larkspur is a quaint little town of two- and three-hundred-thousand-dollar homes that prides itself on maintaining its charm by forsaking streetlights in favor of trees. For all I know, there is a city ordinance against cutting down trees in Larkspur. Trees are everywhere. They grow through holes in people's roofs. They dictate the paths of sidewalks. They are even left standing in the middle of the road, which is all very fine provided you are not looking for the names of streets and the numbers of houses. Dumont refused to be of any assistance whatsoever, even though I alternately offered to let him sit up and threatened his life with murderous pokes of my foot.

By the time we found his house there was a hint of light in the eastern sky. It was a large, boxy redwood place with plenty of odd-shaped windows. It sat on top of a hill and was accessible either by climbing a long wooden staircase that ran up in a zigzag pattern from the driveway, or by scaling a pathless, underbrush-covered slope. A single light was on and that was over the front door. One car was in the driveway, a red Audi.

"All right, Carl," I said. "We're home."

But he did not budge. I tried pulling him up, but he was like dead weight. Finally I leaned across the seat and opened the door and pushed him onto the macadam. That was a mistake. Dumont rolled over as I was pushing him and hit on his feet. Before I knew what he was doing he was racing for the stairs.

I wrenched open my own door, started around the car after him and ran smack into Joyce. "Get the hell out of my way," I said, flinging her roughly to one side and running for the stairs. Dumont was already at the first landing.

By the time I was there he was at the second. I could see at least one new light on inside the house and I could hear Dumont yelling for Helen.

I turned at the second landing, took the last ten or twelve steps that led to a cement pathway, saw the front door at the end of that pathway slam shut, and threw myself onto the ground. Scrambling forward on my belly, I slipped into the shadows and waited for the door to be flung open again and the firing to start. Something landed beside me and I jumped, but it was only ratty-haired Joyce. She was grinning as if we were playing some kind of game.

"What the hell are you doing?" I whispered. "He's got a gun."

"Well, so do you," she said, breathing heavily.

"The hell I do."

"But in the car—"

"You don't think I wanted him to know that, do you?"

"Yikes," she said, but she did not stop grinning.

Lights were going on and off all over the house and then a whole new set of noises, thrashing noises, started up. "Go to the other side of the house and see what that is," I said, and Joyce, like a fool, did as I asked.

For a brief period I heard two sets of noises and then a car door slammed and an engine roared.

"Goddammit, someone's getting away," I shouted to no one and, being almost as big a fool as Joyce, ran for the front door.

It was locked, as I knew it would be, but there was a rock about the size of a basketball at my feet and a window about head high near the door. Without even thinking, I threw one through the other, only to realize as soon as the window shattered that I was not about to hoist myself through any jagged glass opening.

I turned to run after Joyce, but suddenly the door was yanked open and I froze. I waited for an explosion, waited for a bullet to tear its way into my back, and when neither thing happened I looked over my shouder. Standing framed in the light of the doorway, holding a rifle aimed in my general direction, was not Carl Dumont but his wife, the vamp of the Good Luck Motor Hotel.

I faced her and slowly raised my hands. The barrel of the rifle moved and I tensed. "Come quick," she said urgently. "I think he's gone."

I was mutely following Helen inside when Joyce came pounding around the corner.

"He must have jumped halfway down the hill, boss, because he was already—" She stopped when she saw Helen and her rifle.

"Who's this?" Helen demanded.

"Nobody," I said.

"Then tell her to wait out here."

I told Joyce to wait in the car.

"Bull-*shit*," she said, heavily accenting the last syllable. "I want to go with you."

"Well, you can't. Go listen to the radio."

"I've still got your keys," she said, holding them out in front of her. "Maybe I'll just drive off."

I was in no mood to be teased. I ripped the keys from her hand. "Wait any place you damn well please," I told her and walked into the house with Helen.

"You certainly have a remarkable way with women," was all Helen said as she led me through a den outfitted in imitation leather chairs arranged to face a big screen projection television. We passed into a brightly wallpapered kitchen before I responded.

"Yeah," I said, looking around at every hidden corner and closed door where someone could be hiding. "That's what my wife used to say."

"Oh?" Helen said, putting a pot of water on the stove. "I didn't know you were married."

"Hey, what is this?" I said, sweeping the pot from the stove and sending it crashing to the kitchen floor. "I'm not here on any goddamn social visit, you know. If you think we're going to sit around and drink coffee while your old man takes off to God knows where, you've got another think coming."

Helen was furious. "Look what you've done to my linoleum, you sonofabitch." She grabbed a sponge from the cabinet beneath the sink and began mopping up the water that had spilled.

I got down on the floor next to her. "Where's he going, Helen?"

"I save your life and all you do is bust up my house," she said. "Just do one more bit of damage, Hector, just try it."

"Well, you'll pardon my ignorance, I'm sure. But so far I've only had the pleasure of your company three times— one time when a guy took a punch at me, one time when you kicked me in the balls, and now, when you pull a gun on me. I'm sorry, I didn't recognize those as lifesaving gestures. It must be my paranoia."

"I wasn't pulling any gun on you. I had it on him, and I wouldn't have had to do that if it wasn't for you."

Helen gathered in her housecoat and dropped into a sitting position. I was still on my hands and knees facing her and I suddenly felt as ridiculous as I must have looked. I got into a sitting position of my own and the seat of my pants promptly began soaking up the water Helen had missed with her sponge. "What's that mean?" I said.

"Oh, I suppose it was just a coincidence that you two showed up here together. You didn't tell him a thing about me and Jonathan in the motel, did you, you damn trouble-maker."

"I've got a few names I can lay on you too, Helen. Like 'liar,' for one. What's all that crap you fed me about your brother blackmailing you?"

Helen started to come back at me and then stopped. She looked at the sponge she had in her hands and threw it on a nearby table. It landed next to the rifle she had been carrying when we first entered the room and she stared at that for a while. She shifted her eyes above the table to a cuckoo clock that was nailed to the wall and she probably would have looked at every other object in the room if I had not grabbed her wrist and shaken her.

"Hey, watch it," she said, pulling away. "Why should I tell you anything?"

"Why? Because I'm sitting here on your floor at four o'clock in the morning, ripped, bloody, dirty and determined to know if only so I can go home to bed, wake up tomorrow and face life like any other human being who doesn't have to wonder what's going to happen to him the next time he doesn't have an answer to questions he knows nothing about."

"All right," she said, glaring at me from a face that could have been carved from marble for all the warmth it showed. "You want to know the whole story, it goes like this. I married that bastard Carl as a way to get out of dancing. Only all these nice things I think he's got, the club, the house, the car, turn out not to be his. They're all hocked. Everything he's got is owed to or already belongs to somebody else. He works seven days a week, so we don't go anywhere. He's got no money to give me, so I can't go anywhere. All the stuff I been waiting all my life to buy, he tells me we can't afford. On top of that, he sticks me out here in the country with no friends and no neighbors and nobody to talk to except his goddamn kid, who sits around the house doing nothing all day long. Then some asshole gives Carl the line that there was more than just conversation going on between me and Ferrell and Carl comes home in a rage and kicks Ferrell out. Just like that. Never asked me a question, never let Ferrell tell his side of the story. Just said he knew what was going on and told him to get out."

Helen paused long enough to see if the unjustness of what Carl had done was registering. "So Ferrell went off and lived in that dump I told you about. I knew he was bitter, but I didn't think he was bitter at me because I hadn't done anything. Then one day he calls and asks me to go to one of his meetings with him, and I'm so bored I go. He introduces me to the guy running the meeting, who turns out to be Jonathan. We talk and the two of them suggest I spend a day up at the retreat with them. I said fine, I'll go. Only when they come to pick me up Jonathan was by himself. This much of the story I told you before was true, I thought it was just a natural thing that we ended up at that motel until you showed up."

I raised my eyebrows. "Oh, really? Well, somebody

had to tell Ferrell you were going to be there and I have a hard time imagining the Reverend Jonathan Franklin doing it."

Helen stared into her hands. "The day you saw us, it wasn't the first time we had been there. We had gotten to the point where we used to meet whenever Jonathan went up to his retreat on Sunday afternoons."

"And you told Ferrell this?"

Helen Dumont nodded. "That's how we knew it was Ferrell who had sent you."

"And how did you figure out who I was?"

Helen looked up quickly but didn't answer.

"This is where we broke off before, remember? This is where I have to start covering my crotch because the questions are getting rough again."

"I'm sorry about that," she said. "You had caught me in a lie about the license plate and I couldn't think fast enough to come up with any other story."

"What was wrong with the truth?"

"The truth was . . . I didn't know what the truth was. Jonathan was the one who found you. He just gave me your name and office address and told me to get the pictures, no matter what. I had the one story that Jonathan and I made up together, and that was it. Then you started telling me all these other things that were involved and I got scared and ran. I came back here and pretended I was doing what Carl was doing—waiting for Ferrell to show up with the pictures. I thought I was safe until just now when he showed up with you. Then the only thought I had was to keep him from killing me."

"I got the impression from what you said before that it was me Carl was going to kill."

The hard edge returned to Helen's voice as she threw up her hands in exasperation. "Look, Hector, I know you're a private detective and all, but try not to be such a nerd. I woke up from a sound sleep with the two of you pounding up the stairs. I took one look and I knew Carl had lost control. When he loses control he goes crazy, and then everybody better watch out. I wasn't going to take any chances, so I got the rifle and when he came through the door I told him that if he came within ten feet of me I was going to let him have it. He said you were after him and I told him I'd take care of you and that if he kept right on going out the back door everything would be all right."

"And will it?"

"Well," Helen said, her blue eyes scanning my face, "that depends on what you told him, doesn't it?"

The sun was not yet up when I left the Dumonts' house, but there was a grayness in the sky that gave everything a cartoonlike two-dimensional quality. In the stillness of the hour I could hear an occasional automobile moving in the distance, but other than that everything in Larkspur, California, was still.

I walked down to the rental car and found my friend Joyce asleep in the passenger seat. She remained that way until I reached the city. I waited until I crossed the Golden Gate Bridge and then I pulled to the side and woke her up.

"Where we going?" she said, not bothering to look around to see where she was.

"I'm going home," I said. "I'll drop you wherever you want."

Joyce curled up and laid her head on my lap. In my mind's eye I could see grease marks formulating on my pant leg. "You don't mind if I crash with you, do you?" she said. "I've got no place else to go."

"C'mon," I answered wearily, shaking my leg to get her up. "It's five o'clock in the morning, I'm totally wasted and I don't feel like fooling around. I'll give you twenty bucks and you can find a room somewhere. Okay?"

Apparently it was not okay. Joyce pushed off and slid to the far side of the car. In the light of day I noticed again she had fine blue eyes, just like Helen Dumont, and at this particular moment they showed almost as much warmth as Helen's.

"I did you a favor when you needed it, man," she said.

I exhaled and looked away. Even at this hour there was a lot of traffic on its way into the city. I heard the click of the door handle and I turned back quickly and grabbed Joyce before she stepped out of the car. "Where were you going to stay if you hadn't run into me?" I said.

"I've got places."

"Like where? Don't you have a home or anything?"

"Yes, I live somewhere. No, I don't want to go there."

"You're not a runaway, are you?"

Surprise spread over her face. "Mister, I'm twenty-two years old. I'm married, divorced, and living with an asshole and I don't want to get into the whole story with you."

I held onto her and said nothing. My silence came from the fact that I was tired and my mind had locked on empty, but Joyce thought I was trying to force an explanation out of her and, sighing, she launched into some long complicated tale about living with her boyfriend in the Mission and how her boyfriend had taken to smoking "freebase" cocaine which sometimes kept him up for seventy-two hours at a time and made him crazy. On and on she went, until finally I just put the car in drive and told her I didn't give a damn if she stayed at my place or not, but that if I did not get there soon I was going to pass out behind the wheel.

Joyce talked the full twenty minutes it took us to get from the bridge to my apartment. The sound of her voice was probably the one thing that kept me awake long enough to make it there.

"Which way, boss?" Joyce said, and I got out and led her to the concrete stairs that rose from the carport to the rest of my building. We passed two of my neighbors on their way to work. They gave Joyce a thorough checking out, but she only smiled and I only nodded.

"I don't believe it," she said when she first walked into the apartment. I had not yet picked up all the mess that Jarmon had left.

"Neither do I," I said. I kicked some things out of the way. "Damn cleaning lady, I told her this stuff was supposed to go in the closet, but she insists on piling it on the floor."

Joyce looked at me quizzically for a moment and then laughed. "Hey, you've got a good sense of humor. I like that."

"Gee, we'll get along just fine then." I scooped up a towel and tossed it to her. "Here, you can wash up with this. There are two slide-out couches that turn into beds. Take whichever one I'm not on."

Ten minutes later my teeth were brushed, my clothes were off and I was lying down, bone tired and unable to sleep because Joyce was merrily singing in the shower, "Lots of choc'late for me to eat..."

The water shut off and still she sang and still I couldn't sleep. At last she came out of the bathroom with my towel wrapped around her head like a turban, wearing an old Gant shirt of mine that ended halfway down her thighs. The shirt's stiff, buttondown formality gave her an unexpected air of propriety.

"Is it all right to wear this?" she asked sweetly.

"It looks beautiful," I said, and I was surprised at my own choice of words.

The drapes were pulled tight, but there was enough

light for me to see her and for her to see me. With her hair up like that, her features had taken on a new cast. They were stronger than I had thought and her skin was smoother; but her face, her whole appearance, was dominated by her eyes and as she stood there, halfway across the room, I could not stop looking at them. I lay on my back, not moving and, at first, not meaning anything as I watched her watch me. But then she smiled, and I smiled back.

She moved closer until she was just a few feet from my bed and her fingers began undoing the buttons of the Gant shirt. She started at the bottom and as she worked upward the shirt fell open and I saw that she was painfully thin, with a narrow, narrow waist and breasts that were no larger than nubbles. And then I sat bolt upright.

"Jesus Christ, what have you got all over you?"

Joyce shrugged her way out of the shirt and laughed. "They're tattoos, silly," she said and climbed into bed with me.

16

The knocking on the door came about ten o'clock. Joyce had been sleeping with an arm and a leg draped over me and when I tried to jump up we got tangled together so that I nearly dragged her to the floor. The knocking sounded again.

"Just a minute," I yelled. I was searching for a pair of pants and when I could find none I grabbed the towel which Joyce had used for her hair. Holding it pinched around my hips, I ran to the door, calling out, "Who is it?"

For an answer I got more knocking and so I positioned myself behind the door and opened it just enough to see the woman standing there. She wore a long camel's-hair coat, had tightly curled brown hair and large brown eyes which looked back at me with contemptuous familiarity. She held a bag of groceries in one arm. Celery and a package of spaghetti projected out of the top of the bag.

"Oh," was all I said. It was all I could think of as my wife thrust the bag of groceries toward me.

"I brought some stuff," she said. "I don't know whether you're cooking these days or not, but it's all stuff you like."

"Yeah," I said. "Yeah," or something equally meaningful. I tried to reach around the door with one conspicuously bare arm.

Peg pulled the bundle back. "What's wrong?" she said.

"I'm not yet dressed," I told her. "That's all."

Peg pushed the door open. "You're apparently not working, either, if you're still home at ten. I've been calling you for days and you haven't even tried to get back to me, have you?"

I had a quick thought about the answering service and wondered when I had contacted it last. "I've been busy," I mumbled.

"Yeah," Peg said, glancing around. "This place is awful dark."

She walked straight down the hallway to the drapes at the sliding glass doors near the foot of the bed where Joyce was lying. Peg jerked the drapes open and Joyce said, "Hi."

She was lying propped on one elbow and was exposed from the waist up. Peg's mouth had fallen open, but she made an effort to recover. A small effort. "Oh, hi," she said as she stared at the green snake which came down Joyce's shoulder and bared its fangs just above the chocolate-drop nipple of Joyce's tiny breast.

Peg shifted the bag of groceries so that it was clutched to her stomach like a shield. "Who are you?" she said.

"I'm Hector's assistant," Joyce said cheerily.

"Uh, Peg, this is Joyce, this is Peg." I used one hand to gesture between the two women and continued using the other to hold up my towel.

"I suppose you know who I am," Peg said, and when Joyce shook her head she ceased treating her as if she was any longer in the room. "What's that shit all over her?" Peg demanded.

"Tattoos," I said.

"What's she, about fourteen?"

"Twenty-two," I said.

"My ass," Peg said. She strode forward to the bed and wrenched the covers all the way off. Joyce never once moved.

"My God, she's got them all over her. What's that thing going up between her legs, a cat?"

"It's a black pussycat," Joyce said. "I got it right here in San Francisco from Lyle Tuttle. His own son did me just after he had finished putting roses all over Cher's bottom."

Peg bent over to get a closer look, but I grabbed her elbow and steered her away. She twisted out of my grasp and smashed the groceries down on the kitchen counter. "Isn't this great?" she said. "I come to see my husband and he's in bed with the illustrated pubescent."

I made another attempt to grab her arm and she pushed me away. I lost my grip on my towel and it fell to the floor. Before I could grab it again Peg kicked it into the center of the room.

"Mr. and Mrs. Nude America," she said, pointing at both of us.

Joyce continued smiling and I turned away in embarrassment. This was not enough for Peg, who marched over to the wall and flicked the overhead light on. "Is this what you want?" she said, and as I looked over my shoulder she was still pointing at Joyce, who stopped smiling and drew her knees up protectively. I could see the sharp, bony ridges beneath Joyce's skin. Joyce saw me looking at her and her eyes seemed to lose some of their confidence. From where I was standing I could see the blue veins in her long thin hand as it moved to her breast, the one with the snake, and covered it.

"Maybe you should come back later, Peg," I said quietly.

"Oh, really," she said, her voice dripping with sarcasm. "Well, maybe I'm not dressed properly for this little gathering. Apparently in Hector's house we don't wear anything."

Peg threw off her camel's hair coat and stood for a second in her sweater and slacks, glaring at Joyce. Suddenly she crossed her arms in front of her and raised her sweater over her head. Her breasts, which appeared absurdly large in comparison with Joyce's, rose as she lifted her arms and fell back as she threw the sweater toward the bed. Obviously startled, Joyce caught the sweater in one hand and sat up.

"C'mon, Peg," I said, "you're acting like a madwoman."

"Oh, am I?" she answered, her eyes fixed on Joyce, who almost seemed to be shriveling like a piece of bacon in front of me. Peg popped open the button that fastened her slacks and pulled down the zipper. They were tight slacks and she was packed into them. She had to roll her hips to get them to the point where they slipped down her thighs. She was not wearing underwear and in a moment she was standing nude like the rest of us; for Joyce was now on her feet, holding Peg's sweater to her mouth and looking absolutely bewildered.

A lot of things could have happened at that moment which would have made Peg look ridiculous, but she alone had created this scene and she was more prepared than either Joyce or I to play it out. With one hand on her hip, her legs long and firm, her stomach tight and her breasts swelling, she triumphantly scanned Joyce from head to foot. Standing next to Peg, Joyce had little with which to fight back. The snake, the black cat on her thigh, the bluebird on her upper arm, the sailboat on her shoulder, the cherries on her hip, the sun rising through the bed of flowers on her back, all seemed a little silly as she stared at Peg. Her hair, matted and wild from having been slept on while it was wet, almost appeared intimidated next to Peg's orderly curls. Even the blueness of her eyes seemed lost by the uncertainty I was seeing in them.

"I think maybe I better go," Joyce said, turning and patting the bed in an apparent effort to find her clothes.

I said nothing.

"I think they're in the bathroom," she said.

Peg and I remained as we were while the sounds of Joyce dressing came from down the hall. There was a brief time while the water ran and then for a few seconds there was silence. Finally the front door opened and closed and we heard rapid footsteps on the cement walkway. Peg turned to me and opened her arms.

"Come to Momma," she said.

I lay with my head on her chest, staring off toward the kitchen where the grocery bag still rested on the counter, leaning to one side like some free-form sculpture topped by the palm tree of the celery stalk. Neither Peg nor I had spoken in nearly an hour, but with my ear pressed against her, I could practically feel the words building up inside her.

"I'm sorry I spoiled your fun with that little girl," she said at last. Even in her apology, Peg could not resist a dig.

"It's all right," I said. "She's just somebody I met."

"It wasn't what I came here for. It's just that when I saw her . . . you and her, I mean . . ."

"I know." I knew exactly, and I did not want to discuss it.

"I felt so angry with you for not being there when your family needed you."

I raised my head. Peg was not looking at me, she was staring at the ceiling. "What are you talking about?" I said.

"And then I thought he had gotten to you, because all next day I kept leaving messages with your answering service at the office and they kept saying you hadn't called in yet. Finally I made myself think only good thoughts. That's why I went to the store before I came over here. I was thinking positively—and all that positive energy just blew up in my face when I saw what you were doing."

"Peg," I said, forcing her to look at me. "Has something happened I don't know about?"

"A guy was in our house," she said. "He came in Sunday night and I woke up and found him standing there. A huge guy, six-three, maybe, with a red plaid hunting jacket and a woman's stocking over his head. He had a knife that he held like this." She demonstrated an underhanded grip that one might use for ripping something from the bottom to the top. "He said he wanted the pictures."

I went cold inside. Peg sensed it and we sat up together.

"You know who it is, don't you?" she said.

"Did he have curly hair and a mustache? A potbelly?"

She shook her head. "I don't think so," she said, but then she hesitated. "It was hard to tell." She got more helpful after that. "He had kind of a funny accent. Sort of like a cowboy."

"Jarmon," I said.

"Do you know him?"

"He followed me here Monday night looking for the pictures."

"Sunday night he thought you were with me."

I looked around slowly. "You mean after you were asleep? When you were in bed?"

Peg took a deep breath.

"Somebody else was there, wasn't there?" I shook my head. "You're really something else, Peg. You absolutely freak out because I have a girl in my apartment and meanwhile you're screwing everything that's not in an iron lung. Where do you get off?"

"Don't, Hector."

"Don't what? You come over here acting like a goddamn Virgin Mary in front of Joyce and look what you've been doing."

"I was hardly acting like the Virgin Mary when I took my clothes off in front of her. I wasn't trying to tell you not to have other relationships, Hector, I just don't want to be confronted with them."

"So who's confronting? I moved out of the house over a month ago. I'm here in my own apartment minding my own business, you come beating on my door, drive my friend out and start telling me about some sailor or something you've got in my bed."

"Your bed? You've hardly set foot in that house since you left. What do you think I'm supposed to do, use a zucchini until you decide it's time to come home?"

"I've offered to come home."

"You offer when you're horny or you're hungry. Try offering in the middle of the afternoon sometime. But look, Hector, I'm not going to fight about that now. I was there and you weren't. I had been out with a friend and we had too much to drink and I let him stay over and that's all you need to know."

"You could at least tell me nothing happened between you."

"Nothing did."

"Just like with Jerry Seales."

"Goddamn you. You never forgive anything, do you?"

She got up and began putting on her clothes.

"What's there to forgive? Just because my former boss sends a case my way so he can be alone with my wife, and just because my wife lets him screw her, that's nothing to get angry about, is it?" I stopped, knowing I had gone too far. "Oh, Christ. Tell me what happened."

But Peg was already getting into her slacks. She sucked in her breath to button them and said, "The next thing I should tell you is to send me alimony."

"We're not even divorced."

"That can be easily fixed." She finished dressing and turned to me. "The guy came in and pulled my friend out of bed. He called my friend 'Hector,' and he demanded the pictures he said you had taken that day. My friend didn't know what he was talking about and so the guy twisted his arm up behind his back and stuck the knife in his ribs. He said he'd slit him from one side to the other if he didn't tell where the pictures were. That's when I screamed and tried to help, but the guy knocked me away and threw us both on the bed. Then the kids started to scream in the next room and everything got so noisy and confusing that it was hard to tell what was going on, except that we managed to get the guy to look at my friend's wallet and see that he wasn't you. He said he was sorry to have bothered us and he ran out.

"I grabbed the phone and tried to call you and I must have let the phone ring a hundred times, but you never answered. I didn't know what else to do so I called the cops and they sent out these two patrolmen who looked like they were about eighteen years old. They found where the back door had been jimmied and then they treated the whole episode like a burglary. I knew there was something more to it and I tried to tell them about you being a private detective, but they just said they'd get in touch with you."

"I'll expect their call around the first of the year." I lit a cigarette and passed it to Peg. She stared at it as if she thought I might be offering it as an enticement to stay, which I was. "I need to talk to somebody about this," I said, "if you'll sit down."

Peg went over to the kitchen table and sat down warily. I put on a bathrobe, one that she had given me several years before, and sat down with her. Slowly and carefully, I told her all I knew about Ferrell Dumont, his father, his stepmother and his experience with the Temple. I told her about the Reverend and Mrs. Franklin, about Blodgett and his theory, about Franz-Josef and his family and about Jarmon-Harris. I even told her about Grace and Bob and life at the Delphi Apartments. When I was done she nodded as if she understood the situation. I found that infuriating.

"So what is it you seem to know that I don't?" I said between pinched lips.

"Men," she said.

"I'll resist the urge to comment."

"Doesn't it strike you as just a little funny that Ferrell would borrow money and then move out of his apartment on a Sunday night? Obviously he wasn't going to get the film from you, develop it, contact Franklin and get money out of him before dawn. So where was he going to spend the night? He sure didn't go home if his stepmother was still looking for him at the apartment house on Monday. From everything you've said, it doesn't appear that he had any real friends. How much was he able to squeeze out of the neighbors?"

"Ten bucks. That's what Bob said Grace loaned him on Sunday."

"All right. He borrowed money from Grace so he could move to another place and get away from her. He had told her too much already, and he didn't really want her clamoring after him once he made the big killing."

"He moved to another place because he didn't want Helen to find him," I said, trying to keep the exasperation out of my voice.

"Then why did he sneak out in the middle of the night and leave all his stuff behind? If he was just trying to hide from Helen he could have moved out anytime. Take my word for it, he was sneaking away from Grace when he walked out of that building."

"All right, Peg, I'm not going to argue with you. Assume you're right. So what?"

"So where's a guy go with one piece of luggage and a ten-dollar bill in this town?"

"He buys a giant jar of peanut butter and he camps in Golden Gate Park."

"Or he rents a room in the Tenderloin."

The glow of enlightenment was seeping through the cracks in my skull. "You're not telling me to check every hotel in the Tenderloin, are you?"

Peg shrugged. "The Reverend, didn't you say they found him in the Tenderloin? With your gun planted next to him?"

"My gun that Ferrell Dumont had stolen."

"So maybe whoever planted the gun didn't know that it had been stolen. Look at it this way, Hector. What better way to frame Ferrell than to shoot the Reverend with Ferrell's gun, plant the body near Ferrell's room and then leave the gun for the cops to find?"

I looked at it that way and I liked what I saw. I leaned across the table and kissed her. "You're a good woman, Peg."

She smiled, but she did so as she was getting to her feet. There was a brief discussion about her staying longer, but nothing came of it. It seemed we both had other things to do that day.

17

I found Ferrell Dumont late Wednesday afternoon. I had
started my search with the newspaper account of the finding
of Jonathan Franklin's body and a city street map. Then I
went out to the Cannery near Fisherman's Wharf, to one of
those people who earns his bucks by sketching the likeness
of tourists. For twenty dollars this guy in a beret followed
my description and worked out a picture that fairly accu-
rately represented Ferrell Dumont. Ferrell might not have
recognized himself in the drawing, but the result was close
enough to start a conversation.

The newspaper account said the Reverend had been
found in an alley called Turner Place, which ran between
6th and 7th streets. It was the sort of alley that always looked
wet. On one side it received the back doors of some city
government offices, a cafeteria, a stationery shop, two in-
scrutable buildings, a bar and two hotels: the Metropolis
and the Sphinx. Along the other side were the back doors
of a trade school, a bar, Ho Ho Harry's Ribeye (All the

Salad You Can Eat), a pawnshop and four hotels and/or boardinghouses; the Iroquois, the Bat-Swan, Caesar's and one that just said Transients. I found Dumont at the Bat-Swan. It was not my first choice.

Palmieri had told me that he had found Franklin in one trash can and my gun in another, so I walked the length of the alley trying to figure out where the Reverend might have been. A giant blue dumpster was outside Ho Ho Harry's and some smaller gray dumpsters, the kind where you open the top and find barrels inside, were near the doors of the cafeteria and the government buildings, but the only hotel that had more than one actual trash can was the Sphinx. I started there and worked my way around.

The Bat-Swan was my fourth stop. Its name was painted in a semicircle at the top of a glass door which sported masking tape to cover up a crack that ran through the words ROOMS DAY WEEK MONTH SOME BATH. When I pushed the door open it stuck on the pitted linoleum floor. A single naked light bulb burned in a lobby which was about five feet wide and twenty feet long. At the back of the lobby was a fire door which led to the alley and next to that was a ramshackle set of stairs. A tiny office fit like a cupboard behind a counter in one wall, and a sign hanging in the office read:

> To check out leave key in key box. We reserve the right
> to enter the room of any guest who has not paid up or
> checked out by twelve o'clock noon.

No one was behind the counter, but there was a buzzer and in front of that was another sign held to the counter by a hundred layers of yellowish Scotch tape. This sign said to ring if you wanted the manager. I was practically leaning on the buzzer before I got any response.

A door opened behind the counter and a small dark head poked its way out. Its owner grimaced when he saw me. "Cop," he said.

"Come out here," I ordered. "I want to talk with you."

The manager slunk out from behind the door carrying a nasty white Pekinese under one arm. He patted the dog nervously.

"You know me?" I asked him.

"I don't know you. I feel you."

"What's that mean?"

"I read people," he said. He struck me as being very foreign looking. It might have been his manner or dress. He was wearing a light green shirt with dark green piping, baggy trousers, wool socks and sandals. It might also have been his hair, which was black, thinning, laden with grease and combed straight back. In any event, I was wrong. I was to find out later he came from New Jersey.

"I'm looking for a guy," I said.

"You come to the right city, you want a guy."

I placed the drawing on the counter in front of him. "This guy would have come in here Sunday night. He had a suitcase, a briefcase and he wore a raincoat."

The manager glanced at the drawing, eyed me and shrugged. It was the best response I had gotten in my trip around Turner Place. I dropped a five-dollar bill on top of the drawing.

"Private detective," the manager said. He only looked like an idiot.

"The guy just inherited a fortune. I need to tell him."

The manager put the Pekinese on the floor. He stuffed the five-dollar bill in his pocket without looking at it and then hunched over the drawing, thumping his fingers on either side of it. "This don't look like him," he said.

"But you know who it is."

"I know the guy," he said. "He don't belong here, he was too neat. Everything about him was just so." The manager made a hand gesture as if this was a disgusting trait to have. "The guy I know, he got the mustache, the hair, the nose, but he don't look like this. Except that I read guys, I wouldn't know it was him."

"He come in here on Sunday?"

The manager nodded. "Stayed Sunday night. Then he left."

"Where'd he go?"

"Beats me."

"You didn't read that?"

The manager's eyes were slippery little pellets. They slid right over me, went to the front door and then bounced back again. "I read guys when I see 'em," he said. "I didn't see this guy leave. Just found his key in the box when I got up the next day." He thumped a little cigar box with a slit in the top. The box was padlocked and chained to the counter, but anybody who wanted to could probably have carved it open with a Swiss Army knife. "I find a key in here, I know a guy's checked out." He shook the box. "Hard to keep track of what's going on around here since the old lady left. Took off on me. I know who talked her into it, too. It was one of the guests. A broad, if you can imagine that. Had a knapsack and everything."

The manager got a paper coffee cup out from beneath the counter, spit in it and put it back. "I never was any good at reading broads," he said.

"You find anything in my friend's room that might tell me where he was going?"

"Ain't been up there yet."

"Today's Wednesday."

"So? I gotta do everything around this place now, you know. I gotta do the books, the laundry, clean the rooms, do the maintenance. But did my old lady care? Fuck, no. She wants to run off with some broad, doesn't shave her legs. How would you like to wake up one day and find the woman you been married to for sixteen years had gone queer on you?"

"That's tough. When did it happen?"

"I don't want to talk about it," he said. He lifted up the Pekinese and deposited him on the counter between us. The dog flopped on his belly and regarded me as if he found me slightly repugnant. The manager leaned down and began nuzzling him, cooing something like, "But Momma's gonna be coming home soon, isn't she, baby? Huh, poops? Isn't that the truth?"

"Mind if I go up and take a look around this guy's room?" I said.

The manager had his face buried in the dog's back and appeared to be taking little nips out of his hide. The dog looked annoyed, but did not move other than to turn his head and stretch his neck.

I picked up the drawing so that the two of them would not get their slobber all over it. "What number?" I said.

The manager stood up straight and shrugged.

I gave him another dollar.

"Three-oh-eight," he said, descending on the dog again.

In the Bat-Swan, 308 meant walking up not two but three flights of stairs. They were lousy, carpetless stairs that smelled like old subway tunnels. Between the second and third floors I had to step over a used baby diaper and I could not help but wonder what it was doing in a place like this.

The third floor was silent and there seemed to be no one else around until I tried the door to 308 and found it locked. As I rattled the knob, the door to 310 opened and a tall, hairless old man in a wool shirt buttoned to the neck came out.

"He's a-hiding." The old man cackled. "He won't come out."

"There's no one in there," I said.

"Sure there is. A young fella."

"He was here. He moved out."

The old man looked unhappy. "That's too bad. I saw him just the other night at the telephone." He pointed down the hall to a pay phone.

I put my shoulder to the door, but it would not budge, even though the handle rattled fiercely. I stepped back and kicked the handle as hard as I could. It fell off and the old man scurried over and picked it up.

"Here," he said, but I told him I didn't want it and kicked the door again. This time the door flew open.

I knew Ferrell Dumont was dead before I even saw him. The old man knew it, too. I saw his eyes widen as the fetid air from the room wafted over us. From where we were standing we could look in at a small sink with a mirror and a light bulb in a gold half shell. Beyond that there was a closet and then a bureau. I had to step inside to see the rest.

Ferrell was lying face down across a chipped and cracked gray iron bed. He was shirtless. The color had drained from the top of his body and the part of him that was lying closest to the bed was almost a dark blue. The back of his skull had a hole blown in it and there was blood and little tiny bits of bone spattered about the bed and the blankets and the nearby wall.

There was a shuffling sound behind me as the old man turned and ran for the stairs. I shouted at him and he froze.

"You know what happened here?" I said, walking toward him.

"I just sit in my room, I don't know nothing."

"You there Sunday night?"

"I'm there every night. I don't bother no one. Ain't no one bothers me." The old man was beginning to snivel.

"You ever been to the joint, old man?"

He shook his head. "Just once."

"How long were you in for?"

"Twenty-eight years."

"You must be used to hearing things then. What did you hear Sunday night? Say, around midnight?"

The old man's eyes were watery. He looked confused for a minute and then brightened. Barely. "Midnight, I was listening to the Nightcaps."

"That a band?"

"It's a radio program. Folks call in from all over the country and talk. Sometimes they get together and take trips. They got one to Hawaii next spring I might go on. Anybody who wants to can go."

"Somebody went in that room and fired a gun. You hear that?"

"Just the Nightcaps, that's all I heard. Program comes all the way from Kansas City, or is it Salt Lake City? I think it's Salt Lake City. You have to turn the radio real loud sometimes to hear what the people have to say. I got an earplug so I don't bother nobody."

"I want you to remember back. The night you saw this guy at the phone, remember that?"

"Nice fella," he said.

"It was the day he moved in, wasn't it?"

"Sometimes they don't stay long."

"This one came in around nine thirty Sunday night. Went right out, came back an hour or so later. Somebody might have been with him when he came back, or else somebody came knocking at the door later. Which was it?"

"Didn't hear anything. Ten o'clock on, I got me the Nightcaps."

"Did you hear any voices next door?"

"Was gonna call in myself that night. Had all my change. Lady called in from Canada. Vancouver, I think. Maybe Victoria. She knew how to grow geraniums indoors. I went out to call and the fella was there. Only time I seen him. Only time I heard him."

"You heard him? What did he say?"

The old man was trembling. "Didn't hear him exactly. Just kinda heard him while I was waiting to use the phone."

"And what did you kind of hear him say?"

The old man shifted his feet and moved his jaw soundlessly. I leveled a finger at him.

"Police are going to be real interested in you. Dad, I tell them you're a convicted felon living right next door to the dead man. Anything missing and they might start asking where you got the money to buy that radio."

"I had the radio," he said, his voice cracking. "It's mine."

"They might have to take it as evidence. You know cops."

"But I don't know nothing. I was just there when he said—" He stopped and held his hand to his face. "He said, 'Okay, this is,' then he gave his name. Farley, I think it was. 'I got your call, and I'm here at the Bat-Swan.' Then he gave his room number, 'Room three-oh-eight,' he said, and then he hung up, just like that."

"Who was he talking to?"

The old man looked helpless. His hands waved unhappily.

"All right," I said, "you go back in your room and wait. The police will be here shortly. I'll tell them to go easy on you."

The old man sidestepped his way back up the hall, keeping his eyes trained on me as if I might leap after him at any moment. When the door closed I returned to Ferrell's room and began my search.

There was no sign of a struggle. Ferrell had either felt comfortable enough with his murderer to lie down or he had been ordered to do so. The bed he was on had not been slept in, although its covers were mussed. I went out to the hallway, inhaled a deep breath and returned to examine the smashed-in-section of Ferrell's skull. There was just the one hole, larger than I would have expected from a single bullet, but the skull bone had fragmented and collapsed and there was a gray ring around it that distorted the size. My lungs were screaming at me when I finally let out my breath and turned to the rest of the room.

A closed suitcase stood upright on the floor. I wanted badly to open it, but the fear of leaving or smudging fingerprints kept me from trying. The briefcase was a different story. It was both open and empty. I tried the drawers of the sole bureau in the room and found nothing. Ferrell's shoes were neatly arranged beneath the bed, his shirt was fitted over the back of the room's only chair, and his raincoat was draped carefully across the seat of the chair. In one pocket of the coat I found a quarter, a couple of dimes, and a cheap paper napkin on which the name and address of the hotel had been written. The other pocket was empty. Steeling myself, I went back to the body and ran my hands into Ferrell's pants pockets. It was the first time I had touched him, and the first time I realized that he was limp. Rigor mortis had already passed.

Satisfied that there was no roll of film to be found, I went down the hall to the pay phone and called Palmieri. I told him I had found the first dude in my defense.

18

Palmieri was hacking and wheezing and sucking on a cigarette all at the same time. His little toady, Mellon, was running around making noises as if he was giving orders to evacuate a ship. Shepard was not there because he had called in sick. Palmieri said it was because it was getting close to the end of the year and Shepard had to use up his sick days or lose them.

Mellon came bounding out of Ferrell's room like a seal emerging from the surf. "Looks like a hooker, Ed," he said with an air of finality. "John's lying face down on the bed with nothing but his pants on. Hook pretends she's giving him the back rub, pulls her piece, blows him away, takes his money from his wallet and she's gone."

"His pants still buckled? His watch still on?"

"Yeah."

"You see any signs at all a hook was there?"

"Thought I'd run the mug book past the manager."

"Lot of good that will do you. That stick of slime hasn't

got the first idea who's in his hotel. I gave a shit, I'd get a warrant and search his apartment for heroin, that's what I'd do. But you go ahead. Take him down the Hall and show him the books and see what you get out of him."

"Figured this situation might come up, Ed. Took the liberty of bringing a couple of the books along with me. Thought it might save time. You know, whore might still be around here."

"You were so sure it was a hooker."

"Has all the trappings, Ed. Young, middle-class white guy wasted in a fleabag hotel. All I needed to find out was if his money was gone."

I butted in. "Pretty astute, Mellon, except your nice young white guy is a paroled convict involved in armed robbery, blackmail, arson and murder. He's got a gambling debt he couldn't pay to a crime figure known as Jimmy the Dog and half the city would like him dead, including his father, his stepmother, his girlfriend's husband and an entire religious movement."

Mellon flushed red. "Yeah, well I'm not forgetting about you either, you prick."

Palmieri gently pushed Mellon toward the stairs. "Bill, you go get your books and talk to the manager. If he's got anything more to say than 'ah-bubba,' I'll be surprised, but it's a good idea."

When Mellon was gone Palmieri coughed out his last bit of cigarette smoke and turned to me. "He's pushing for inspector, you know. Work twenty-four hours a day if he could get away with it. Wants Shepard's job, so he's always running around slipping me these little stories about him. Problem is, he's as subtle as a glass of tequila. Last time Shepard calls in sick, this guy, he spies on Shepard's house, watches him come out with the plaid pants, the Ban-Lon shirt, the old soft hat and the golf bag. The next day, Mellon waits until the three of us is together and says something like 'So what did you shoot yesterday, about ninety?' Shepard says, 'If you're talking about my temperature, it was a hundred and one.' Mellon, the meatball, says, 'Yeah, you look kinda pale. You oughta get out there on the links more often, get some color.' Jesus Christ, I thought Shepard was gonna kill him right there."

The photographer was done in Ferrell's room and the body was being loaded onto a stretcher. A print man was still busy brushing everything in sight and a deputy coroner was rather casually jotting down notes. The deputy coroner was a thin man with reddish hair and a very high forehead and he pursed his lips into a fish mouth when he wrote. He agreed that rigor mortis had passed and said that meant Ferrell had been dead at least thirty-six hours. I asked him if Ferrell could have been dead since Sunday night and he said, "Could have. He's got maggots."

Palmieri asked him if he thought the weapon might have been a short-barreled .38 and he said he wouldn't say no. "Hole looks to be about the right size," he reasoned, "but you'll have to wait until we pull the bullet."

Palmieri took me by the elbow and led me downstairs. "Today is your day, Hector. Today I look at everything just the way you tell me and I look at everything in the best possible light for you. Starting back last Sunday night in your office, I see this guy Ferrell comes in and he gets something from you. Takes something. Takes the film. I still don't got the building guard who's gonna tell me about that, tell me what time the guy left your office and so forth, but I take your word for it that it's late at night. I talk with the manager here and he tell me, yeah, the guy checks in nine thirty or ten or so and that's the last he's seen of him. I talk with the old man next door and he tells me, yeah, he seen Ferrell on the telephone sometime after that, and he heard Ferrell tell somebody where he was."

Palmieri saw the diaper on the stair and kicked it aside. 'Do you believe this?" he said. "What kind of person would bring a baby in here? It's a wonder Mellon didn't scoop this up and tell me it was a clue." He threw a glance at the stairs above him. "You know, I should have this whole fucking place closed down. I think I'll call the Department of Health or something.

"What was I saying? All right, I got it. Whoever Ferrell was talking to on the telephone comes here to see him. Ferrell feels good about this person, feels close enough that he doesn't mind waiting around with his shirt and shoes off. Or maybe he feels good enough to take that shirt off when the person arrives. There's a distinction there and I think it's important. In the one case he's probably waiting for a guy. Guys don't care their buddy's got a shirt on or not. But if he takes the shirt off when the friend arrives, then the friend's probably a girl. I mean, I don't see him taking his shirt off in a little room in front of another guy and keeping it off unless he's a fag. This guy, Ferrell, he wasn't no fag, was he?"

I shook my head. "Ladies' man."

"That's what I thought. So now I try to figure out how hot it was that night. Old man next door tells me it was cold, but he's got the bad circulation, he looks like he's always cold. The manager tells me everybody's got his own heat, and he's right, Ferrell had his own little radiator in there. I check it out. Right now the room's not too hot, it's not too cold. But it's in the middle of the goddamn afternoon. Supposedly nobody's been in the room from the time the murderer left until you kicked the door open. So I go to the radiator and it's turned up full blast. For three days the radiator's been going, it's afternoon now and it's still not hot in there. I figure it sure as hell wasn't so hot Sunday night that Ferrell had to take his shirt off to cool down. I mean, you're hot the first thing you do is turn off the radiator, right?"

"So you think the murderer was a woman?"

"Maybe it was Mellon's whore."

"I don't think he had any money. He gave me three hundred bucks on Thursday, and he apparently had to borrow some from his girlfriend to do that. On Sunday he went and borrowed another ten bucks from her. Said he didn't have enough to eat, but within a matter of hours he checked in here."

"Price of the room was eight fifty. Think a whore blew him away for a buck and a half?"

"Think he'd call one if that's all he had in his pocket?"

Palmieri patted me on the shoulder as we reached the lobby. "Probably didn't even have that much. There was an empty can of bud and an empty package of Twinkies in the wastebasket."

Ahead of us Mellon and the Bat-Swan's manager were huddled over an open picture book. The manager was eagerly scanning one face after another. He seemed to be quite enthusiastic about helping the law with this particular aspect of its investigation. "Hey, here's another one that's good-looking," I heard him say. Mellon noticed us coming and barked that this wasn't any beauty contest.

Palmieri walked over to them. "So," he said. "I think we can assume the murderer is familiar with this hotel since he or she told Ferrell to come here, if we can believe what the old man tells us. We also know that the murderer came right down these stairs just like we done and came over and dropped the key to Ferrell's door right in this box." He tapped the cardboard box so forcefully that both Mellon and the manager flinched. "Now why would she—humor me, and call the murderer a 'she'—why would she do that?

Obviously she knows the way handsome, here, works. She knows he don't check the rooms as long as the key's been dropped off. How long you been doing that, sport?"

"Hey, I'm here all by myself," the manager protested. "I gotta get to the rooms one at a time. I got a party coming in, needs a room, I'll clean it up. But right now it's the slack season and I got plenty of rooms. There hasn't been no need to get up the third floor before today."

"What did you do when you found the key to three-oh-eight?"

"I checked the guy off my book and I put the key on this board over here, shows I haven't cleaned up the room yet. I clean it up, I put the key in one of these slots over here; means the room's ready for the next guest."

He started to reach for the key, but Palmieri's command stopped him.

"Don't touch that key again. Mellon, you wait till Victor comes down and then you have him dust that key for any prints our friend, here, might have been kind enough to leave us. Meanwhile, friend, you keep looking through those books and I want you to point out every one of those girls who's ever set foot in this hotel."

Palmieri turned toward the back of the lobby and I followed him. "I thought we decided it wasn't a hooker," I said.

"We agreed he wasn't buying no hooker. But what other kind of woman would be familiar with a shithole like this?" Palmieri reached the fire door where a sign said that an alarm would go off if the door was opened. Palmieri pushed it open and nothing happened.

We stepped out onto Turner Place and looked around. Palmieri kicked a metal trash can that stood just a few feet from the door. "This is where we found Franklin," he said. "He was folded up like an envelope and his ass was jammed in here. Everything else, his arms, his legs, his head, was sticking out, so it wasn't like anybody was trying to hide him or anything."

He began walking toward the closer end of the alley and when he reached the blue dumpster outside Ho Ho Harry's he stopped and patted it with his hand. "And this is where we found your gun, Hector."

I went over and stood next to him. The dumpster was at least six feet tall and at the moment it was nearly filled with refuse. "If I wanted somebody to find a gun, I don't know that I'd throw it in there. I thought when you told me you found Franklin in one barrel and my gun in another you were talking about two barrels side by side. I look at this, I figure whoever killed Franklin may very well have been trying to hide the weapon. It wasn't real smart, but it was an effort."

Palmieri nodded. "No reason to look in this unless you got a dead body a few feet up the street. I think it's a reasonable place to ditch a weapon if, say, you shoot somebody in a hotel who's not likely to be found for a few days, you walk down a couple of flights of stairs, exit out a back door onto an alley and just happen to come across this big baby while you're sprinting for home." Palmieri paused. " 'Course, you wouldn't do it if there's a body already in the street."

I got up real close to Palmieri while he was lighting another cigarette. I got up so close I could feel the heat from his match. He looked at me evenly. "What are you telling me, Artie?" I demanded.

"Just looking at things in your best possible light, Hector."

"Bullshit, Artie, you got a lab report on my gun, didn't you?"

"That's right."

"The report shows my gun didn't kill Franklin."

"That's right. Ballistics ran some tests on your gun. They fired it into the cotton box and ended up with a bullet that had different rifling marks from the one that killed the Reverend."

"So now you're going to accuse me of killing Ferrell Dumont, since you said my gun had blood and hair on it and Dumont was shot in the head at close range."

"Oh, that," Palmieri said, at last stepping away from me. "I kind of owe you an apology on that one. What they found was steer blood. You can understand what happened there. Your gun was lying around with all the garbage from the rib-eye joint and we just assumed the stuff we saw on it was human blood until the lab did a precipitin test and found out different. The hair was cat fur."

Palmieri spoke through clouds of smoke. "The way I see it, a guy's got nothing on but his pants, he's bound to have his gun—or maybe even the gun he took away from you—lying around some place. Murderer picks it up; victim don't know, he's lying around face down on his bed, waiting to get his back rubbed or something like Mellon says; she fires on him; goes out the back door and throws the gun away the first place she sees. She maybe had no idea she was setting you up. You like that, Hector? Is that in good enough light for you?"

Palmieri turned and gazed thoughtfully back up the alley. "You know, I said a moment ago that you probably wouldn't throw your gun in this thing if there was a body already lying in the street and you didn't say nothing, but I want you to run that around the track."

"You think somebody came along with Reverend Franklin's body and left it outside the hotel after Ferrell had been killed. You think maybe it was just a coincidence the Reverend's body was there and the gun was here."

"Now I didn't say that, Hector. Coincidence is what you're left with when absolutely everything else is eliminated. I don't think we got coincidence here. I think we got mistake." Palmieri picked at his teeth and tugged at his collar while I waited patiently for an explanation. He looked up after a moment and acted surprised when he saw that I did not understand what he was saying. "Whoever dumped the Reverend here did it because he knew Ferrell was inside. What he didn't know was that Ferrell was dead."

Having something explained by Arthur Edmund Palmieri was rather an unusual experience for me. I had always assumed he was just bright enough to know that when he left a room he was supposed to use the door and not try to go through the wall. I was beginning to learn that, in his own inarticulate way, the big guy was a master at his craft. I made half an attempt to thank him and he responded with something along the lines of "Ah, blow it out your ass."

Palmieri bounced the butt of his cigarette off the side of the dumpster and leveled a finger at me. "You ain't shown me nothing yet, except maybe that you didn't kill both the Reverend and Ferrell Dumont. I told you that looking at it in your best light I figure it was a woman who killed Ferrell. I'm also going to start looking at Jimmy the Dog, since you brought his name up. But that don't mean I can't make a case against you. Now the first thing I'm gonna do is run a check on the bullet in that boy's squash and if it matches up with your gun you're in trouble all over again. Just so's there's no misunderstanding, Hector, I want you to know that I think that's what I'm gonna find and when I do you better be able to produce that building guard to support your story about the gun being stolen from you. Got that?"

"I'll find Franz-Josef for you, don't worry."

"Good. Now if you'll excuse me, I gotta go help Mellon keep that dumb fuck manager from jacking off over all them pictures of pretty girls."

Palmieri strode off in the direction of the hotel while I made a vow to myself never to be civil to the sonofabitch again.

19

My efforts to find Franz-Josef Moore began in earnest with an unanswered phone call to his wife late in the afternoon of the day I found the body of Ferrell Dumont. Convinced that all the members of a family the size of the Moores could not be away for very long, I took time out for a couple of hits of Turkey and then, with my insides nice and warm, tried again. By seven o'clock in the evening I had tried calling half a dozen times without success. By quarter of eight, buoyed by bourbon bravado, I was rapping on the Moores' door.

This time there was no roar of a radio, no sound of children's voices. I shouted, "Yo, is anybody home?" and somebody from one of the neighboring units shouted back, "Why don't you shut up?"

I returned to my car and waited and in a few minutes a young boy wearing shorts, heavy wool socks and ankle-top sneakers came streaking out of the building.

"Hi," I said, jumping out of the car and intercepting him on the sidewalk.

The boy slowed into a kind of bouncy walk and tried to move around me.

"You seen Tyrone Moore?" I said.

"He gone," the boy said.

"You mean he won't be back until later?"

"I mean he gone for good. Mr. Moore come home with a trailer and they all move away." The boy got around me by feinting one way and then scampering off the other and then he, too, was gone.

I got in my car and drove to the office. The building guard this evening was an old man named Ralph who walked with a limp and liked to listen to big band music. Ralph was the sort of guy who always made comments about the weather.

"Hello, Mr. Gronig," he said when I came in, "looks like we're in for another night of rain."

"Yeah, the wind's picking up," I said, and sat on the corner of his desk.

"Yeah, well, I guess we need it . . . the rain, I mean."

"Sure, the farmers and all. Listen, Ralph, anybody heard from Franz-Josef the last day or so?"

"Nope. This is his shift I'm doing, you know. I'm not supposed to be doing these night shifts. Doctor's orders, but I'm pitching in to help out." Ralph looked a little uncomfortable. "I heard what he did to you, Mr. Gronig, and I'm real sorry about it, but you know them colored guys."

"I take it you weren't good friends with Franz-Josef."

"Aw, it's not that, Mr. Gronig. He's a good enough guy, it's just that, you know, them people think different than you and me."

"Well, I heard he was under a lot of pressure, working two or three jobs and all."

"I know he worked over the Baghdad Club as a doorman, but I don't think that was too tough a job. Just stand there in a big coat like Robert Preston in *The Music Man*. You ever see *The Music Man*, Mr. Gronig?"

I told Ralph I had missed that one and excused myself before he could run through the entire story line.

The Baghdad Club teeters precariously on the edge of Nob Hill. It is a businessman's club, staffed with dozens of aliens and near-aliens who scurry about in starched jackets, seemingly ignorant of the English language and yet able to respond to the slightest request with an unerring accuracy of production. It is a club filled with overstuffed furniture and the clack of dominoes.

I left my car parked in a white zone in front of the door and mounted the steps until I came face to face with a barrel-chested doorman. He was looking out to the curb with some concern and he told me I was sure to get a ticket if I left the car where it was. I told him it was all right, it was a rental car, and his look of concern turned to one of dismay.

"May I ask, are you a member, sir?"

"Not really," I said. "I'm here looking for one of your cohorts."

"My what?" The doorman wrinkled his face to show he was confused.

"Franz-Josef Moore. He working today?"

Now the doorman's look changed to surprise. "Franz-Josef's been missing all week. I think they've had to replace him."

"Were you a friend of his?"

"Well," the man said, inclining his head slightly forward, "I am the head doorman and Franz-Josef was one of my crew."

"How many in your crew?"

"Well, there were three. If they've hired another, they haven't told me yet."

"Who's they?"

The doorman thought I was putting him on.

"Look," I said, "I don't mean to bother you, but it's rather important that I find Franz-Josef right away. If he's not here I'd like to talk to any of his buddies who might know where he is."

"May I ask who you are, sir?"

"Yeah. I'm from the San Francisco School District." I let it go at that and the doorman, after having waited an exceptionally long time for me to continue, suddenly began nodding his head.

"Ah, I see," he said. "A school problem, is it? Well if you're trying to find Franz-Josef, Theotis Watson from the kitchen would probably be the first to know where he is."

"Is the kitchen this way?" I said, pointing inside.

"Well now, sir, I'm afraid that it would be that way only if you're a member."

"Gee, I guess I'll have to serve you with a warrant."

The doorman seemed to know as much about warrants as he knew about cohorts. He grew very flustered and took his hat off to run his fingers through his silver hair. "Well, I'm pretty sure that Theotis isn't in there. I saw him working this morning, I know, and usually if they work in the morning they don't at night. We're basically a luncheon club, you know, sir."

"Right. So where can I find Theotis?"

Unfortunately, there were limits to the help the Baghdad's head doorman could give the long arm of the San Francisco School District and I ended up finding Theotis Watson only by reverting to the private investigator's most indispensable tool, the phone directory. It told me to go to a second-floor apartment off a garden courtyard on Fell near Golden Gate Park.

It was nine o'clock when I arrived. The lights seemed to be out in Watson's apartment, but I leaned on his bell anyway and in a moment or two I was rewarded with the sound of shuffling steps on the inside. A leathery brown man with long sideburns that flared up just short of mutton-chops greeted me with some uncertainty.

Theotis Watson had a friendly manner and a natural energy that made me feel even more slovenly than usual as I slumped about on his doorstep trying to explain my presence. I told him that Franz-Josef had been involved in some sort of disturbance at one of his jobs on Sunday and Theotis Watson's eyes widened. I showed him my card as if it were a sworn affidavit of everything I was saying.

"I knew something was wrong," Theotis Watson said.

"What do you mean?"

"I could tell . . . well, it was like he was agitated about something when he came over here that night."

"What night?"

"Why, Sunday night. Isn't that what we're talking about?"

"Yes, of course. Please go on."

"It was just lucky for him that I had been out doing some tripod shots, because usually I'm in bed by midnight. But on Sunday night I'd been doing time exposures from the top of Diamond Heights, catching the moon as it rose over the city, and I couldn't wait to get them developed, so I was still up when Franz-Josef came over."

"You have your own darkroom?" I asked him.

"It's really just a pantry that I've sealed off."

Suddenly it was all too obvious. My heart quickened.

"Franz-Josef had some pictures he wanted you to develop that night, didn't he?"

"That's right. How did you know?"

I looked into Theotis Watson's anxious face and groped for the correct line. "Those pictures may have gotten Franz-Josef into trouble. They didn't belong to him and they may be the reason he's been missing these past couple of days. If you developed them, you know what I'm talking about."

"Oh, no," Watson said, "the film he had was Kodacolor prints. I'm not set up to do that kind of thing. I told him that, but Franz-Josef, he said he had to get those pictures done that night. He practically begged me to help him and even though I probably shouldn't have done it I sent him to Harold Rose down in the Mission."

"Harold Rose?"

"You know him."

I shook my head.

"Yeah, well . . . he's a guy who does specialty work, if you follow me." Theotis Watson fiddled with his doorknob and looked sheepish. "He was the only guy I could think of who might be able to help Franz-Josef at that time of night."

I told Watson I didn't understand what he meant.

"Rose, he drives a tour bus for one of those companies that caters to Japanese tourists. He takes them around to all the encounter parlors and strip joints and then when he brings them back to their hotels he offers to sell them his own pictures."

"What kind of pictures?"

Theotis Watson grimaced. "C'mon, man, you know what I mean. He's got a little studio set up in his flat and he's always looking for people to pose for him. Men, women, kids, old ladies, anything. He does all the shooting and all the developing right in his apartment and then he sells the pictures to his customers, just like I said. Everybody knows about Harold Rose."

I spent a minute or two more with Theotis Watson trying to assure him that he had done nothing wrong in sending his friend to see some conniving porno-monger in the middle of th night. When I left I took the same set of directions he had given Franz-Josef and headed for the Mission district.

Harold Rose lived in an unrestored Victorian on a side street off Valencia. It held three separate units, but at shortly after ten o'clock at night the middle flat, the one belonging to Harold Rose, was the only one with lights on. I hit the bell and a man yelled over the sound of his stereo, demanding to know who I was, I yelled back that Theotis had sent me and that I needed something developed.

After a moment the door opened and I was faced with a skinny little guy in a red fishnet T-shirt and stiff new blue jeans. He looked me up and down and skeptically asked, "Who did you say sent you?"

I planted my hand in the middle of his chest and shoved him back inside. He staggered in surprise and there was a tense moment when it looked as though he might leap at me. Then he saw that I was looking past him and down the short hallway to a yellow-walled room where a woman sat on the floor amid several large decorative pillows. I had seen her from the porch, but she was still straining to identify me.

"Hello, Joyce," I said, and she literally jumped to her feet.

"Hector?" she said.

"The world-famous detective, at your service."

Harold Rose's beady little eyes had gotten as wide as they were going to get. "You mean this is the guy? This is the guy you were with, Joyce?"

"How did you find me?" Joyce said, ignoring Harold Rose.

He did not like that and stalked back to confront her, his small fists clenched white by his sides. I followed him and when we were all standing in the yellow room I locked my hand on Rose's shoulder and forced him to sit down on the floor.

"Hey, watch who you're mauling," he said, but he was not big enough to argue.

I motioned to Joyce to sit down next to him, but I remained standing, looking around at the dozens and dozens of photographs that lined the walls. They ranged from the coy to the downright vulgar, pictures of naked human bodies in various poses with various people, things and objects. I recognized Joyce with her tattoos in one shot, cuddled with what appeared to be a midget in baby's clothes.

"I think you and I can make a deal, Harold," I said.

"For what?" His tone was defiant.

"A black man came by here around midnight last Sunday. He had a roll of film he wanted you to develop right away. You charged him some exorbitant fee, went in the darkroom and made two sets of prints. You kept one for yourself and I want it."

"Who says I got it?"

I smiled and nodded my head toward Joyce. Harold never even gave her a chance to deny it. He swung from where he was sitting and busted her right in the eye.

Joyce screamed and grabbed her face. "Goddamn you, Hector, I never told you any such thing."

"She's right, Harold," I said. "Don't hit her again."

Harold looked at his dirty little hand. "Yeah, well, she deserved that for other stuff."

"Like what?" Joyce demanded.

"Like screwing him," he shouted, jabbing his finger in my direction.

Joyce began to cry and Harold looked at her disgustedly. "You want to know what I did?" he said to me. "The guy comes in, dressed like a cop or something, says he's desperate. Has to have the film developed right away. Can't even wait till morning. I says, I'm too tired, I won't do it for less than a hundred bucks. All he's got is fifty. I don't even know the guy, but I do it for fifty. Only, once I develop his prints, I see they're of a guy and a broad in bed, and for Chrissake I know who both of them are. It's this minister I seen preaching in Golden Gate Park and this broad I used to see stripping on Broadway. So I figure, I'm practically working for charity anyhow, I might as well get something out of the deal. What am I supposed to do? This maybe gold mine just fell in my lap, but I don't know what this guy's gonna do with the pictures, either. So I wait and keep my ears open.

"Yesterday I wake up and here's the fucking paper on my doorstep telling me Franklin's been shot. I figured I had to get to the broad real fast or what I got's practically worthless. My problem is, the only thing I know about her is that she used to dance under the name of Danielle and she's married to a guy named Carl Dumont, who owns the place she used to dance at. Now about twice a week I bring a bunch of zipperheads into Dumont's place, so he knows who I am. Sometimes when I got people in there and they're spending some money, he comes over and shoots the shit. So we're almost, but not quite, friends.

"The thing is, I know he always goes out to Marvella's for breakfast after he closes up. So me, I get the bright idea, I'll send Joyce, who he doesn't know, out to Marvella's. Maybe she can follow him home. All she's supposed to do is find out where the dude lives so I can go after his wife, maybe turn a yard or two."

"That's what I did," Joyce whispered.

"What you did," Harold Rose said, his voice rising once again, "was to run into Smokey and get high with him so that when this cat comes along he steals your show and you have to go running out and join with him when you should have been on your own."

"What are you saying, Harold? This guy's a real pro. If I hadn't joined up with him I never would have found Dumont's wife."

"Lots of good it did me, Joyce," he shouted. "Maybe if you'd have come right home instead of staying out all night with Batman, here, we could have caught up with the bitch before she split."

"Helen Dumont's gone?" I said.

But Harold was still berating Joyce and I had to grab him by the hair to get him to listen to me. "What happened to Dumont's wife?" I said.

"How the fuck do I know? She's just gone, that's all."

I let go of his hair and Harold Rose patted it back into place. "How do you know that much?" I said.

"Because I was out there in Marin County watching that goddamn house and waiting for Carl to go to work so I can hit on his old lady. Instead, he stays home all day, working in his yard. I called Gil at the club see if it's his day off. Said I had a big party maybe coming in tonight and I wanted to know if Carl was going to be there personally. Gil says to me like it was a big secret that he didn't think Carl was coming in because his old lady took off on him."

I looked to Joyce for affirmation and got it. She attempted to smile at me, but I did not respond.

"Don't do that, Hector," she said softly. "I didn't do

anything to hurt you." She began running the palms of her hands up and down her tight-fitting blue jeans, smoothing out wrinkles that did not exist.

"Yeah," I said and then I turned to Harold. "All right, Harold, now that you've told me all this, what good do you think it's going to do you?"

"I just want you to know what I've been through with that set of prints so you'll understand what it's worth."

"Fair enough," I said. "Let me see them."

Harold Rose stood up until the top of his head was about five feet four inches off the ground.

"No, Harold," I said, holding up my hand. "Tell Joyce where they are."

I reached down and pulled Joyce to her feet. She looked to Harold for her orders, but he said nothing. I put my hand on Joyce's thin buttocks and clamped it there.

A moment passed and then Joyce, her eyes on Harold, her voice cracking, whispered the word "Please," and Harold muttered that the prints were in the brown box on the first shelf in the bedroom. I let go my grip and Joyce left the room. Harold watched me sullenly. He was nervous and I could smell his perspiration across the room.

When Joyce came back she handed a white envelope to Harold. He looked inside, nodded and held the envelope open toward me. "These are them," he said.

"How much do you want?"

Harold Rose's eyes glazed with uncertainty for less time than it would have taken to blink. He dragged his thumbnail across the top of the prints. "Five hundred bucks," he said.

I stepped up close to him and smiled.

"Four hundred," he said.

I gave him the back of my hand instead. The envelope dropped to the floor and I grabbed it. The little rodent tried to recover, but I took hold of his fishnet shirt and drove him up against the wall. "The only reason I don't break every bone in your pus-covered body is out of respect for your lady friend," I told him and then let him crumple to the floor.

"You're not going to pull this off," he gasped. "I've got friends."

"I doubt it," I said and let myself out.

20

There is nothing quite so creepy-cozy as the tight, shadowy atmosphere of a big-city building late at night. I liked the feeling enough to shut off all the lights but my desk lamp. Its lone bulb cast a moonlike image in my coffee, reflected off my nearly empty bottle of Wild Turkey, and left everything beyond its reach in twisted, silhouetted caricatures of their natural figures. I leaned back in my chair until all but my legs were covered with darkness, and I worked on my cigarette. The building creaked and groaned. A hum of electric motors breathed so subtly and constantly that I was conscious of it only in those brief moments after an especially sharp noise had filtered its way up from the street.

Spread out on the blotter of my desk were the photographs I had taken from Harold Rose. Now I understood Franz-Josef's nervousness, his strange behavior on my return to the building Sunday night. He had been the one who had broken into my office. He had done it quickly, thinking he had all night to cover things up—and I had come back before he had had a chance.

Somehow he had known the film would be there, and he had known what to do with it once he got his hands on it. By morning he had disappeared and so, too, had his daughter Patsy, released from the mysterious grip of the Temple. Had Franz-Josef made a trade? Of course he had. But with whom? And how had he known about the film in the first place?

I leaned forward and sipped at my coffee. It was getting cold and had almost reached the point where it was too awful to drink. For some reason, the taste of the cold coffee brought back a memory of a road I used to walk down with my brother in the autumn when we would go to buy jugs of apple cider. There was a woman who used to stand behind the screen door of a house on that road and watch us to make sure we didn't steal the gourds from her roadside table. The memory meant nothing, I had not thought of the road or the woman in years, and it had no connection with what I was working on, but it made me feel inexorably lonely. Lonely enough that I called Peg on the telephone just to talk with her.

She answered sleepily, her voice carrying the tiniest note of fear because it was late. I answered her hello and then could not think of anything else to say.

"Hector?" she said. "Hector, are you all right?"

"Do you have a minute?"

"Are you in trouble or are you just waking me up? Because if you're drunk or something I don't want to hear—"

"I wanted to talk with you. Are you alone?"

"I've got the baby in bed with me. She was having nightmares."

"Is she okay?"

"Hector, you can ask me that in the morning. Now what is it you want?"

"I got a break in the case I've been working on. I did like you suggested and searched the neighborhood where Franklin's body was found. Ferrell Dumont was in one of the hotels nearby. He had a bullet in his head."

"Oh, my God...." Peg's voice faded from the phone and I knew she was sitting up in bed. "Hector, everyone involved in this case is being killed, one right after the other."

"There's still Helen Dumont. But now I hear she's disappeared."

"Oh, my God," Peg said again.

I laughed—a little. "Are you scared?"

"Jesus Christ, I'm scared to death. Aren't you?"

"How can I be scared? I'm a private eye. Private eyes don't get scared."

"The smart ones do."

"There you go, comparing me with Jerry Seales again. Hey, Peg, that was a joke."

There was no response.

"It's supposed to show you how I'm not angry any-more."

"Why are you calling me at this hour, Hector?"

"To get a little support."

"I didn't seem to be much good at that when we were living together." It wasn't an apology. It was just another way of asking me why I was calling.

"Hell, you got me started on this road to fame and glory, Peg. If it weren't for you I wouldn't be where I am today."

"I seem to remember you were a private investigator before we even met, Hector. In fact, I seem to remember that's how we met."

"But you got me started on my own, setting up an office for me out in the garage and everything...."

"It's still here, Hector."

"I've got my own office now, Peg. You should see it. It's a real beauty. Wall-to-wall flooring, a window, a door with a jerry-rigged lock—"

She cut me off. "Don't you ever want to come home, Hector? Don't you ever want to see your kids?"

"They make me sad."

"Your own kids make you sad?"

"Kevin acts like I'm there to steal his mommy away and Karen doesn't even know who I am."

"You know what the cure for that is, don't you?"

I was silent.

After a moment, Peg sighed. It was a long sigh, a sigh of resignation. "Do you want to come over here? Is that what you want?"

"I don't know. Maybe it's not safe. The way it looks, maybe you're right in what you said a minute ago. Maybe somebody is trying to wipe out everyone connected with this whole blackmailing scheme."

I could feel her girding herself for what she was about to say. "Hector, I want you to come over."

I realized that I had been holding my breath and slowly I let it out. "All right," I said. "Let me go through a few more things and I'll be over in a little while."

She hung up and I went back to my pictures. Franklin and Helen at the motel-room door. Franklin with his hand on Helen's hip. Two snapshots of the motel with Franklin's Mercedes in the yard. Four more of Franklin and Helen in bed, and one out-of-focus shot of the Reverend coming at me. I lit a new cigarette and let it burn between my fingers while I went from one shot to the other and when I was done I returned to those that should have been the least interesting and went over them again. The license plate of the Mercedes was clearly the focal point of one shot, but there in the foreground, the lower right-hand corner, seemingly marring the picture, was the blue hood of an automobile.

The grotesque marquee of the Good Luck Motor Hotel was the subject of the next print, but the print also told me something more about the blue car. It told me it was a late-model Plymouth sedan, that it was stopped near the entrance to the motel and that it was occupied by a white-skinned driver whose blurred hand resting on the steering wheel was the only human feature discernible. I searched both pictures with a magnifying glass and then I sat back. I knew where I had seen that blue Plymouth before.

I reached for my coffee, remembered how cold it was and dropped my cigarette butt into it. Thomas Blodgett had given me a ride in just that type of blue Plymouth. The same Thomas Blodgett who, on at least one occasion, had taken a special interest in Ferrell Dumont. The same Thomas Blodgett who had sparred with Franz-Josef Moore over Franz-Josef's daughter. As First Assistant Reverend, it was possible that Blodgett not only knew what Franz-Josef did for a living but where he did it; and if he knew that, then it was also possible he knew about me. If, for any reason, Blodgett had wanted to get rid of the Reverend, he could have utilized both Ferrell and Franz-Josef. He could have taken the one—a parolee, son of a strip-show owner, a street-wise young man—and used him to set up Franklin. He could have told Ferrell specifically to hire me to photograph the scene in the motel. Then he could have used Franz-Josef, the security guard and his distraught father, to get the film from me before Ferrell had a chance to pick it up. Done correctly, Franz-Josef, would have never known what was on the film he was trading for his daughter; and

Ferrell and I would have blamed each other for its disappearance. Suspicions would have been directed everywhere but at Blodgett.

I rubbed my eyes wearily. The story made sense up to a point, but it didn't tell me why anyone would shoot the Reverend or, for that matter, Ferrell Dumont. I tried to think about both of those questions, but my mind was too tired. My eyes drifted shut. I opened them again and they closed again. Giving in, I turned off the light and tipped my chair back. I was only going to rest for a moment and then I was going to Peg's.

Somewhere in my subconscious I became aware of the whine of the elevator. I heard the asthmatic wheeze of its door opening on my floor and I instantly became awake. The room was filled with the grayness of early morning. I checked my watch. It was seven thirty.

A single set of footsteps came down the hallway, rapidly at first, then slower, until at last they halted in front of my door. There was a moment when nothing happened and then a fist pounded on the opaque glass. Almost immediately the handle of the door was roughly shaken as someone tried to come in. I never moved.

A shadow passed back and forth across the glass and then dropped straight down like a man going underwater. I waited. Something was being done to the keyhole of my door and I knew that my patched-up lock would not hold for more than a few seconds. Slowly and carefully I eased open the center drawer of my desk and closed my hand around the only weapon I had, a pair of scissors.

With a snap, the bolt gave in the lock and the door waved open. So still was I sitting that the young man who came into the room did not even see me until he had taken a full two steps. Then he saw me. He reared back.

"Don't go for a gun or anything, kiddo, or I'll shoot you where you stand." I tried to make my voice calm and even, but instead it was hoarse and broken from my few hours' sleep. The intruder stared. He put his hands up, palms out, fingers spread, and said, "I'm not carrying a gun." He was a handsome guy, in a smashed-up sort of way. Short and powerfully built, he had curly brown hair, sharp features and a cleft chin from which you could have quarried stone. He was dressed in blue jeans and a conglomeration of athletic gear that included a blue windbreaker, a football jersey with a number on it, heavy white athletic socks and white Adidas running shoes with green stripes.

"You just come to rip the place off," I said, "or you here for some other reason?"

The kid got up on his tiptoes and tried to look into the drawer where my hand was. I made a sudden motion and he quickly sank to his heels again. "I come to see Hector Gronig, the detective."

"Well, he's not here," I said.

The kid cocked his head.

"I'm his night watchman. Mr. Gronig's tired of people like you breaking in here all the time. He told me to shoot the next one who did it."

The kid weighed what I was saying. "Bullshit," he said uncertainly, lowering his hands a bit.

"Eees no bullsheet," I said. "What did you want to see Mr. Gronig about?"

"I got a message for him. I figured I'd get here before he did. Just sit around and wait for him. Kind of a surprise, you know?"

"Hey, just like in the Bogart movies, huh?"

The kid licked his lips. "Yeah," he said.

"What was the message?"

"My boss wants Mr. Gronig to join him for breakfast."

"Well, isn't that nice? And who might your boss be that he can't just call Mr. Gronig up on the phone?"

"James Coble. He sent me because he wanted to make sure that Mr. Gronig was able to attend."

"Mr. Gronig doesn't know any James Coble."

The kid was no Einstein, but he caught on after a while. "Jimmy the Dog," he said. "He'd like to see you, Mr. Gronig."

"Ah ha," I said, dropping the scissors noisily onto the bottom of my drawer and withdrawing my hand empty. "I was wondering when he was going to get around to me. What time does he want me there?"

"I'm supposed to bring you as soon as I find you."

"It will take me about an hour to clean up."

The kid put his hands down and looked at his watch. "He's waiting breakfast on you now."

"Suppose I didn't get in until ten o'clock like I usually do?"

The kid turned around and closed the door. He came back to my desk, dropped both fists on it and leaned forward. "Listen, scout," he said menacingly, "I don't play little word games the way you do, sitting there in your chair trying to make me look stupid. When I play games sometimes people end up not feeling too good. My boss, he just wants to talk with you. You don't want to talk with him now, that's okay, he'll talk with you later on. Maybe he'll come here himself, maybe he'll come visit you at your house, maybe he'll just bump into you on the street, but he'll get around to talking with you. Thing is, though, you made me mad. First you pulled a gun on me, and nobody pulls a gun on me, they don't pay for it. You dropped that gun in that drawer, you know, I could have dove right across this desk, I could have gotten you by the throat and beaten your fucking head against the wall until it was a bloody pulp, but Jimmy don't like me doing stuff like that. He says, get them when they don't know it's you. They know it's you, but they can't prove it, that's what he means. Sometimes a guy does something to you, you say you'll get him later, but it's a little thing and you don't see the guy again and you end up forgetting about it. Right now, that could happen between you and me. But you don't come with me, you make me look bad, and then that's two things I got to pay you back for."

I stood up. The kid's eyes followed me. He was taking rapid little breaths and had himself pumped up enough to fight a bear.

"What did you say your name was?" I said.

"Nicholas," he answered. "Nicholas Glenn."

I remembered what Palmieri had said when I told him the name Ferrell Dumont had first given me and I was not surprised. "Oh, I heard about you, Mr. Glenn. Armbreaker, aren't you? No matter, I'll come along. If good old Jimmy the Dog has any complaints about my odor and appearance, I'll just refer him to you."

Nicholas Glenn's eyes flashed. "You saying I stink? I take two showers a day, jerkoff. I brush my teeth after every meal. I don't smoke cigarettes, I don't drink liquor and I don't drink coffee. So what have I got that stinks?"

"It's your underwear."

The kid snapped upright and his face flushed. "Yeah? Well, I'll have you eating lunch out of my underwear before I'm through with you."

"Ah, knock it off, Nicky," I said, heading for the door. "We haven't even had breakfast yet."

21

Nicholas Glenn drove a Grand Prix that seemed far too big for him. He had to take off his windbreaker to drive the car because, he told me, it restricted his arm movements. The car had power steering and it appeared about as tough to manipulate as the magic-eye door at Safeway, but that's what he said. He kept the radio on various Top 40 stations and punched the buttons every time he did not like a song that came on. Commercials, most of which seemed to be for waterbeds or stereo equipment, did not seem to bother him; and the only thing that saved me was that the drive out to South San Francisco—South City—was mercifully short.

We got on and off the Bayshore Freeway, went by several blocks of warehouses and truck terminals, passed around a shopping area, drove through a working-class neighborhood and entered one of more expensive, but still unpretentious, homes. My driver stopped in front of the last house on a dead-end street.

The only thing that distinguished our destination was the Cadillacs in the driveway. There were two of them, one black and one blue, and they stood out like crystal at a barbecue. We walked around them and entered the house with a key that Nicholas Glenn produced from his front pocket.

For what appeared from the street to be just another stucco bungalow, the house was surprisingly plush inside. A sunken living room held leather couches and chairs and a huge flagstone fireplace occupied most of one wall. A country kitchen with a butcherblock center table and every conceivable appliance was just to the right of the main door and beyond that was a well-stocked pantry where a young man with short hair and a neatly groomed mustache was scurrying about. He was wearing tight pants and a tapered T-shirt and I thought to myself that he was an awful strange sort to be in the home of a gangster.

"Follow me," Glenn said and together we skirted the sunken living room by following a ridge of highly polished pinewood floor that led us to a formal dining room with gold carpets and an elaborate chandelier. Drapes were shoved aside, a sliding glass door was thrown open, and we walked out to a backyard patio surrounded on three sides by the house itself and on the fourth by a fifteen-foot-high fence. Attached to the fence was an outdoor shower and next to that was a large redwood tub. From where I first entered the patio my view of the tub was obscured by a tree, but I could hear voices and as I got closer I could see steam rising from the tub and three people seated inside. Two were men, one blond and barely out of his teens, the other middle-aged and bald as a light bulb. The third person was a fleshy, apple-cheeked woman, at least sixty years old. Her gray hair was bunched haphazardly on top of her head and her very large, very droopy breasts seemed to be floating on top of the water. I looked quickly at her and then looked away again. All three were nude and all three were sitting on some sort of bench beneath the swirling water.

"Oh, Nicky, you've got him already," the bald man called out when he saw me. He rose and waded toward us. "William and I just got up and we didn't expect you for hours." He leaned a pair of burly forearms on the redwood decking that ran around the edge of the tub and inspected me curiously. "You are Hector Gronig, aren't you? I mean, you're not just some little surprise Nicky brought home to me for breakfast?"

"A hot cross bun, perhaps," William said, taking great care to enunciate every single syllable.

William was thin and sullen looking. His muscles, what there were of them, were as soft and white as if they were made of Crisco. His lips were thick and turned slightly outward and his eyes were large and watery. By contrast, the bald man had a frank and forceful presence. He had broad shoulders and a thick, well-defined chest that made his dramatically bald head seem too small for his body.

"I'm Gronig." I told him, "and it wasn't my idea to be here this early. Nicky woke me up and threatened me."

The bald man laughed. "Just one of Nicky's jokes. Why don't you jump in the tub with us? William and I just got in."

"No thanks," I said.

The bald man stopped laughing. "Aw, Nicky," he said, looking directly at me, "I think our friend is afraid to take his clothes off around my mom. Or maybe it's William, what do you think?"

"Maybe he thinks that the only time you get in a tub with some fruits is when you bob for apples," William said in his affected little manner.

The bald man laughed and looked back at William

affectionately. "Or maybe he thinks this is a wine tub and we'll squeeze his grapes."

"Or that you'll bust his cherry with your banana." William tittered. Hearing him pronounce the word "ba-nan-a" was worth the drive out from the City all by itself.

The bald man's eyes glistened from the fun he was having. "Give me one good 'raisin' why he shouldn't come in," he gasped and then slapped the side of the tub in mirth.

"Because he 'cant-alope' with you, I suppose," William fired back.

I turned to Nicholas Glenn. "Hey, this is just great with the two stooges and all, but I thought you were bringing me to see your boss."

Nicholas Glenn smirked and held his hand out in the direction of the bald man.

"You're Jimmy the Dog?" I asked incredulously.

"Maybe you should show him how you got your nickname, Jimmy," William sniped, but Jimmy the Dog was done playing for the moment.

"You didn't really call me a stooge, did you, fuckface?" he said.

I told him I didn't.

Jimmy the Dog grumbled to himself while I stood rubbing my unshaven chin in the middle of the courtyard. "All right," he said, "I want you to come on in this tub. I've got some business to discuss with you." He sloshed back to William and sat down. When I did not move he grew angry. "I didn't ask you to come in, I told you to come in and if you don't do it on your own I'm going to have Nicky and Frank throw you in with all your clothes on."

I looked to my right where Nicky was cracking his knuckles. I heard a sound behind me and turned to see a V-shaped, railheaded man with a neatly trimmed beard. He was wearing a motorcycle outfit, complete with multi-zippered jacket, leather pants and visored hat. I told myself that I could have fought my way past either of them, but that was not the reason I was there. I had come to see Jimmy the Dog and to hear what he had to say and if he only wanted to talk while we were sitting in a wooden bucket full of hot water, that was his prerogative. Or so I told myself. I took off my jacket.

"Be sure to get in the shower before you come in here," Jimmy the Dog said, speaking through a cupped hand.

I folded the jacket once or twice, then refolded it again before I laid it on a redwood bench. I unbuttoned my shirt and looked around. The only one who was watching me was Nicholas Glenn and his major interest seemed to be sizing me up for a place he could punch. With half a thought to discouraging him, I held my stomach just a little tighter than normal as I took off the rest of my clothes and stepped naked under the outdoor shower. A moment later I slipped over the side of the tub and into water that must have been 110 degrees.

"Like heaven, isn't it?" Jimmy said as I took a seat on the subsurface bench as far away from him as I could get.

"It's nice," I said noncommittally.

Jimmy tilted his head back, closed his eyes and smiled. "I want you to be comfortable now, because I've got some questions to ask you."

"I'm comfortable," I said. I felt as if I was sitting on a radiator.

"Good," he said, his eyes still closed.

I took the opportunity to inspect the old woman, who had been sitting silently to one side. She was smiling almost idiotically at me and she nodded her head when I tentatively smiled back.

"Are you a friend of Nicky's?" she asked sweetly.

"No, ma'am," I told her. "Nicky has no friends."

"This is my mom," Jimmy the Dog said. "She takes a hot tub every morning for her arthritis, and it does wonders for you, doesn't it, sweetheart?"

"That's right," she said. "I get up every morning and come out and get in the tub for my arthritis."

"Okay, Mom, that's enough gabbing out of you. Hector's here on business."

"I hope you don't mind my asking," I said, "but just what kind of business am I here on?"

Jimmy's eyes stayed shut. "The business of Ferrell Dumont, of course. I want to know why you been asking so many questions about him."

"It's my job. I'm a private investigator."

Now Jimmy's eyes opened as he swiveled his head and stared at me. "I know you're a private investigator, asshole. I want to know who you're working for, who hired you."

"I'm helping the police," I said. It was the best I could come up with on the spur of the moment.

That brought a snort out of my host. "The police don't need twerps like you helping them out. How come it was you who found the kid's body? Ferrell's. How come it was you?"

"He owed me some money. I was looking for him to collect."

"Yeah? Well, he owed me money, too."

"So I heard."

It was not the right answer for my host. It sent him bursting to his feet so quickly that the water began sloshing over the sides of the tub. "So you heard?" he shouted. His mother giggled as Jimmy pushed his way through the water and slopped down next to me. "So you told the cops to start checking me out, is that what you're saying?"

My face was awash with sweat from the heat of the tub. I splashed water on it in a vain effort to cool down.

"Look at me," Jimmy demanded.

I looked at him. His eyes were as thin as postage stamps. "If it was me who killed him, that would be the surest way to guarantee I wouldn't get anything back, wouldn't it?"

I agreed because it was what he wanted me to do.

"Besides, it wasn't him I was interested in, anyhow. It was his father."

I was still agreeing. "Of course," I said.

Jimmy the Dog came ominously close to striking me. I threw up my hands protectively and when I dropped them again Jimmy had crossed back to his little friend William. His mother continued smiling as though she thought we boys must be having a wonderful time splashing around in the tub.

"You lousy fart," Jimmy snarled when he had seated himself again. "I shouldn't have let you in here. I think you're making my water all dirty." He groused about for a minute or so, firing me nasty looks while his mother clucked her tongue in sympathy. "Do you have any idea what's been going on with the Dumonts or are you just running around with your finger up your ass?" he suddenly screamed.

"Well . . ." I said, the word sounding like the off-key chime in a rundown clock.

Jimmy took my answer for what it was worth and the aggravation drained out of his face. "If I'm going to have to explain the whole thing to you I'm going to need a drink." He rose and scanned the yard until his eyes came to rest on Frank, the leather freak. "Hey," he said, snapping his fingers, "bring us something to drink. Some champagne and orange juice cocktails."

He dropped back onto his seat and sent a new cascade of water pouring over the sides. As far as I was concerned, he could have emptied the tub and I would not have minded one bit, except for the fact that I would have had to look at his mother's misshapen body in all its awkward fulsomeness.

Jimmy regarded me across the water. "I don't really give a shit what it is you think you're doing," he said, "as long as it doesn't involve me. The problem is, you start messing around with the Dumonts and there are people who automatically start thinking about me. So I'm going to help you out, Mr. Private Investigator, and I'm going to put things in perspective for you. And when I'm done, I'm going to expect a little favor out of you, all right?"

I was in no position to bargain. I was losing perspiration at an alarming rate and my stomach was slowly, but definitely, flipping over. I nodded.

Jimmy grunted. The deal was sealed.

"First of all," Jimmy said, "you got to understand it wasn't the money I wanted. It was Carl's nightclub. In order to see my problem here, you got to understand Carl, and I'll take it for granted you don't."

I didn't argue. I was trying to cool myself with long, steady breaths.

Jimmy the Dog leaned forward. "The man's like a department store mannequin. He looks just great until you get up close and see that nothing about him is real.

"Couple of years back, Carl approached me to borrow some money because Ferrell had gotten himself into a peck of trouble. Up to that point Carl'd never so much as talked to me in my whole life. I mean, he had his big-shot buddies, his North Beach crowd to run around with, he didn't have to deal with guys like me. He really needed it, he could tap the goombahs in San Jose. So I knew he had to be played out all over to come to me. What I didn't realize until later was that his very important friends were the very guys he had to pay off. Seems they were sick of getting stiffed by his kid."

"Every man's dilemma," William chimed in brightly. He turned expectantly to Jimmy the Dog for a sign of recognition, but all he got was a command to shut up. Jimmy, as he had told his mother, was talking business.

Suddenly Jimmy was on his feet bellowing toward the house, "Where the hell is my juice?"

William, his long, thin fingers pressed to his cheek, his eyes rounded in mock surprise, coyly exclaimed, "Why, I think you've spent it all, dearie."

Frank came scurrying out the back door with a tray holding a bottle of Korbel, a pitcher of orange juice and four stem glasses. He put the tray down on the deck next to Jimmy and retreated as Jimmy poured champagne into three of the glasses and orange juice into all four. "No champagne for Mom," Jimmy said. "She gets too tipsy and might start taking advantage of all the handsome young men around here."

"Oh, son, I'm too old for that." She giggled and I began to wonder if she had noticed anything at all peculiar about her son's playmates.

Jimmy handed two glasses to William. "Bring one to the fisheater," he said, nodding at me. Whether it was caused by the order or Jimmy's failure to laugh at his earlier joke, William was clearly upset. His face bore an unmistakable pout as he made the movement across the tub seem like a never-ending trek across the Gobi Desert.

By now my head was virtually throbbing from the heat, but I still waited until Jimmy had downed his glassful before I tasted mine. I would have waited for William to sample his as well, except that he was staring morosely into the water.

Jimmy returned to his lecture about Carl Dumont.

"When he first came to me the only thing he had for an asset was his club, which wasn't worth shit the way he was running it, but I was interested in the possibilities—as a business venture of my own, I mean."

William made the mistake of making one more try to be funny. Holding his glass like a microphone, he announced, "Jimmy the Dog from the Dirty Dawg, giving the place a whole new image by having a bevy of beautiful boys bopping blissfully for all the boring bastards from Blue Earth, Minnesota."

Not even William's daring, innovative pronunciation of the word "Minn-e-so-ta" could save him this time. Jimmy the Dog's hand slapped down hard on the back of William's neck with a sound like a gunshot. The young man's face was driven into the water and he only had time to give a quick cry of shock before all that was visible of him was the bony ridge of his spine, expanding and contracting and racing back and forth like an electrified eel. Seconds ticked by and the roar of the water jets melded with the sounds of William thrashing about. Jimmy bared his teeth and pushed down all the more.

"Jim-mee," his mother said at last, "you're going to get in trou-ble."

Jimmy shifted his grip to William's hair and jerked his head out of the water with such a vicious motion that he had William's chin almost pointing to the sky. "You're lucky my mom's here, William. Don't you ever interrupt me again."

William, his face mottled red and ghost white, burst into a paroxysm of sobs and coughs. Jimmy let go of William's hair and once more turned to address me. William threw his arm around the bald man's shoulders and clung there like a monkey.

"Aww," said Jimmy's mother, delighted that everything was back to normal.

"All right," Jimmy said, huffing and flexing his shoulders so that William's head bounced up and down. "I was telling you about when Carl first came to see me and how all he had to put up was his club. I decided it was something I might like to get involved in and so I gave him the money he needed to pay off Ferrell's debts. I agreed to take a second mortgage on the club because I know this guy Carl, see. I know he's going to start missing payments as soon as the next emergency in his life comes along." Jimmy struck himself in the chest and let his hand ricochet off his forehead. "Carl Dumont thinks with his balls and his heart. But that doesn't mean he's stupid and I learned that the hard way. I got impatient, you see, and I made the mistake of telling him that I was interested in buying his club. Ever since he found that out he's made sure he's never been a day late in his payment, no matter what else he had to let slide."

Mother Coble had grown bored with our discussion. "I think I'll get out now, son," she said, and when she stood up the water line in the tub dropped at least a foot. The flesh hung off her in sheets as she turned her back and crawled onto the deck. The crack of her ass was pointed straight at me, but I tried not to look until Nicky arrived with a bathrobe and helped her into it. She turned and waved cheerily. "You boys have fun now. I'll see you at breakfast. Toodle-ooo."

We all called out "Toodle-ooo" and things like that and she waddled off toward the house.

Jimmy's eyes followed her fondly. I directed his attention back to the matters at hand by asking why Carl had not wanted to sell.

"Ah," he said, still watching his mother, "you've got to know the guy. I've never seen anybody in my life so hung up about being taken. You can't reason with him, either, because he loses his damn temper and then it's all over. So I just backed off for the moment. I knew that if he was working that hard to protect his club he was bound to leave himself open some other way. Believe me, between his new wife and his big house in Marin County and his cars and his kid, Carl's always in need of money. So I started checking around and you'll never guess what I came up with."

I did not immediately realize he was waiting for my response. At that particular moment I was far more concerned about the itching that was developing all over my body. I had begun to worry that the tub was giving me hives.

"You listening to me?" Jimmy demanded.

"Yeah, right," I said. "I give up. What did you find?"

"That suddenly Ferrell's got markers spread all over town again, just like a couple of years ago. What's wrong with you now? You don't look so good."

"You mind if I get out for a minute and cool off under that shower?" I said, and while I was pointing across the yard I suddenly realized that my clothes were gone. I looked back at Jimmy in alarm, but he pretended not to notice.

"Just stand up," he said, making a lifting motion with his hand. "You'll feel better. That's it. I want to finish what I was saying about Ferrell's debts. I started buying them up, half, three quarters of the price, whatever I could get them for, and after I had enough I took them to Carl and demanded payment. The fucker refused. First he claimed they were fakes and then he claimed he wasn't covering for Ferrell anymore."

Jimmy the Dog's mouth twisted at the memory. "Sure, that's all right, Carl. You paid off Ferrell's debts to those other guys in the Sansabelt pants, those fucking big-shot turkeys you like to hang around with, but you don't have to pay off Jimmy Coble. He's just a fucking fairy anyhow."

I sat down again. Fast. Jimmy was getting himself dangerously worked up and I did not want to be in his path. Unfortunately for William, he chose that moment to attempt to drape his leg over one of Jimmy's. A bolt of furious annoyance shot across Jimmy's already tense face. He dipped his shoulder and brought it up sharply against William's jaw. I heard a crack and there was a flurry of hands, arms and bodies that ended with William on his feet and bent at the waist, his fingers covering his mouth and trying to stem the blood that was flowing into the pool.

"You don't listen, do you, William?" Jimmy screamed, his voice unmercifully shrill.

William shook his head and the blood flowed more freely. The commotion had brought Nicky running out of the house and Jimmy greeted him with a shrug.

"Get him out of here, Nicky," he said warily.

Nicky grinned malevolently and practically pulled William out of the tub. Poor William stood well over six feet tall but could not have weighed more than a hundred and thirty pounds. He looked like a long-legged plastic doll as Nicky threw a towel over his quaking shoulders and led him off to the house.

"Don't you put your hands on him, either, Nicky," Jimmy called after them.

For my part, I sat silently and watched the blood William had left behind swirl through the water. The red color sank, resurfaced, sank again and was lost. I was still trying to follow its traces when Jimmy splashed down beside me.

Now we were completely alone. I looked once more for my clothes, hoping they would somehow magically reappear, and when they did not I looked for some means of escape. The fence that held the shower was clearly unscalable, while the house itself stood like a fortress, with no door other than the one through which Nicky had led me an eternity ago.

"I tried to warn Carl, you know," Jimmy said, resting his arm on the edge of the tub behind me. "I had to tell him there would be problems if somebody didn't pay me back. Anybody else would have tried to work something out, but not Carl, the big macho asshole. Instead, he stages a fight in front of all the help at his club and pretends to cast Ferrell out into the wilderness. That was all for my benefit, you know. Trying to show me that they were separated.

"Now do you see the real reason Ferrell was hiding in that crummy apartment house? Oh, don't look so surprised, Sherlock, I knew where he was all the time. But like I said, it wasn't Ferrell I was interested in. What Carl would really have liked was to get Ferrell the hell out of the area, but he couldn't do that because of his parole, so he was just trying to keep him hidden until he could scheme up some way to pay me off. Real sharp, Carl. Shit. What he came up with was this plan to blackmail the minister and I found out about that soon enough."

It was like overhearing a conversation at the opposite end of a hallway. I could tell what was being said, but I didn't know why. I must have looked confused bacause Jimmy banged me none too gently on the back.

"His wife, Gronig. She called me right off the bat, told me what was going to happen and asked what it would be worth to me to keep Carl from getting his hands on the pictures he wanted of her and the Reverend."

"What did you tell her?"

Jimmy acted shocked. "I told her I wasn't interested. For all I knew, it was Carl's idea for her to call me. I mean, how was she planning on getting the pictures away from Carl and Ferrell, I asked her. She wouldn't answer me. I could just see Carl scheming the whole thing out: getting me to give them the money they owed me, then laughing his head off. Besides"—Jimmy sat back—"I'd just as soon see him try the blackmail. If he gets caught, I get his club anyway. Am I right?"

"That's right," I said, momentarily unsure of what I was agreeing to, but nonetheless glad that I was bringing a look of relief to Jimmy's face.

"Good," he said. "Then you can explain to Artie Palmieri that I wouldn't have had any reason for wanting Ferrell dead, and you can get him to stop messing around with this stupid investigation he's conducting of me and my business."

I glanced up in alarm, wondering now if I had missed something. Apparently my expression was too revealing, because Jimmy suddenly rapped me smartly on the back of the head.

"The reason you're here, hotshot, enjoying this tub with me, is so that when you leave you'll be able to explain to Artie that if Carl denied any connection with his son's debts when he was living, he's sure not going to admit them now that the kid's dead. I want you to tell Artie that I can't even keep the pressure on Carl anymore because he's got his big-shot buddies all feeling sorry for him and I'd have every greaser in the Bay Area down on top of me if I did. You think you can do that?"

I realized that the weight I was feeling on my back was coming from Jimmy's hand. I also realized that if I leaned any farther forward my nose was going to be in the water, and so I nodded eagerly and told Jimmy I would tell Artie. I was willing to say anything that was going to get me out of the tub and away from this bald-headed bizarro.

Jimmy the Dog rose directly in front of me, his genitals dangling dangerously close to my face. "You understand what I'm saying, don't you? The kid died and I not only lose out on my chance to get his father's club, but I lose out on the debts I bought. They don't issue insurance for stuff like that, you know. If Palmieri's got to have a suspect, I can think of plenty others better than me."

I sat upright, my back ramrod straight against the wall of the tub. Slowly Jimmy lifted his hand out of the water and with his fingers held tightly together jabbed me in the chest. "Like Helen Dumont," I repeated.

Jimmy nodded. "With Ferrell dead and her disappeared, it looks like maybe I was wrong about her when she called. Maybe killing him was how she planned on getting the pictures all along. You think about it, it makes sense. She took the pictures, sold them to somebody else and beat it. Think about who she was and what she had to put up with. Think of the way Carl treated her ... keeping her stuck at home, never giving her any money and then all of a sudden asking her to spread her legs for some guy she doesn't even know just so he can pay off his son's debts. Put yourself in her place. You'd probably try to cut the best deal for yourself, too. Besides"—and here Jimmy's little sailboat of a mouth bobbed around, moving first one way and then another, until finally it stretched into a broad, toothy smile—"you always suspect the one who runs away, don't you?"

22

Jimmy the Dog Coble finally let me out of the tub after that. There was no mention of the breakfast that had been promised me, but I was not much interested in eating with that crowd anyway. My clothes were returned to me in a neatly folded pile along with a luxuriously soft Turkish towel. I took a quick shower, savoring the sparks of feeling that the needles of water were igniting in my skin. All the while Nicky stood by, shaking his keys at me like they were a pair of dice.

We drove back to the City without speaking, Nicky and I. My thoughts were on what Jimmy had told me about Helen Dumont. If she had killed Ferrell, that would explain why she pulled the rifle on his father the night she saw me chasing him up her stairs. It would even explain why she had disappeared that same night. She couldn't, after all, be sure how much I had told Carl, or how much he could piece together himself.

But if she had killed Ferrell, how had she managed to

get him out of his apartment and into the Bat-Swan? Had he agreed to doublecross his father with her? He might have if he and Helen really were lovers. If that were the case, then it would only make sense that they would meet some place on the night the pictures were taken.

I thought of the death room: a man, a woman, a bed ... the man flushed with the excitement of having gambled successfully, carelessly leaving a gun, my gun, out in the open.... I shuddered and Nicky's head swiveled suspiciously. I told him his driving was making me nervous and he told me not to make him mad and floored the accelerator.

On Sunday night, neither Helen nor Ferrell would have known that the film he had taken from me did not contain the pictures of the motel. Helen probably wouldn't have even known by Monday morning, when she went to the Delphi Apartments. She could have caused a scene just to prove she did not know Ferrell was gone from there. I smiled at the thought of the lengths to which she might have gone to set up an alibi for herself. Nicky wanted to know what was so fucking funny. I shook my head and looked out the window.

I thought of Helen going to my office and then tracking me down at my apartment and again I thought in terms of cover-up. Could she have known by then that Ferrell had gotten the wrong film? I remembered her reaction when I told her that the film Ferrel had taken was not the one that contained the pictures of her and Jonathan Franklin. It was the only time I had seen her glacial composure shaken; and yet, to be fair, that was not the only thing I had said that might have set her off. I sighed. I had to find out a whole lot more about Helen Dumont before I could be sure that she had shot Ferrell Dumont in the Bat-Swan Hotel.

Nicky went rocketing onto Market Street and I told him to let me off at the 24 Hour Donut Shop about a block and a half west of my building. I went inside, picked up a large coffee, a coconut, a raspberry and a glazed, and leisurely strolled the rest of the way to my office. It was a low-ceilinged day in San Francisco. A chilly wind was blowing and those people who were out at quarter after ten in the morning were bundled up in scarves and coats that gave them the appearance of being armored as they scurried over the bricked-in sidewalk with their heads slightly turned and their chins tucked into their chests. They might have been protecting themselves as much from marauders and muggers and unwanted companions as from the elements. I was the only one who was different on the street that morning. My limbs were loose from soaking and my mind was sharp with the prospects of my new leads. I was feeling extraordinarily good and even the sight of Bill Mellon, S.F.P.D., leaning against my door did not cause more than a fleeting moment of distress.

"You shouldn't eat all that sugar," he said, following me into the office and bullying his way into one of the captain's chairs. "It'll make you depressed."

"Not me, pal," I said. I walked around behind my desk and inspected my sack of doughnuts. I dug out the glazed one and tossed it to Mellon. He caught it and immediately got gook all over his hands. "What have I got to be depressed about?"

"You might start with the ballistics report on the bullet they found in Ferrell Dumont. It's from your gun all right."

Even that did not faze me. I had expected it and I said as much to Mellon.

"Yeah? Well, tell it to the judge," he said.

"Oh, Jesus, it's the Eliot Ness routine again. I suppose you're going to take me down to the station now."

"Nope. I'm here on my own." Mellon looked at the sticky object in his hand and said, "Goddammit, I don't want this thing," and he threw it at the alleyway window. Maybe he thought the window was open, but it wasn't. The doughnut hit square in the middle of the glass, seemed to hang there for a moment, and then slid to the floor, leaving behind a rather large, opaque slick.

"Hey, don't worry about it," I said. "You can eat it next time you come." I took my coffee out of the bag, eased the plastic lid off and threw it on the floor next to the doughnut. Mellon regarded me strangely.

"So you're just here on extra credit, is that what you're telling me?" I asked him.

Mellon got out his handkerchief and carefully wiped each of his fingers. "Something like that. I've got an idea or two and I'm following up on them."

I sipped at my coffee. "What are your ideas?"

He weighed my question while he folded his handkerchief back up and put it away. "I think it was a girl who done these killings. That's why I took that hotel manager through the whore books. We didn't come up with anything, so I decided to talk with you. See what you thought. I figured you might want to help."

I took another sip of my coffee. A good loud sip. "Sure, Bill, anything for a buddy."

"Help me, help yourself."

"Never thought of it that way, but by golly I guess you've got a point there."

Mellon's pudgy little features wrenched themselves into a most unpleasant contortion. "You jerking me around, Gronig?" he said. His mouth was somewhere up along the side of his jaw.

"Perish the thought," I said.

Mellon squirmed in his chair. His hand drummed against the arm support and his lips worked soundlessly.

"What's that you say, Bill, 'please'?"

"I don't have to say please to you," he said contemptuously. "You're a suspect."

"Yes, but I might know who really killed those people."

"Tell it to—"

"I know, I know, tell it to the judge. But if I told it to you, Bill, you might be able to make inspector."

Mellon's ears glowed red. "What's that supposed to mean?"

"I know all about you, Bill," I told him between chews on my coconut doughnut. "Hard-working guy, never quite able to get a break. Every time your number comes up it seems they have some new minority quota or something and a couple of guys get vaulted right past you. That's why you're here on your own, isn't it? I mean, this is probably your day off or something, but you figure if you can break open a big murder case like Jonathan Franklin's they won't be able to ignore you anymore."

"And if you're withholding information from a police officer you can go to jail, buster."

"Information? Who's got information? I'm working on a case and I've developed some ideas, some suspicions, and maybe a few neuroses, but I'd be remiss in my duties if I went around spreading rumors before I had the facts to back them up."

Mellon kicked one of his short fat legs over the other so that his ankle was resting on his opposite knee. His trousers slid up, exposing a lot of shin the color of bleached flour. "Working on a case." He snorted. "You don't even have a client."

"Ah, Mellon, there's the rub, and that's why I'm willing to help you by sharing some of my ideas. Thing is, if I tell you anything that helps you bring in the killer I want to make damn sure I'm going to get some credit out of it. That means publicity, and publicity means business, and business means money and right now I have two households burning up my money like it's gasoline."

"Hey," Mellon said, spreading his stubby little hands magnanimously, "you get me anything I can use and I'll see you get your publicity—"

"Good."

"—jerk me around and I'll see you get your ass fried."

I took a vicious bite out of my raspberry doughnut and glared across the desk until I realized that the wetness on my chin was red jelly ponderously creeping toward the floor. That was the end of the doughnut as far as I was concerned. I used the bag to wipe my chin clean and threw the whole mess into the trash. Mellon sighed and shifted his weight. I picked up my coffee and eyed him over the rim of the Styrofoam cup.

"You got anything to say or am I just supposed to sit here and watch you slop shit all over yourself for the rest of the day?" Mellon said at last.

"We've got two different deaths here, Bill," I said.

"Three if you count the old hag in the motel in Sonoma."

"All right, three if you count Agnes Luck. But I don't think we can afford to assume that they were all killed for the same reason or by the same person. I admit your theory about a woman killer is good as far as Ferrell goes. In fact, it's remarkably similar to a theory your boss has. Did you know that? Sure. Now what kind of woman would be familiar with a young stud like Ferrell and a craphouse like the Bat-Swan Hotel? Well, you guessed a prostitute and I'd have to say you were in the right ball park. But you struck out."

"The game ain't over yet."

"Way to maintain the analogy, Bill, but let's get serious. You went through all the books with the manager of the hotel and you didn't get anything, so now you've got to try something else. Other possibilities. You could maybe try some of the encounter girls, or you could try the next step up, maybe some of the topless dancers."

Mellon grappled with what I was telling him for a moment and when he caught on his whole face blossomed with delight. "Ferrell's father owns a topless club on Broadway."

"Now you're cooking."

"You got somebody particular in mind?" Mellon was growing cagier with each passing second.

"Let's put it this way. If you were Ferrell and you needed a woman to set somebody up for blackmail, who would you use?"

Mellon jumped to his feet and even though that was not a very long jump it made a great deal of racket. "I should have thought of that," he said. "The woman in the motel room who claimed she was Ferrell's sister, that's who you're talking about, right? She could have been partners with Ferrell, then killed him off and tried to work the blackmail by herself." Mellon carried his new ideas around the room with him as if they were balloons. Suddenly he wheeled and punched his hand into the air. "In which case," he said, "this woman who killed Ferrell would have had no reason for killing Franklin. She would have wanted him alive so she could sell him the pictures." With that, Mellon's expressway to elucidation came to an abrupt end. He looked at me expectantly. "So who killed Franklin?"

"You're not the only one asking that question. Me, I was thinking we might look at someone who was hurt by what Franklin had done."

Mellon leaped at that. "His wife," he said.

"Or maybe one of his devoted followers. Someone who thought he had brought shame on the Temple."

Mellon looked crushed that there might be an alternative. He scuffed the floor, kicking the carpet into little hills; then he got out his notebook and began writing things down. He got only so far and stopped. "Wait a minute," he said. "In order for anyone to know what Franklin had been up to, they would have had to have seen the pictures, wouldn't they?"

I shrugged, as though that were something I was still working on.

Mellon jammed his pencil in his mouth and stared at his notes. He took the pencil out, pointed the eraser end at me and then stuck it back in his mouth again. "On the other hand," he said, the pencil clipping the tops and bottoms off his words so that I almost had to anticipate what he was saying in order to understand it, "whoever killed Franklin must also have known where Ferrell was or they wouldn't have brought Franklin's body there. How could anybody but Ferrell's killer have known that?"

Satisfied that he had stumped me at last, Mellon slapped his notebook shut and retreated to the door. "Thanks a million," he said. "I'm gonna go check out some of these leads."

I had to move quickly to get out from behind my desk and take the doorknob from Mellon's hand. "I'll tell you what, Bill, you go get that hotel manager from the Bat-Swan and meet me in front of the Dirty Dawg at three thirty. We'll go in and see Carl Dumont together and get him to show us the stills of all the girls he's ever had dancing there. Maybe he's even got them for the waitresses and the hostesses. Whatever, we'll get him to show them to us and if the hotel manager picks out the woman I saw with Franklin you'll know we're in the money."

Mellon hesitated. He studied his watch and saw that it was barely ten thirty. "I suppose I could go home for a couple of hours. The wife had some things for me to do. How about you? What are you going to do until then?"

"Hey, I've got other cases I've got to work on, you know."

Mellon looked around the office and I fully expected him to make a derisive comment, but I think his mind was already elsewhere. "Yeah, well, I'll see you at three thirty."

"Three thirty."

23

The doorknob was still wet from Mellon's perspiration when I left for the Temple.

The heavy cloud cover in the downtown area turned to ground fog as I drove out past Van Ness Avenue and proceeded through the Western Addition and into the Richmond. By the time I reached Thirty-fourth Avenue it was cold enough that I wished I had worn something other than my old suede jacket.

The Temple itself was almost obscured by the fog. Bits and pieces of it stuck out surrealistically, as if they were floating on air. The effect was no less strange inside the main entrance, where the corridor was draped in black bunting and a rather amateurish watercolor painting of a bushy-haired man who bore some resemblance to the late Reverend was propped on an easel set amid what was literally a pile of fruits and flowers and breads. Hanging beneath the painting was a sign that read *Behold, I stand at the door, and knock*. It meant nothing to me, but it seemed of immense import to the several women who were kneeling on rope mats before the easel.

I skirted this assemblage and walked into the office where Miss Toy had taken me the first time I had come. As I stepped through the doorway a short-haired, long-necked figure rose up in front of me and I was intercepted by young Peter Riordon, Mary Franklin's assistant.

"Can I help you with something?" he said, just as if he had never seen me before.

"Hey, Peter, how are you?" I said, clapping him on the shoulder.

He winced at my lack of decorum.

"Can't tell me, huh, boy?" I winked at him. "Well, that's okay, I didn't come to see you anyway. How about finding Thomas Blodgett for me?" He didn't move, so I spun him around and patted him on the rump. "Hurry now, quick like a bunny," I said and he went straight out of the office without a backward glance.

I stuck my hands in my pockets and waited. I did not move for fully five minutes and I only went out to the main corridor after that because a noise had started up like the hum of an electric generator and I wanted to see what was causing it.

The people in front of the picture had begun to chant, but even up close I could not make out what they were saying. Feeling obtrusive, I swung away from them and walked to the end of the corridor. Once again a figure appeared out of nowhere to block my path. This time I was confronted with a very large, very dark-skinned man who exhibited all the friendliness of a strange city on a winter's day.

"Only the front hall is open to visitors," he said, his lips moving just enough to reveal an extraordinarily wide gap between his two front teeth.

"It's all right," I said, "I was here before." And when that did not move him I added, "I'm a friend of Thomas Blodgett."

"All men are friends of Thomas," he answered and there was such a note of finality in his voice that I did not bother to argue.

"Yes. Well. Perhaps you could tell him I'm here. Hector Gronig. He'll know who I am."

The dark-skinned man smiled patiently and, with the sound of chanting voices reverberating around me, the simple act seemed almost eerie. "Perhaps," he said, cupping my elbow in his very large hand, "you could wait in the front hall. There are benches there for our guests."

I went back to the office where I had found Peter Riordon. He was there again, his face flushed, his breath coming in spurts. "Mrs. Franklin will see you now," he said.

"That's nice," I said, "but I came to see Blodgett."

The young man's eyes began journeying around the room. "I couldn't find him," he said.

So I followed Peter Riordon and this time we were not stopped by the guard in the hallway. We went down one corridor and up another. We went outside the building and crossed the courtyard. We entered the second building and took the stairs all the way to the top-floor apartment of Mary Franklin.

She was seated on the edge of a couch when I came in and she looked smaller than I remembered. She was wearing a shapeless black dress, the sort that fat women often use to hide their size, and she looked lost in it. Her feet were bare and she had on neither jewelry nor makeup. Her hands were clasped together and she looked up at me like I had come to break her heart.

"You've found out something," she said.

I nodded and the fear on her face turned to pain.

She started to speak, lost her voice, backed up and tried again. "Do you know . . . have you found out who killed my husband?"

"We found Ferrell, you know."

Mary Franklin's eyes were on the floor, not that part of the floor directly in front of her, but a part off to one side and some distance away. "Yes, I heard." Then, growing bolder, she said, "Does that have anything to do with why you came to see Thomas?"

"I came to see Thomas to show him the pictures I told you about."

It was not the answer Mary Franklin expected. Her face stiffened. "There are no pictures," she said.

I took the envelope which contained them out of my pocket and dropped it onto the couch next to her. She looked at it for a long time before she picked it up. When she slid the pictures out she did it carefully, as if they were fragile. She forced her eyes downward and looked at the top picture. It was one of the shots of her husband's car in front of the motel and she stared at it unblinkingly as if it were the page of a book. "Damn you," she said.

"I'm sorry, Mrs. Franklin."

"Oh, I bet you are," she snapped and this time when she looked at me her eyes were brimming with tears. She shuffled through the rest of the pictures, stopping here and there, but generally moving faster than I had expected she would, and when she was done she thrust them back into the envelope. "Is that all?" she said.

"That's all I took."

"And how many other copies do you have?"

"That's it. I don't have the negatives, if that's what you mean. These came from the man who developed the negatives, Mrs. Franklin. He was keeping them for himself, but I believe he gave everything else to Franz-Josef Moore."

She did not react to the name. She only wiped her eyes and said, "And how many other people have copies, I wonder."

"Maybe you can tell me."

The woman's handsome face was contorted with misery. Her hair had begun to work itself loose from the braids that were bunched on top of her head and her natural brown coloring was flushed a pale pink. Her mouth was held so tight that her skin was crevassed from the strain when she said, "What do you mean?"

"I think Franz-Josef Moore traded those pictures to get his daughter Patsy out of the Temple. There were only two people who were in a position to make such a trade with him, Mrs. Franklin. You and Thomas Blodgett."

As if on cue, the apartment door flew open and Thomas Blodgett bustled in as best he could in his long white robe and sandals. Peter Riordon leaped in front of him and was half bumped, half shoved to one side as Blodgett made straight for the couch. Mary shrieked uncontrollably as Blodgett threw himself on his knees in front of her and tried to hug her resisting body to his shoulder.

Riordan, quite obviously unused to being in a position of having to decide things on his own, looked to me for guidance. I jerked my head sharply toward the struggling couple. He hesitated at first and then suddenly made up his mind and flung himself on Blodgett's back. Blodgett went over like a demolished building, pulling Mary down with him so that all three people were floundering around on the floor. The billowing cloth from their garments tangled their arms and legs so that every time one moved another was twisted and dragged until at last Mary screamed at them to leave her alone. And then all the action came to an abrupt halt.

I got down on my stomach and searched around the pile until my eyes met Blodgett's. "What are you doing, Thomas?" I asked him.

Blodgett blinked at me. "I heard Mary crying and I thought she needed help."

Mustering her dignity, Mary slowly disengaged herself and got back to her feet. She was no longer sobbing. She looked more embarrassed than anything else. "I didn't need you," she said. "Peter was here."

Blodgett, too, got to his feet. "Yes," he said, looking at the younger man with obvious disapproval as he straightened out his robe. "Well, Peter, perhaps you can excuse us for a few minutes." He waved his hand toward the door.

Peter, who was the only one still sitting on the floor, looked at Mary questioningly.

"He'll stay right here," she said emphatically. "And you might just explain what it was you were doing outside my door in the first place, Thomas Blodgett."

He produced a handkerchief from the folds of his robe, mopped his face and said, "I was told that this man was back bothering you again and I thought you would be in need of some assistance. I was coming up the stairs when I heard you—"

"And you were afraid of what I might be telling Mr. Gronig, is that it, Thomas?"

The First Assistant Reverend took a quick swipe with his handkerchief at the steam which had formed on his glasses. His eyeballs seemed to bulge through the clean spots he had made. His mouth quivered, but no words came out.

Motioning to me, Mrs. Franklin said, "Show him what you have."

And I, feeling rather like a dutiful soldier, passed Blodgett the envelope that had been lying on the couch. Blodgett shook the pictures into his open hand and slowly shuffled through them, staring at each one in its turn.

"Mr. Gronig thinks one of us traded Patsy Moore for those pictures," Mrs. Franklin said to him. "Tell me, Thomas, was it you?"

Blodgett looked up cautiously, as though almost willing to believe this was a monumentally bad stab at humor, and then he saw the way Mary Franklin was watching him and said, "I didn't do that." Then, turning to me, "I didn't. Why would I do that?"

"Perhaps," I said, taking the photographs from his hand and separating out the two images of the motel with the blue car in the foreground, "because you didn't want anybody to see that."

Blodgett studied the two photos. He looked from one to the other and then he flipped them over and looked at the backs. "To see what?" he said.

I used my forefinger to point at the two blue splashes. "Isn't that your blue Plymouth, the one you once gave me a ride in?"

I knew from the way the atmosphere in the room suddenly changed that I had said the wrong thing. But I did not know why until Blodgett very primly handed the pictures back to me.

"Mr. Gronig," he said, "I do not own an automobile. The Temple owns nearly a dozen vehicles. Except for the Reverend's Mercedes, all are identical blue Plymouths."

I did what Mellon had done. I got out a notebook and pen and began writing furiously. I was buying time, trying not to lose the offensive. "So," I said, "you admit that somebody from this Temple was watching that motel while the Reverend was inside."

Blodgett's face virtually shimmied. "I admit nothing of the kind. I admit that some sort of blue car was passing by when you took the pictures. And that is all."

Blodgett was so busy bristling with indignation that he did not immediately notice I was no longer looking at him. I was staring at Riordon, and Riordon was staring at his shoe tops.

"How about you, Riordon?" I asked him. "Do they allow you to drive one of those blue Plymouths?"

Mary Franklin let out a gasp. She covered her mouth with her hand and gazed in horror at me, as if I were a truly awful creature, a two-foot-long garbage slug that had just slithered into her living room.

Blodgett's reaction was to her, not to me. "Now see here," he said and advanced until he was within an arm's length of me. He would have advanced farther, but my hand was on his chest and my fingers were curling around the cloth of his robe and pinching at the bones of his sternum.

"No, you see here, Blodgett. I think these pictures are evidence. If I find out which one of you received them from Franz-Josef Moore, I think I'll know who killed the Reverend and why."

It was intended to be my exit line, the little thrust that was going to leave them eyeing each other nervously, maybe even pointing fingers or shouting accusations, but it didn't work. It was spoiled by Blodgett, who waited until I was nearly out of the room and then said, "Everything you say is dependent on your assumption that one of us obtained those pictures in exchange for Patsy Moore, isn't it?"

I turned slowly and retraced my steps. "I'd like to know how else she could have gotten out of here," I said.

Blodgett, his voice now smug, said, "I would like to know myself because, you see, Mr. Gronig, it wouldn't be the first time that someone had been taken out of the Temple proper without any of us knowing about it."

"How can that happen with all the guards in all the hallways?"

"I'm afraid you're going to have to ask Henry Willis that."

"Henry Willis?" The name drew me up short. It was familiar, but I could not immediately place it.

"Henry Willis calls himself a deprogrammer. He is, in fact, a kidnapper who specializes in stealing children from our home."

And suddenly I remembered who Henry Willis was. He was the one Franz-Josef had gone to see about Patsy. The one who had wanted too much money for Franz-Josef to be able to hire. "Where, ah, can I get hold of this Henry Willis?"

It was, after a long moment, Mary Franklin who answered me. "We don't know where Willis is. He operates in secret and if you want to reach him you have to call a number in the San Francisco phone directory. *Henry Willis* is all it says. No address. You speak into a recording machine and leave your own number. If he wants to meet with you he'll call back."

This time it wasn't each other they were eyeing nervously as I made my retreat. It was me.

24

"You bastard," Peg said. "I stayed up half the night waiting for you."

I held the receiver away from my ear as Peg ripped me from top to bottom about what a self-centered, irresponsible good-for-nothing I was; and when at last she ran out of breath I said, "Peg, I'm sorry. What happened couldn't be helped and I'll explain the whole thing later to you. But right now I need an awfully big favor."

Peg was not so easily mollified. "Oh, you do, do you? Well, I need the mortgage money, the money for the gas and electric bill, the money for the water, the telephone, the garbage and God knows what else. Kevin needs new shoes. I think he's going to need glasses, the school nurse tells me today. And on top of that I've got a husband who stands me up. What happened, Hector, you find the little bitch with the tattoos again?"

"Peg, I was kidnapped."

She stopped yelling. "Kidnapped?"

"Practically," I said. "But don't worry, I'm all right."

"You were kidnapped and you're all right."

"Peg, I'm within an inch of breaking this case wide open. I swear to God, Peg, I'm that close and if I can do it my career is made. I'll pay all your goddamn bills, I'll take you to Acapulco, I'll fill your head with drugs, I'll do anything you want."

"My bills?" Peg screamed with surprising unconcern for someone who had just learned that her husband had been practically kidnapped. "Who do you think you're talking to? I'm the one taking care of the kids you never get around to see and you're the one who's supposed to be paying the bills."

"Peg, I love you. I love the kids. All I need you to do is make one little telephone call. Honest, Peg, I've got all the parts to the puzzle now. I just need your help in putting them together."

"Hector, you couldn't put two halves of an English muffin together."

"Please, Peg."

She sighed. She was good at sighing and this time she sighed loud enough to blow my ear off, loud enough to let me know just how big a favor she was going to do for me. "All right," she said. "What is it this time?"

I was in front of the Dirty Dawg five minutes ahead of schedule. Mellon showed up ten minutes late, arriving with all the subtlety of a Boeing 747. His unmarked car came tearing up the street with a red light flashing on its dash and he never once braked until he was practically past the club. The car swerved and was wrenched to a halt with two wheels up on the curb. Mellon slammed the gearshift home and tore the keys from the ignition. The car doors were flung open and its occupants came bolting out.

The Bat-Swan's manager was closest to me, and I grabbed him by the collar to stop his pell-mell rush for the door. "I don't think we're in that much of a hurry, brother," I told him.

"Leave me alone, I've got to look at some pictures," he said, struggling to free himself from my grasp.

It became glaringly evident that things were not going to proceed quite as I had anticipated. That much, at least, was confirmed when I got a look at Mellon's face. Something, apparently, had not gone well at home, for Mellon was in a foul humor. He brushed past us and began tugging furiously at the nightclub's doors. When he finally accepted the fact that they were locked he began pounding on them. He pounded for a long time.

One door opened a crack and a slicked-back head of hair gradually revealed itself as belonging to Gil the bartender. He blinked at us in the sunlight and it was like watching some prehistoric animal stir himself from a millennium of sleep. "Shaddup," he said. "We're not open."

With a quick draw that would have impressed an old-fashioned gunslinger, Mellon had his badge out and was hollering, "Police business!"

"You got a warrant?" Gil asked.

"Don't need a warrant."

"The hell you don't. We open to the public in ten minutes." And with that Gil slammed the door, leaving Mellon puffing with anger.

We went back and leaned against Mellon's car. "I can read that guy and he's trouble," the Bat-Swan's manager said, evidencing the uncanny knack which he had earlier disclosed to me. "I betcha he's gathering up all the evidence and running out the back door right now."

"This place got a back door?" Mellon asked.

"Hey," I reminded them, "we're only here to look at pictures."

"Of course it's got a back door," Mellon answered himself. "It's fire code. Maybe I should check it out."

"Maybe we should go," said the manager.

"Maybe we should all just wait a minute," I said.

"You know the guy's name?" Mellon demanded. "I should maybe run a make on him."

"I seen guys like him before," said the manager. "They got this weird image of themselves. They think the whole thing in life is not to get pushed around. Me, I don't care. People push me all the time. I don't care."

We were spared further enlightenment when the Dirty Dawg's doors were thrown open and a young woman in shimmering hotpants beckoned to us. "Hey there, officers," she said. "You can come in now." Smiling, she escorted us into the almost total darkness of the club. The Bat-Swan's manager shied back, but I grabbed his arm and thrust him in front of me. Whatever cover he might have provided was lost as soon as we stood inside the club, trying to accustom ourselves to the lack of light.

"Hey, detective," a voice called out, "I hope for your sake that's a real cop you brought with you."

Gil was standing behind the bar and he was rubbing his big hands together. Mellon made right for him, bearing his badge like it was a note on a silver tray. "You don't like cops, is that it, big boy?" Mellon snarled. As I said, he was in a foul humor.

Gil leaned over the bar and pointed at me. "I don't like him."

"What was the idea of keeping us waiting out in the street after I'd identified myself?"

Gil did not seem intimidated by Mellon's official attitude. It's possible he had seen the same movies Mellon had. "Boss's orders," he said. "Don't let nobody in until four o'clock."

"Your boss here now?" Mellon asked.

"He's not here."

Mellon looked at me.

"Ask him," I said, gesturing to Gil.

"I'd like to take a look at some of your publicity shots for your dancers. I'd like to make an identification." Mellon seemed a little unsure as to exactly what it was he would really like.

"No can do," said Gil.

"What's that mean?" Mellon said testily.

"What that means, fella, is that I'm just the bartender here. I gotta serve the customers. You want to look at some pictures, you gotta see the boss and the boss ain't here."

Things might have gotten nasty at that point if something had not suddenly happened to divert our attention. The Bat-Swan's manager had been eagerly scouring the club and I saw him start. I tried to follow his eyes and when I looked over a few tables I gazed directly into the face of the woman I had been with in the parking lot.

"Hello, creepo," she sneered.

Before I could answer, the Bat-Swan's manager said, "Hello, Missy."

I grabbed his arm in what was beginning to become a habitual action on my part. "You know her?" I said.

"Sure, she used to live at the Bat-Swan."

Mellon jumped on her like a catcher going after a passed ball.

"Hey, what is this?" she said, pushing him away.

"I'm Mellon, S.F.P.D.," he said, flashing his trusty shield.

"Then what are you doing with these weirdos, trying to find their keepers or something?"

"You know these gentlemen?"

"Gentlemen, my ass. The one guy doesn't like girls and the other one likes to look through keyholes at them."

"You said you used to live at the Bat-Swan?"

Missy pretended to retch. "That's right. Three whole lousy weeks, during which time, I would like to add, this so-called gentleman never once changed the linen, cleaned the bathrooms, brought new toilet paper—"

"That's it," said Mellon, looking at me.

"What's it?" Missy asked, also looking at me.

"It's not it," I said. "Will you come here for a second, Mellon?"

Mellon told Missy not to move and stepped over next to me while she turned in the direction of her co-workers, most of whom were gathered near Gil at the bar, and threw up her hands to tell them she didn't know what was going on. I put my arm around Mellon's shoulders and drew him close enough to speak directly into his ear.

"She's not the one, Bill," I whispered.

"Not the one what?" he said, not whispering. He glanced back over my arm at Missy before grudgingly lowering his voice. "I was looking for a girl who knew Ferrell and knew the Bat-Swan. I've got her and that's all I care about."

"Bill, believe me, she didn't kill Ferrell. She's got no motive. Just because you find A and B doesn't mean you have the alphabet."

"You trying to tell me how to do my job? I'm looking for a type, she's the type, now I'm going to question her."

"You're wasting your time. Look." I turned and called back to Missy. "Did you ever tell anybody else at the club about the Bat-Swan?"

"The place was a joke. I told everybody about it."

"Joke?" said the Bat-Swan's manager. "I'd like to see

how much money you made last year." But nobody paid him any attention.

"Helen Dumont? You ever talk to her about it?" I demanded.

"Probably. I probably told everyone who works here about it."

"Helen Dumont?" Mellon whispered incredulously. "The dead guy's mother? That's who you think did it? Oh, you're a cookie, you are."

"Mellon, all three of them, Ferrell, his father and his stepmother, were supposed to be working a blackmail on Jonathan Franklin. Helen was doublecrossing them, trying to get the film and sell it herself. This Missy here, she didn't do anything more than tell Helen about the lousy hotel where they never even cleaned up the room when people moved out."

"Well, we'll find that out, won't we?"

"How you going to do that?"

"I'll take her downtown. She'll go voluntarily; she doesn't want me to come back and arrest her as a suspect."

On that much, at least, Mellon was right. Gil shouted from behind the bar that she didn't have to go anywhere, apparently having had some experience with police himself, but after a few words from Mellon, Missy nodded her head and went with him. The unsavory manager from the Bat-Swan went along too, and I, remembering Gil's warning from the last time I was in the Dirty Dawg, decided not to stick around any longer by myself.

25

The woman at the answering service was giving me a hard time. It seemed I hadn't called in for several days and there were messages dating all the way back to Sunday. Many of them were from Peg, but I was only interested in those that had come in today. There were enough of those all by themselves.

Peg, the woman said, had called in at one o'clock, asking me to telephone her at home. At three o'clock Peg had called again, saying that she had made an appointment for me and that if I did not get back to her within the hour she was going to cancel it. At half past four she had told the service that she had not been able to cancel and that I was to meet her at the Royal Exchange on Front Street by quarter to six or this was positively the last time she was ever going to go out of her way for me. "I guess you'll have to hurry," the answering service concluded and I heard the sound of stifled laughter as I hung up because it was almost six o'clock already.

Why Peg would want to meet at the Royal Exchange was

a mystery to me. It was not her kind of place. It was a Financial District singles-type bar that catered almost exclusively to the after-work, three-piece-suit set who liked to hold their drinks chest high and make charmingly pithy remarks to the parade of young lovelies who passed up and down the aisles in slit skirts, semi-high heels and fixed-eye expressions of studied preoccupation. Peg, I was sure, would be lost in a place like that—almost as lost as I was when I charged through the door at ten minutes after six calling her name.

Scores of the city's most eligible young professionals parted like the Red Sea and left me with a virtual path to the end of the bar where a curly-haired woman in an all-too-flimsy blue blouse was surrounded by a group of gangly dorks in pinstripes. Peg saw me coming and broke her conversation in mid-sentence to greet me.

"Where the hell have you been?" she demanded. She did not wait for an answer, but dragged her open hand across my cheek. "Jesus, when was the last time you shaved? You look like you've been living in a sewer."

Suddenly everyone within a ten-foot radius backed up to stare at me. For a moment I was alone, an island of dishevelment, the only person in the bar who had slept in his clothes, the only person with a bruise on the back of his head as big as a billboard. "I can't be too bad," I said. "I spent a good part of the morning in a hot tub."

A waitress came banging her way through the crowd and the people who had moved away closed in again, perhaps assuaged by the fact that I took hot tubs, perhaps just subjugated by the limitations of space. Peg shut her eyes in a demonstration of infinite patience and when she opened them again she introduced me to the nearest dork, whom she called Rory. She said, "Rory, this is my husband," and he was gone before I could even finish asking him where the hell he had gotten a name like Rory.

"What are we doing here?" I whispered to Peg, looking around suspiciously. "What have you done with the kids?"

"My mother's got them."

"Why?"

"You wanted to meet Henry Willis, didn't you?"

"Tonight?" I said, dancing out of someone's path.

"We're already late," she said. "I was supposed to meet him at six o'clock next door at Harrington's."

"But I can't do that now. I'm not prepared."

Peg gave me a weary smile. She had shown me patience and now I was testing the very limits of her endurance. "Hector," she said, "I called the number just like you told me to do. I got a recording where you get a little beep and then so many seconds to spill your message. I said our son had run off and joined the Revelation Temple and I said I had to meet with Mr. Willis as soon as I possibly could. I gave my maiden name and the unlisted phone number and this afternoon someone called back and said Mr. Willis happened to be in the city and would meet with me at six o'clock. I said I would have to check with my husband and I was told it was six o'clock or nothing at all. What could I do? You said to make an appointment, so I did. When you didn't call me I tried to cancel, but they said they couldn't reach him and that if I wasn't there by quarter after six he'd just leave. I called my mother and I got down here as fast as I could."

I looked at my watch. We had about thirty seconds to come up with a plan. Peg was scrutinizing me to see if I had one. I smiled confidently and told her the first thing that popped into my head.

Harrington's formed an interesting counterpart to the Royal Exchange, spurning the beautiful people catered to by its neighbor in favor of the serious drinkers, who didn't need any catering. Harrington's was actually two parallel bars, each sharing a common wall with a broad connecting archway at the back. Peg's instructions were to enter through the right-hand set of doors, walk the length of the "old" bar, pass through the archway, go out through the "new" bar and then complete the circuit a second time. If she was not stopped on the second trip through she was to assume Mr. Willis had decided not to meet with her.

Figuring that whoever was watching for her would be seated facing the doors to the old bar, I chose to enter the other way. I went straight to the back and took up a station in the archway, at the one spot from which I could watch Peg from entrance to exit. It meant that I practically had to join in a circle of three men and a woman who were gaily conversing about some hilarious matter of legal research, but by draping myself over a cigarette machine I found that I could make myself at least partially inconspicuous.

Peg, on the other hand, was noticed the moment she pushed open the doors to the old bar. A well-tanned gentleman with a semicircle of white hair and a white goatee swept her into a waltz as she went past him and tried to move her about to the undanceable melody of some vintage Cole Porter tune. She disengaged herself gracefully and walked toward me, passing the hunched backs of the major league drinkers at the bar and entering the rear area of booths and wooden tables. Several people looked up, but no one intercepted her. She walked past me as though I were an inconspicuous bum draped over a cigarette machine.

She did the whole routine again and the reaction in the old bar came the second time she passed by me. A broad-shouldered man in a dark suit suddenly got to his feet. He had been sitting alone in one of the booths facing the door, and the moment he stood up I knew who he was. I grabbed a long-necked Budweiser beer bottle from a nearby table and as the man started to step away from the booth I moved in behind him, pressing close, with the neck of the beer bottle poking roughly into the seat of his pants.

"Sit down," I said in a whisper calculated to carry up to his ear and no farther, "or you'll be tying on a colostomy bag for the rest of your life." It was the kind of colorful image I thought Mr. Jarmon might appreciate.

Mr. Jarmon hesitated. He moved his hips almost imperceptibly and then he said, "With what? That little old beer bottle?" And before I had a chance to respond he spun around and rabbit-chopped it out of my hand.

The bottle hit with a splat and the glass shattered, bringing all conversation around us to a sudden and undeniable halt. Even the whump and clatter of dice cups was stifled as the players at the bar looked over to see what had happened. What they saw was Jarmon glaring down at me from his several-inch-high advantage. What they heard was short, concise and to the point. "You don't ever want to fuck with me, boy," he said.

While I was searching for some comeback I failed to comprehend the slight dip of his shoulders, the swinging movement of his arm. He came at me like a handball player whipping the ball toward the back wall and I never had a chance to react. The moving hand seemed to explode as his palm made contact with the skin of my cheek. I went hurtling into a table of confounded beer guzzlers who scattered as if they had been blown out of a cannon.

The table I hit tilted crazily and I hung on to it with both hands, trying to keep my feet in some contact with the floor. I was clinging like a drowning sailor to a piece of wreckage and somebody had to grab the table to keep it from going over. Somebody else's hands seized my waist—small, firm hands. It was Peg and she was trying to pull me up. Beyond her I could see the back of Jarmon's head as he fled through the doorway, but I couldn't get after him because Peg was pinning my arms to my sides and hugging herself to me. My face was flooded with stinging, searing pain, but I refused to touch it because everyone in the bar was staring at me and because I was too busy struggling to get out of Peg's grasp. I made it just as the piano player launched into "Happy Days Are Here Again."

"Hector!" Peg screamed as I ran for the door, but it was a wasted effort and I knew she knew it.

There were a dozen people on the sidewalk and I could tell by the way they were all standing still and looking back over their shoulders toward Clay Street that Jarmon had run off in that direction. I raced to the corner and caught a glimpse of Jarmon running east on Clay, toward the Hyatt Regency.

Jarmon had stayed on the sidewalk and he was bouncing in and out among the steady flow of pedestrians he encountered. I ran in the street against the traffic. A horn blew at me, and then another and another. The noise made Jarmon look back. He saw me coming and picked up his pace until he hit the street in front of the Hyatt. It was filled with buses and cabs, but Jarmon took to the crosswalk like a man with divine immunity, and everybody, even the cabs, slammed to a halt. Moments later I tried the same thing and nearly got run down by a young tourist with orange New York plates who leaned out his window and called me an asshole.

The crowd around the entrance to the Hyatt was swelled with women in bobby sox, poodle skirts, tight sweaters and ponytails. There were men who were dressed in black with their hair slicked, and others who were wearing saddle shoes, chinos and letter sweaters. There was, I gathered, a sock hop going on inside and the costumed people on the sidewalk were so busy modeling their clothes that passage into the hotel seemed virtually impossible. People shuffled this way and that. Some stood with hunched shoulders and arms folded across their chests, just as they must have stood in high school. Some stood with hands in pockets and looked about for friends. Some clogged the doorway. Some gathered in groups, and some didn't seem to be doing anything at all.

Slipping and sliding, I fought my way into the lower lobby and up the nearest escalator until I reached the atrium of the Hyatt Regency, a different scene altogether. Here a large fountain dominated the open floor; diners lounged at outdoor-style cafés; and lighted glass elevators whooshed silently skyward, their occupants staring grimly down at those of us left below. There was nobody on this level of the Hyatt Regency who appeared to be in a hurry. There was only a sound, far off, an incongruous slap of shoe leather on tiled floor, that sent me running toward the Market Street doors. I spotted Jarmon, a full head taller than anybody else, just as he went down the stairs; and I followed.

Out on Market Street the sidewalk was wide and made of red brick. It would end in a few hundred feet as Market Street ended, but first there was a broad open plaza that spread all the way to the blocky maze of the Vaillencourt Fountain. Jarmon slowed when he saw the plaza. He looked at it and then looked straight ahead, where there was a walkway leading to the busy waterfront street known as the Embarcadero. On the other side of the Embarcadero was the tower of the Ferry Building, its lighted clock glowing in the darkness. Jarmon took a step toward the plaza and then looked over his shoulder and saw me. I stopped and so did he. Once more he looked at the plaza, and then he turned and ran for the Embarcadero.

We went one behind the other across the southbound lanes, then through a parking area and over some never-used railroad tracks. Jarmon crossed the northbound lanes in front of the Ferry Building and went left, and I was stuck in the middle of the Embarcadero, my heart pounding, the sweat rolling down my neck while the northbound traffic blew past me at forty miles an hour. By the time I got across, Jarmon had expanded his lead to a hundred yards.

He was running in front of the piers and the warehouses that covered them, heading in the direction of Fisherman's Wharf. He was hugging the contour of the waterfront buildings, looking back every half dozen steps. Then he rounded a corner of a building and was gone. I slowed to a half jog, half walk, and as I reached that same corner I swung wide just in case he tried to jump out at me. But there was no one there.

Looking north, there was no one all along the Embarcadero. To my right, sticking out into San Francisco Bay, was an open pier that was used as a parking lot. I approached it cautiously, my eyes scanning the dimly lighted rows of cars until I saw what looked like Jarmon's shiny red Datsun pickup way at the end, on the outside, its nose pointed to the water.

I walked softly toward it, watching for movement, listening for sounds other than my own tortured breaths, pausing every twenty or so yards. I thought I was being careful until I heard Jarmon's voice behind me.

"I was worried there for a minute," he said.

I turned around as he approached.

"Ain't right," he said, speaking without any of the air-sucking sounds that were coming out of my mouth. "Makin' a man my age run all that way."

"I just want to talk with you, Jarmon." I gasped, holding up both my hands, palms out in front of my chest.

"Name's Willis," he said, still coming on, "and I got nothing to say to you, 'cept this." He never broke stride; he just let me have it right in the face.

But this time I saw the punch coming. My head was already rolling backwards as his fist made contact. It barely hurt, but I fell anyhow and lay there on my back, still trying to get my breath.

His arms akimbo, Jarmon-Harris-Willis stood over me.

"Persistent sonofabitch, I'll say that for you." He nudged me with the pointed toe of a huge cowboy boot. "You got a little whore for a wife, you know that?" He cupped his hands to his chest. "Nice titties, though. It was worth bustin' into your house jest to get a look at them."

He leaned down, almost squatting, dropping his hands to his knees. "Only you shouldn'ta thought I was so stupid, sending her out to meet me with some cock 'n' bull story about recovering a kid from the Temple. Woman got titties like that"—he demonstrated again, wagging his ass back and forth—"I remember what she looks like. Give me a little something to think about some night when I'm whackin' my peepee." He straightened up and prodded me again with his foot. "You can't sucker me, boy. I invented suckerin'."

I squirmed on my back, catching the kick on the soft part of my hip. "I didn't know it was you," I yelled up at him, covering my head in case he tried to kick me there. "I didn't know Henry Willis was the same guy who was going around tearing everybody's house apart."

Willis had been aiming another kick at me, but suddenly he stopped. "Well, what you doin' comin' after me, then?"

"Mary Franklin. Thomas Blodgett. They said Henry Willis might be able to tell me how a girl named Patsy Moore disappeared from the Temple this week."

Willis laughed, as though he were happy I had asked the question. "Well, sure I can. I'm the one got her out."

I spread my elbows wider to get a better look. "What did Patsy's father use for payment, those pictures you've been looking for? The ones he took from my office?"

The laugh ended. "What you know about Franz-Josef, boy?"

I said, "I know Franz-Josef stole the pictures. What I don't know is how he knew about them in the first place."

Willis grimaced. "Well, I told him about them, boy."

"And how did you know?"

Willis contemplated me for a moment. Then he said, "I don't think you're rightly in a position to be asking me that," and he drew back his foot to exemplify what he meant. It was the last kick he would try.

As his boot left the ground I swept my arm up and caught him underneath the heel. Willis fell as if he had been shot and I dove on top of him, slamming my fist into his face and feeling it bounce off his jaw as if I had hit concrete. I knew then that I had made a mistake. Willis was about twice as strong as I was. His hand grabbed the hair on the back of my head and wrenched until I thought my neck was going to snap. I punched blindly at him and missed and then he flung me away.

We scrambled to our feet at the same time, both of us crouched, our hands out in front of us like wrestlers. I leaped in closer, faked a left to his groin and started to come across with a right hook when Willis clocked me with a punch of his own. I spun away, suddenly seeing double, and by the time my eyes had focused again he had me in a headlock and was slamming me into the side of his Datsun. I got a shot into his kidney that straightened him up and then I reached in between his legs, grabbed whatever I could and squeezed for all I was worth. He screamed and tried to club me with his arm, but the distraction allowed me to break his hold and shove away from him.

We were between cars now and Willis's back was to the edge of the pier. He took a step toward me and I retreated. He grinned and took another. I stepped back, stepped forward and charged into him as hard as I could go. The move took Willis by surprise. My forehead hit him smack in the chest, a near-perfect tackle that carried him straight off his feet. He grabbed onto my belt, but his heels caught on a railroad tie used to block the tires of parked cars. We fell together, and after a split second I knew we were falling a lot longer than we should have. Willis knew it too. He was frantically clutching at my shirt, my jacket, my pants. His voice was screaming in my ear and I was insanely trying to hold him up. And then we hit.

Willis's back broke most of the fall for me, but the coldness of the water was like being zapped with electric current. We had gone into San Francisco Bay and it was as dark as if we had gone into a can of paint.

There was an instant when nothing assimilated. It was as though my brain had short-circuited and all the sensory signals it was receiving were scrambled. I was stinging. I was cold. I was lost. And most of all I was wet.

I kept sinking down until my legs fought back on their own, kicking, trying to stop my plunge. And then all my reflexes took over and I threw out my arms, swirling them around me, pushing down on the water until at last my descent ended and I started surging back upward again.

I broke the surface barking for air and furiously treading water. I saw the pilings to the pier not more than ten yards away and the noise I was making changed. I didn't need air. I had all I could possibly want. I was only making noise because I was cold, bone-numbing cold. So I stopped. And the sounds I was hearing kept right on roaring in my ears.

I spun in a circle and remembered Willis only when I saw him. His arms were flailing in every direction, his head was dropping below the surface and then surging up again just long enough to emit choking, bubbling cries. It was obvious from my first glimpse that Willis, the cowboy, didn't know how to swim.

"Hold on, you bastard," I yelled to him; and Willis, in his brief moment above the water, turned his face in my direction and rolled his eyes unseeingly, like a condemned man fighting cyanide gas.

I swam to him, breaststroking, calling out to him as his head broke above the water again. He saw me now, and almost crawled across the surface to get to me. I sucked in a deep breath and dived down out of his reach.

I came up behind him and saw nothing but his hand as it tried futilely to grab onto something. Then his head soared free again, and I lunged for him and clamped my arm over his shoulder and down across his chest. I got a handful of his coat and jerked him into a floating position so that his legs would not beat into me as I frogkicked to safety.

"Here, Hector, here." It was Peg calling to me. She was lying flat on her stomach, hanging over the edge of the pier ten feet above us and pointing down for no good reason other than she was trying to help. Somehow she had managed to follow us along our labyrinthine path from Harrington's to the Hyatt to the waterfront.

I planted Willis up against the first piling we came to. He clung to it with both arms and legs, like a monkey on a pole, and I pushed away from him.

Suddenly realizing that stretching her arm over the side was not going to do either of us any good, Peg raised herself up and looked around. "You're going to have to swim for shore. There's a little dock and some steps there at the end of the pier."

"Shit," I said.

"I can't make it," Willis screamed, and any thought of annoyance at having to swim to shore disappeared from my mind.

"You're goddamn right you can't make it," I said and then I left him there and stroked for the stairs Peg had pointed out.

It took me a couple of minutes to get out of the water, up

to the street and back along the pier to where Peg was standing watch. She threw her coat over my shoulders and I pulled it tight. Willis, by this time, was howling like a wounded animal. The immediacy of terror was gone from his voice and he was yelling more to attract attention than anything else, but he wasn't yelling for fun. His life depended on his dwindling ability to hang onto a thick and slimy wooden log and we were far enough away from the Embarcadero that, unless someone happened to come out to get his car, Peg and I were the only people in the world who could help him. I told him that.

Willis stopped his hollering long enough to consider what I was saying. "What is it you want?" he shouted up. Then a wave hit him unexpectedly in the face and he began hollering some more.

Even with Peg's coat, I was shivering, hugging myself to try to keep warm. I wasn't going to be able to play this game long and I was already sick of the noise Willis was making. "You tell me how you knew about those photographs and we'll see about hauling you out of there," I said.

Momentarily encouraged, Willis shouted, "Git a rope, okay? There's one in my truck. Then I'll tell you."

"I'll get the rope as soon as you talk."

Willis did not argue. "It was the two of them," he said. "Ferrell Dumont and the girl."

"Which girl?"

"Helen. The one you took the pitchers of. They came to me last week, said they knowed how I bin doin' some work with the Temple and asked me how I'd like to git some pitchers that would he'p me."

Willis ducked away from a new wave, lost his grip momentarily and had to crawl back up the piling again.

"They told me Ferrell had fixed her up with Franklin.

That Ferrell was gonna hide up at the motel and take some pitchers of them together."

I got down on my knees and peered through the darkness until my eyes met Willis's. "And you agreed to buy any pictures Ferrell could get, is that it?"

"Hell, Gronig, I didn't need no goddamn pitchers. But they was gonna do it, see? And I didn't want nobody else buyin' 'em and messin' up my business."

Suddenly Willis's voice was lost and then it came back more shrilly than before. "Gronig? Gronig, you still there?"

"I'm here, Henry, keep talking."

"I said I'd take them, they jest had to change a few things, that was all."

"Change things how?"

"Gronig, get me outta here."

"Keep talking. Tilt your head back. You don't have to hold on so tight."

I could see him trying to do what I said. "I told 'em it was crazy, Ferrell takin' those pitchers hisself, gittin' recognized."

"That's it. Keep going, Henry. Talk your way back up."

"I told them to hire you."

The words came through as though they were in some foreign language that I didn't quite understand. They brought Peg down on her knees beside me. Together we stared into the water at the clinging figure of Henry Willis.

"Explain yourself, Henry."

"Franz-Josef'd come to me once, begging me to he'p him git his daughter out of the Temple. I wouldn't do it for the money he had, but I remembered him when this situation come up and I told him I'd git the girl out for nothing if he did me a favor."

"And why did you need Franz-Josef?"

"Because you was in his building."

Painfully conscious of the fact that Peg was next to me, I took a deep breath and asked the next question. "Why me, Willis?"

"Because you was a P.I. and could take pitchers, and . . . because you was alone, I suppose."

I huddled on the edge of the pier, my knees drawn to my chest to keep them from knocking. "And you figured I'd do whatever they wanted, is that it?"

"I was jest tryin' to make it as easy as I could for Franz-Josef to git in someplace, git the film and git the hell out. It wasn't nothin' personal."

I glanced over at Peg. She leaned forward, poised like a mermaid I used to see on boxes of gelatin when I was a kid. "How did you know Hector would bring the film back to his office?" she demanded, and Henry Willis yelped with irritation.

"Well, I didn't, dammit. That's why I was waitin' all night at your house. That's why I jumped all over that fella who come home with you, figgerin' it must be him."

"We're separated," Peg yelled down.

"Well, I know that now, ma'am," Willis said with solicitous exasperation. Water washed over him once again and he sputtered before he went on. "But you can't hardly blame me for thinkin' different back then. It was still a simple plan at that point. . . . I hadn't figgered out I was dealing with a bunch of crazy people."

I said, "What was the plan, Henry?"

And Henry, trying hard to hold his head above the waves, said, "The plan—the plan was that I was s'posed to give Ferrell the money he needed to pay you. I told him to promise you a lot, see? That was how I was gonna control everything . . . only Ferrell didn't do it right. Instead of working things out ahead of time, he jest set up the deal on his own. Calls my service Sunday morning and says he needs the money right away."

A swell, larger than the others, came in and we temporarily lost Willis to a great deal of splashing as he struggled to find a new position. He came up coughing. "Jesus, Hector, git me outta here."

"Tell me about the meeting on Sunday first, Henry."

"Well, there wasn't none. I figured if I wasn't there to give him the money he needed, he couldn't meet with you and that would give me and Franz-Josef a chance to git that film without paying nothin'."

"So you just didn't show."

"I tried to let him know. I left him a message."

"How? Ferrell didn't have a phone."

"I had a number to reach Helen at."

A tingling sensation started in my heart and radiated out to my limbs. "Helen wasn't home that day. She was up in Sonoma with the Reverend."

Willis hesitated, sensing trouble. "I knew that, Hector. But it was the only number I had and there was this guy answered her phone so I asked him if he knowed Ferrell and could tell me how to git in touch with him."

"And he said he could?"

"He asked me what I needed him for and I said to give him a message and he said, 'What message?'"

"What did you tell him?"

Timing the waves before he gave his answer, Willis said, "I didn't tell him what was goin' on, if that's what you're thinkin'. I just said, 'Tell Ferrell that Henry Willis can't git him the money for the pitchers till the banks open on Monday.' Somethin' like that."

"Holy shit."

Henry Willis took my reaction as criticism. "What else could I do?" he complained. "Put yourself in my place."

I looked over the side. Willis's face appeared to be disembodied. It seemed to be floating alone, like a dish, like the famous photograph of Mao in the Yangtse River. "No thanks," I said. I signaled to Peg and stood up. The water that had accumulated in the folds of my clothes poured into my shoes.

"Wait, Hector," Willis cried, jerking upright so fast that he lost his grip on the piling. "I got more."

I stood still long enough for Willis to understand that I was listening.

"I was lyin' about me gittin' Patsy Moore outta the Temple, what I told you before."

"Why did you lie?"

"I tell you and you promise you'll throw the rope right then?"

"Promise."

Willis did not even pause long enough for a breath. "Tom Blodgett," he said. "He called me this afternoon. Offered me a deal. Said he'd he'p me git to anybody I wanted in that Temple if only I'd tell you when I seen you that it was me abducted Patsy Moore."

Peg turned, looking to see if I wanted her to go to the truck. I nodded and she went back and fumbled around for a few seconds. When she returned she had a coil of rope that was thick enough to tow a car.

I leaned over the edge of the pier one last time. Henry Willis stared up at me, sure now that his long ordeal was finally at an end.

"Here's your rope," I said and threw it over the side.

He watched the whole coil fall. He watched it hit the water and then he screamed.

"Take it easy, Henry," I called to him. "You can always tie yourself to the piling and hope the tide goes out."

26

"I suppose," Peg said, "you think that's funny, what you just did."

We were walking briskly along the pier, I with Peg's coat still pulled over my shoulders like a cape and Peg with her fists clenched by her sides. I had been thinking she was holding herself like that because she was cold. Now I knew better. "It is funny," I said.

"What if he drowns?" she demanded. "Is it still going to be funny then?"

"He won't drown. Haven't you ever seen garbage float on top of the ocean? That's what will happen to him." We were close to the Embarcadero now and I spied a lighted phone booth. "Besides," I said, veering toward the booth, "there's a fire station within six blocks of here."

The booth was the size of half an orange crate, and just big enough to cover my head and shoulders. Peg waited next to me with her arms crossed while I reported that a man had fallen into the Bay and was calling for help. Within seconds of hanging up we heard the cry of sirens and I grabbed Peg's elbow and hustled her across the street and back in the direction of the Financial District.

"You just better hope they get there in time," she said, keeping her arms so stiff that I felt as if I were walking an ironing board.

"Peg, he's a mean, rotten scumbag who deserves anything bad that can happen to him. He's busted open my head, slashed my tires, wrecked my apartment, broken in on you, slapped me, insulted me, lied to me and caused me no end of trouble. Do you think I give a damn if he stays cold and scared for another few minutes?"

She stopped. We were in the middle of a mini-park, a half block of green grass that the city planners had forced some Canadian or Hong Kong developer to dedicate to the public in exchange for prime high-rise property that blocked everyone else's view of the Bay. Peg positioned herself so that she was directly in front of me. "What *do* you give a damn about, Hector?" she said.

It took me an instant to respond. Then I threw up my hands and grinned. "What do you mean, what do I give a damn about? I give a damn about a lot of things. I give a damn about you and the children. I give a damn about doing my job—about making money—" I waved my hands faster, trying to recall what else I gave a damn about. Finally, annoyed both with her and with me, I said, "It's an unfair question, Peg. In case you haven't noticed, I've been kind of busy the last hour and I really hadn't been thinking about what I give a damn about."

"Tell me what it is you think about, then. We'll start from there."

"Peg, this isn't the time or place for analysis. It's pitch dark, I'm soaking wet, and you, you're as cold as I am. Here, let me give you back your coat."

"Stop it, Hector. This is the time and place because we're both here and we need to talk."

There was urgency in Peg's voice that made me stop arguing with her and wait for the onslaught.

It came subtly. "You're a loser, Hector. And the reason you're a loser is because you don't stand for anything. You do whatever the people you're dealing with do. You stoop to whatever level they're on. You never try to be better than them, and as a result you never are better. That makes you a loser."

Petulantly, I said, "I stand for plenty, Peg—"

She snapped at me before I could finish. "What? Tell me what it is. It's not me and the kids, so don't give me that. You don't stand for us when you choose to live by yourself in some blank-walled studio apartment that looks like a Motel Six. Doing your job? What is it about the way you do your job that shows you stand for anything? You said something about making money, but you don't really ever make any, so it can't be that."

Angrily, I snapped back. "Maybe it's seeing justice done, Peg. You ever thought of that?"

She reacted as if I had just hit her in the face with a cream pie. "Justice? Is that what you're doing in this case? Who are you seeing it done for, Hector? Because it seems to me that everybody involved is as much of a scumbag as this guy you've just left floating in the Bay. That wasn't justice I just witnessed, that was revenge." Peg drew herself up short before she could say anything more and we both stared at each other. She went for a long time without blinking, her mouth set firmly, as though she were the one whose shortcomings were being so intricately detailed.

"You can't let people push you around in this business, Peg," I said, and she started off again.

"Oh, you and your tough-guy image of yourself. Look,

Hector, you're not a tough guy. The Hector Gronig I married was brave and smart and funny and determined. He was also a good, kind man who started out in his career thinking he was going to help other people—not hurt them. Somehow this business has changed you, Hector, and you've become so busy trying to show how tough you are that any time anybody challenges you it becomes a personal crusade."

"Between him and me it was personal, Peg."

"He said it wasn't."

"Yeah? It wasn't personal when he slapped me in front of a room full of people? It wasn't personal when he kicked me all over the pier? You didn't see that, did you, Peg?"

"It wasn't personal because in his mind it was all part of his work. He wasn't hitting Hector Gronig, the boy who grew up in San Francisco and went to Lincoln High and was co-captain of the baseball team. He wasn't hitting the man I married or the father of my two children. He was hitting some professional rival who was voluntarily competing for the same thing he was."

"There was no volunteering, Peg. You want to talk about what he said, what he said was that he purposely got me involved—"

"You didn't have to take the job when it was offered to you. And when the film was stolen you didn't have to go chasing around looking for the thief."

"I told you what Palmieri did, bringing that Sonoma cop into my office—"

"You didn't have to agree, Hector. If you didn't burn down that motel there was no way they could prove you did. You let them use you."

Peg put her hand on my arm and squeezed. The act made both of us realize how tense I had become. The squeeze became a caress, and when it did her voice softened.

"If you think about it, Hector, you'll realize that you've let everybody use you in this case. Everybody you've told me about, anyhow. Palmieri, this guy in the water, Blodgett, Ferrell Dumont, Helen, Ferrell's neighbor in the apartment house. In a sense, even Franz-Josef and his wife. Maybe some have been more up-front about it than others, but they've all done it—and the reason they've gotten away with it is because they at least have a plan or a purpose for what they're doing. You don't. You're just reacting to whatever happens, and as a result you've got no control over anything. Not your situation, not your case, not even your own life."

I scuffed one soggy shoe into the soft turf and looked up at the sky. Somehow I hadn't noticed how heavy the cloud cover had become. I wondered if it actually was going to rain or if the fog was just lower than usual.

"I know, Hector," she said softly. "I know from personal experience."

Off to the side and slightly behind us, some of the fire department vehicles were already leaving the pier. A bright light that had been shining briefly at the end of the pier was shut off. An ambulance came out of the parking area, but its siren was not going and it appeared in no particular hurry. Back on our side of the street the conversation had taken a decided turn.

"You had a right to be mad at me, Hector. What I did with Jerry Seales was as bad a thing as I could have done. But I'm sorry for it. I was sorry then and in some ways I'm even sorrier now. I can't blame you for storming out like you did, but now that you're out there, Hector, you don't seem to be able to find your way back. Neither one of us seems to. And now it's no longer just a matter of you being mad at me. The separation itself is keeping us apart, almost as if it's taken on a life of its own.

"I know you can't possibly be having such a wonderful time with your Joyces and your Chinese take-outs that you're happy with the way things are." She waited a moment. She had been confident enough to say it, but she wasn't confident enough to leave it alone. "Are you?"

And I, despite using every muscle in my body to restrain myself, lost the battle and shook my head.

Peg put her hand up and touched my hair. "You've got to be freezing," she said. "Suppose we go home and make up some soup? Maybe if we talk about what you've uncovered it'll help you decide what to do about it. It's helped before, you know."

My head was working on its own now. It bobbed up and down like there was a goddamn spring in my neck. I silently cursed it for betraying me. And then I cursed my fingers for wrapping themselves around hers as she led me off in search of my van.

27

At shortly after nine o'clock on the following morning I was standing on the steps of the Delphi Apartments leaning on the bell to apartment 409. The clouds that had been threatening ever since I climbed out of the Bay were still obscuring the sky and I was dressed for the rain I knew would be coming. I had prepared a story for Bob and another for Grace, depending on who answered my ring, but neither of them said anything over the loudspeaker. I was simply buzzed in without question.

I went past the manager's office on a dead run and I was partway up the stairs before she could get out much more than a croaking sound of exclamation. The door to 409 was closed when I got there, but Bob answered my tapping. His flowered boxer shorts were pulled up about two inches above his baggy brown pants, and he wore no shirt, no shoes, no socks.

The man was built like a mudslide. His chest and his arms might have had some definition at one time, but now the flesh seemed to drip off him, as though it were straining to hit the ground.

I tried to look him in the eyes, but he was regarding me with such despair that I shifted my gaze to other things. The apartment seemed to be in even worse condition than the last time I had seen it.

I told him I was looking for his wife.

"She's sick," he said.

"That's all right," I told him, "I've had my shots." He made no effort to stop me when I walked into the apartment.

In the kitchen several days' worth of dishes overflowed the sink. In the living room open bags of potato chips, cans of Pepsi and pages of newspaper covered with ballpoint pen scribblings were everywhere. The shades were pulled down and the curtains were closed. The television was on, as it probably always was, and while I glanced at it Bob furtively scooped up one of the newspaper sections as if he was afraid I might try to read what he had written on it. I smiled at him and turned through the only open doorway. I went past a bathroom where a faucet was in a state of drool and where a dozen amber vials of pills stood on the top of the toilet tank.

The bedroom was worst of all. Its only bureau was old and cheap and home painted in a most unnatural ivory color that was visible only in patches because of the numerous articles of clothing piled on top of it. A pink vanity table was covered with perfumes, lipsticks, brushes, eyebrow pencils, nail polishes and hair curlers. The table's mirror held a couple of newspaper clippings and a series of photographs that seemed to be arranged chronologically. There was a smiling young girl, round-faced and busty in a tight skating outfit. Three boys were shown in outdated football uniforms, their hands stretched menacingly in front of their fiercely serious faces. In one snapshot a couple stood in front of a vintage Pontiac and in another a dark-haired young man stared out from beneath a low-slung army cap. The last picture was of a stout old woman on a veranda looking apprehensively into the camera.

"That's the story of our lives, right there," Grace said from the bed.

I turned to look at her. Pink sheets and pink blankets were pulled to her chin. Her grayish-blond hair was pinned carelessly on top of her head. There was a night table next to her and it was covered with cups bearing spoons and tea bags. There was a clock on the table, but it had stopped.

"And now it looks like that's all there ever will be," she added.

"How are you feeling?" I asked.

"Bob, you go make us some tea," she said because he was hovering around in the doorway. When he left she motioned for me to come over and sit beside her. I gathered up the tails of my trench coat and sat down gingerly. She reached out and held my hand in hers.

"I knew you would be coming," she said. "I took to bed right after I found out and a lot of things have gone through my mind. You were one of them."

I glanced quickly back at the doorway.

"Oh, don't mind Bob," she said. "I can handle him. He's so afraid I'm going to die and leave him with nobody to cook that he wouldn't say a word if I pulled you right in this bed with me."

My stomach turned at the thought, but I let her continue to hold my hand. "How did you know I'd be coming?"

"Because you were Ferrell's friend and you know how much we meant to each other." She put the back of her hand to her brow and stared at the ceiling. "He tried to hide it from me, that's why he left here and went to that hotel. He didn't want me to see it when it came."

"See what?"

"The trouble that was after him."

I was begining to get the feeling this woman had never uttered an original line in her life. I needed her, though, and I was gentle with her. "I think he was playing a dangerous game," I said.

That was the kind of talk to which she could relate. She hoisted herself up onto one elbow and looked deep into my eyes. "He was doing it for us. He was getting money for us to go away with. I told him I didn't care about money, but he wouldn't listen and now . . ." The way her voice tailed off told me she could not bring herself to say the words. So I helped her.

"And now he's dead. Murdered by some heartless bastard who didn't give a damn for you or him." I almost thought I had gone too far, but the expression that lit up her face told me how glad she was I understood, so I continued. "I was the one who found him, you know. I'll never forget the way he was—"

"Don't say it," she cried, tightening her grip on my hand.

"I'm going to find whoever did it," I said. "I'm going to find whoever blew the back of Ferrell's head off."

"Oh, my God," she whimpered.

"What I need to know, Grace, is . . ."

She looked up, wanting desperately to be of service.

". . . did you ever take any phone calls from anybody for Ferrell?"

Her face fell. "The phone doesn't work," she said dejectedly. "It's been shut off."

"It was shut off on Sunday?"

She nodded. "It's been that way for weeks."

"So if somebody was going to get a message to Ferrell, how would he do it?"

"He never got any." And then she checked what she had said. "At least none that I know of."

"But we know that someone got him a message, Grace. We know that someone got him to leave here and go to that hotel."

"Maybe it was something he knew about ahead of time and he just never told me."

"You don't want to believe that and neither do I. If he had known where he was going ahead of time he wouldn't have had to come to you at the last minute to borrow the money he needed. Somebody got him at least one message on Sunday, Grace."

She bit down softly on her knuckle and shook her head.

"The name of the hotel he was at was in his pocket," I said. "It was written on a paper napkin."

She caught her breath. "Rubio's," she said. "He must have gotten it at Rubio's." She pushed herself into a sitting position and was as excited as if she had just brought Ferrell back to life. "It's the coffee shop he used to go to. They knew him there."

"And you think they would have taken his phone calls for him?"

"Why not?" she said. "They do it for a lot of their regular customers. . . . Do you want me to go over there with you?"

"How far away is it?"

"About a block. It's on Hyde."

"I'm sure I can find it." I got to my feet.

Her hand leaped after mine. "But—" Her voice broke. She was poised for something more and when it did not come she dropped her hand back to the bed and turned her face into the pillow.

Impulsively, I reached down and stroked her hair. This time her hand caught mine and held it pressed close to her ear. Slowly, barely making a sound, she moved onto her side and peeled back the bedcovers. The pink nightgown she was wearing was short; it came only to her hips. Her belly, soft and slightly rounded below the navel, poked out between the bottom of the nightgown and the top of her tiny pink underpants. There was no mistaking the invitation as she held back the covers for me. I looked down. Her white, white thighs were firmer and more slender than I expected. Once again I looked through the door.

"Don't worry about him," she whispered. "He won't come back in here."

She reached for the belt on my trench coat and unfastened it. She quickly undid the buttons until the coat fell open and then she reached inside and began unzipping the fly to my pants. With her other hand she began easing down her panties. The white of her underbelly grew even whiter and the first gray-blond curls of pubic hair began to show.

"No," I said suddenly, surprising even myself as I pulled away from her. I backed toward the door, my eyes fixed on her as she stretched her arms silently after me.

I pulled up my zipper and held my coat tight as I made my way out of the room, trying not to make any unnecessary noises, trying to keep her from saying or doing anything that would attract her husband's attention. But she said nothing as I turned the corner into the hallway. Then I stepped through the doorway into the living room and something moved next to my shoulder.

It was Bob. He was plastered against the wall, on his tiptoes, his arms spread. His mouth hung open, his eyes were impossibly wide and I did not see the blade at first. But it was there, held far away from him, nine inches of carving knife pointed straight to the floor, its grip nearly obscured in his fleshy hand.

Backing up, my eyes fastened on Bob's face, my knees

bent because they wouldn't straighten, I felt my way along the wall until I bumped into the doorknob. As his wife had done a moment earlier, Bob watched me go without speaking. We were both glad to have me out of there.

28

Later in the day I found Bill Mellon, S.F.P.D., at the Hall of Injustice, on the fourth floor, behind a door with a hand-lettered sign that read HOMICIDE. I asked him how his interview with Missy had gone and he insisted that he had learned all sorts of new and exciting things, none of which he could disclose to me because it all constituted evidence in an official police investigation. I told him that I thought we were cooperating with each other on this case and he told me we were cooperating when I had information, not when he did. I ground out the cigarette I was smoking and then, speaking slowly to keep from screaming at this repugnant little man, I told him that everything he knew was wrong.

The rear door of the Dirty Dawg opened onto a half alley that dead-ended against the back of a Chinese shirt factory. It was a meaningless little alley and in a city where space is at a premium it seemed particularly wasteful for it to be holding nothing but the red Audi I had seen parked at Dumont's house in Larkspur. At two thirty in the morning the Audi crouched like a faithful dog beneath a single naked light bulb.

There was one window set in the nightclub's wall. It was covered with an iron grate and grime so thick that it allowed no details. From where I stood, the only way I could be certain someone was still inside the Dirty Dawg was by listening for the tempered throb of rock 'n' roll music seeping through the door.

I looked up at the clouds that had been hanging over the City for more than thirty hours. They seemed lower than ever, but they still hadn't broken. It was chilly and I pulled my collar closer around my ears and sank my chin beneath the top button of my coat. I stepped quietly around the Audi to the side that was away from the club and resumed my waiting by scrunching down with my back against one red-rimmed tire.

From somewhere I could hear the roars and blips of a video machine played against the jabbering background of youthful Chinese voices. Cars were still passing up and down Columbus Avenue at the end of the alley, but they were few enough that I could distinguish the sound of each one individually and after a while the intervals between them became longer and longer.

The luminescence of my watch dial refused to work and I practically had to screw the crystal to my eye to learn that it had become three fifteen. I shifted my position and let my legs stretch out straight. The video game stopped, and now I could make out other sounds. A man was shouting drunkenly, his words rolled up in each other. A woman laughed.

Later, I shifted again. My back was sore where it made contact with the automobile and parts of my thighs seemed to be falling asleep. A cat landed a few feet away, dropped from nowhere. It stared at me with eyes the size of quarters. I saw something in its mouth, and then it ran by me, leaping gracefully and contemptuously over my legs. I went back to waiting.

The opening of the nightclub's door, when it finally came, startled me. A foot shuffled, stumbled, fell back. There was silence for a moment and then the door closed. A raindrop splatted next to me and I flinched. My shoe dragged across the tar.

"Who's there?" Carl Dumont said. His voice was low and seemed to be coated with phlegm.

I put my hand on top of the car's fender and slowly pushed myself up. "Hello, Carl," I said. Rain splattered against the windshield.

Carl's lips were pushed outward, still framing the question. He had his key ring looped over one finger, but he was holding his hand poised in front of his chest with his fingers pointing inside a jungle-colored sport coat. "Oh," he said, "it's you."

He spoke as if he would have been surprised to see anybody but me. Slowly his hand dropped to his side. He looked up at the sky and the rain hit him hard and made his eyes wince shut. When he brought his head down again he was blinking and his upper body was swaying just a little bit. "What do you want?" he said.

"I want to let you know that I found out who killed your son."

Carl Dumont did not respond right away. He measured me from where he was and then in a herkyjerky motion he pushed his hand through his hair. Long oily strands sprang up from his head and waved about uncertainly until they were beaten down again by the rain. He swayed once more and this time he lost his balance and had to put his arm out to the side like a tightrope walker. "Whoops," he said, casting a quick apologetic glance toward me.

He made an effort to straighten himself out and tugged forcefully at the lapels on his coat.

"Ferrell's dead," he said at last, as though that somehow refuted what I had just told him.

"Yes," I said, and the word hung in the space between us. I had the feeling that Carl Dumont would have been willing to remain suspended in that moment for the rest of his life. His expression never changed, but I knew he was silently begging me not to say anything more. "The police have been acting on the theory that it was a woman, Carl. They think that because Ferrell was lying face down on his bed with his shirt off when he got shot. You wouldn't think that a little thing like him having his shirt off would be that important, would you?"

Carl Dumont fingered the collar of his own polo shirt and looked at me in confusion.

"But Ferrell was obviously waiting for whoever had told him to go to that hotel. There's no other reason why he would have been there. We know he hadn't planned to go there himself because he had to borrow the money to pay for the room. And the room was cold, Carl. Too cold to be waiting around barechested. So he must have taken his shirt off after his visitor arrived. That's why the police figure it was a woman."

Dumont was groping for sobriety. He had a long way to go. "Helen," he said, his voice breaking. "It must have been Helen."

"She was the logical one to suspect, wasn't she? Since you said yourself that they were lovers."

I waited to see if Dumont would bounce at that last remark, but he didn't. He nodded. Sadly.

"So everything pointed to Helen and it didn't help

matters for her when she disappeared."

"Goddamn whore bitch," Dumont said. "If I ever find her I'll kill her."

"What do you mean, if you ever find her? You know where she is, Carl."

At that moment, Carl Dumont, even in the drunken state he was in, no longer had any doubt as to why I had come. He stepped closer to me, inadvertently banging into the side of the car. The reverberations shimmered across the hood.

"Wherever she is, you sent her there," I said.

"You're . . ."—Carl hesitated, perhaps searching for just the right word—". . . nuts."

"Am I, Carl?"

"Last time I saw her she was with you. In my house. She pulled a gun on me." He demonstrated, holding an imaginary rifle with his hands.

"And how did she get away from there? She was way out in the country. There was only one car"—I thumped the Audi with the palm of my hand—"and you took it."

"Taxi—"

"At that time of night? Where would she go? I can't see Helen catching a Greyhound, there's no train station nearby and it's a fifty- or sixty-dollar ride to the airport. Besides, she had no money. No, Carl, her chasing you out with a rifle was all staged for my benefit. She didn't realize you had already discovered that she and Ferrell were doub-lecrossing you. She didn't know that you had already shot your own son and were setting her up to take the fall."

Carl Dumont stared at me. "He was shot in a cheap hotel. By a woman."

"You sent him there, Carl. You could have learned about the place from Missy just as easily as Helen could have and you could have met him there. Nothing strange about a guy taking his shirt off in front of his own father, is there? Especially if the father made him do it so that it would look like a woman had been there."

Dumont's face twisted until it was almost unrecognizable. He was trying to speak as he stepped back, as he planted himself, as he fell forward again. "He would never have met with me. We were fighting. We weren't even talking." A sudden inspiration came to him and he virtually shouted it at me. "He wouldn't have met me because he was trying to cheat me. We were supposed to use the money we got to pay off what we owed Jimmy, but he was going to keep it—him and Helen." Carl drew himself up short, unsure if he should have said that or not.

The rain was coming harder now, hitting the metal of the car between us with a steady, solid tapping sound. I spoke over the din. "I agree, Carl. Ferrell never would have met with you. But he would have met with Henry Willis."

"Henry Willis," he repeated. He licked his lips. His face relaxed. "I've never heard of him."

"Oh, yes, you have. You talked to Henry Willis on Sunday afternoon when he called your house to leave a message for Ferrell. And when you found out why Henry was calling, you suddenly knew what your wife and son had been doing behind your back. That's when you came up with your own plan to take care of everybody at once. You left a message for Ferrell to meet Henry Willis at the Bat-Swan Hotel. And Ferrell went. And so did you. You shot Ferrell, and you arranged things to make it look like Helen had done it."

Tenseness had come back into Dumont's face. I watched to make sure his hand did not start inside his coat, and while I watched I talked.

"Nobody's blaming you, Carl. I mean, there had to come a point when even you would get tired of being jerked around by that boy. How many times did you pull his ass out of the fire and how many times did he turn right around and kick you in the balls? God almighty, man, you put everything on the line for him and he paid you back by trying to skip off with the money and your wife along with it. Thing like that happens and a guy's got to change his priorities. When it's every man for himself you'd be crazy not to play the same way. Like those debts you were talking about, I don't know whether they were really Ferrell's or not, but by getting rid of Ferrell you got yourself off the hook for them. Jimmy said so himself."

Dumont's hands had gotten as far as the lapels of his sport coat. They were clutching the lapels down low, where the buttons and buttonholes were. His snake of a nose quivered. His thin lips bubbled with saliva and his eyes were so narrowed I wondered if he could see at all. "You're sick," he said suddenly. "People like you shouldn't even walk around the goddamn streets, you scurvy bag of shit. You moron." One side of his mouth lifted and stayed that way, forming a huge ugly ridge on his cheek. "You think I killed my boy over a bunch of lousy debts? Is that what you're accusing me of, you douchebag? Hah!" His voice changed, twisting into a sneery sort of whine. "Well, I didn't even know where he was. I didn't even know how to get ahold of him and anybody who tells you different is a goddamn liar."

It took a few seconds before Dumont realized I was grinning at him. It wasn't a fun grin on my part, but it served its purpose.

"What?" he said. "What are you looking at me like that for?"

"I've been to Rubio's."

Carl Dumont slowly came unwound. He pushed himself away from the car and his hand left a smooth trail in the pattern that had been made on the car's hood by the raindrops. A croaking little laugh escaped from his mouth as he stared at me in disbelief. "So what's that supposed to mean?" And then he gave himself away by laughing again, loudly and unspontaneously.

"There's a piece of paper in my pocket, Carl. It's got a note on it from Sunday afternoon, says Henry Willis telephoned Ferrell Dumont to meet him at the Bat-Swan Hotel. It tells Ferrell to check in and call 452-7194 to leave his room number. Does that message sound familiar to you, Carl?"

"Why should it? It's from Henry Willis, isn't it?"

Now it was my turn to laugh. "Well, one person we know didn't leave that message and that was Henry Willis. If he had known to call Ferrell at Rubio's he wouldn't have had to call your house like he did."

Dumont began to cough. It was a choking kind of cough that came from deep in his throat and left him bent over at the waist, hawking a huge gob of something into the street. He straightened unsteadily, and dragged his hand across his mouth. "That number isn't mine."

"No," I agreed, "of course it isn't. But it's no secret that Henry Willis takes calls on a machine with one of those tape-recorded messages, and a machine like that can be plugged into any telephone. I called that number this afternoon and I asked for you. A man answered and said you weren't there. Didn't say I had the wrong number or anything like that, just that you weren't there. I told him I was from Pacific Telephone, the fraud prevention unit, and that on Sunday a whole lot of long-distance calls had been billed to that number by someone identifying himself as Carl Dumont. The guy I was talking to said that was all right, he'd take care of it. I said that was fine, and that I needed his name to close out my investigation. You can imagine my surprise when I learned I was talking to Gil, your bartender."

A strained stillness enveloped the alley. Dumont's jaw shifted from side to side and for the dozenth time he ran his hand through his hair. He was taking too long to answer and he knew it. "It must have been him then," he said. "It must have been Gil."

I shook my head. "The message that I quoted you, it's written on a piece of notebook paper that Rubio had on a clipboard hanging next to his phone. It's covered with notes on calls for Rubio's customers, but the only ones that ever came in for Ferrell are from you and Helen. Unless you can tie Helen and Gil together, you're going to have a tough time getting anyone else to take this beef."

The skin stretched taut across Carl Dumont's skull. A noise like clattering rocks came up from his chest and through his clenched teeth, sending a paroxysm of color bursting into his face. With it came the movement of his hand that I had been watching for. His coat billowed and with an awkward, wrenching motion he pulled his gun. It could not have been trained on me for more than a second, but it made my entire body turn ice cold.

And then the barrel of the gun moved because a voice behind me, an excited, anxious, but very commanding voice, said, "Drop it, Dumont, or I'll blow you away."

A lifetime passed while Dumont looked at me almost as if he expected me to help him, and then he fell back on his heel and fired in the direction of the voice. There was a return flash in the darkness and a bullet flew across the alley. Dumont grunted as if he had been punched in the stomach. His body jackknifed and when his gun went off again it was aimed at his own feet. I saw the blood spurt through his shoe as he toppled over onto the pavement.

I was on my knees beside him in an instant. I was there when his mouth filled with blood. The voice behind me was yelling, "Gronig, get away from him," but I ignored it. I was bent down close, trying to hear what Dumont was saying as he soaked my ear and my hair and my coat with blood.

"You were wrong . . . Gronig," he gasped. I tried to clean his mouth, but he shook his head away from me. "I never meant to frame Helen. . . . I didn't even know she was lying to me till you showed up."

Dumont's eyes went dull and I was afraid he was gone, but then he began to choke and I managed to lift his head and prop it on my knee. The blood was coming out of his nose now and this time he made no effort to stop me as I wiped it away and kept it from going into his mouth.

The sound of footsteps splashed toward us as a stocky figure emerged from the shadows. Bill Mellon arrived breathless, his gun still in his hand.

"What's he saying?" Mellon demanded.

"He says he's dying. Get an ambulance."

Mellon started to go and stopped. I could sense that he was thinking I should be the one to go. "Jesus, Bill, hurry, or we'll lose him." This time Mellon turned and ran for the end of the alley.

Dumont's hand grasped my trench coat. He gripped it so tightly I felt the shoulder seam rip open. "Jesus, God, don't let me die," he said.

"I won't," I promised. "We'll have someone here in no time. You'll be fine."

I don't know if he understood me. I don't know if he even could see me, but he was moaning and choking and trying to talk all at once. "None of this was supposed to happen . . ." he was saying.

"I know, Carl."

A flicker of awareness passed through Dumont's eyes. "You stupid bastard," he said, "with your stupid shirt." He tried to laugh, but the sound came out wrong. "He only took it off to lie down."

Carl Dumont's grip winched tighter on my coat. I let him pull me closer so that I shielded his face from the rain.

"He didn't want to wrinkle it . . . and I wouldn't let him . . . leave till he told me . . . so he took off his shirt . . . and he lay down . . ."

Again I thought he was gone. His eyes closed and I shook him, I rubbed his heart. His eyes flew open again.

"I don't feel nothing, Gronig," he said, his voice filled with panic. "I don't feel nothing at all."

"It's okay, Carl." I held him tighter. I found myself rocking him back and forth and then I was afraid that would hurt him more and so I stopped. "Your body's just in shock, that's all."

"I only wanted to know why he was doing this to me . . . when everything I was doing was for him . . . and that's when he smirked at me . . . ."

Dumont gasped as a spasm ripped through him. Then he coughed and a small clot of blood came out and rested on his chin and he seemed to be all right. His eyes opened and they were momentarily calm and clear. I could feel his body relax in my arms as I said, "Is that when you shot him, Carl?"

"He was laughing at me, Gronig . . . laughing at his old man . . . and I didn't know why . . . ."

"So you shot him."

"Gun was just there . . . on the bureau."

"And Helen, what happened to her?"

"She was lying to me, Gronig . . . come back from the motel and told me Ferrell got the pictures . . . then you show up . . . tell me it was you . . . and I knew . . . she'd been the one . . . made him do that to me."

"What did you do with her, Carl?"

Dumont stared up at me. Fifty yards away Mellon appeared at the mouth of the alley.

Squeezing Dumont just a little bit tighter, trying not to hurt him and yet scared he was going to die, I said, "You killed her, Carl. What did you do with her body?"

"The hill behind my house..."

"You buried her there?"

"She was the one, Gronig...made me look so stupid...." Suddenly his eyes flared. "I would have just hit him...if only he had stood up."

Mellon crashed into a squat beside us. "What's he say?"

Something had happened to the figure in my arms. He was still staring straight ahead as he had a moment before, but now when I moved him his limbs flubbered as if they were attached by wire. I shifted my knee so that I could pat his face and his head fell back the same way. I felt for the pulse in his neck and there was nothing there. Carl Dumont was dead.

"What did he say?" Mellon insisted.

"He said he did it."

"Ask him—"

"He's dead, Mellon."

Mellon stared at me in disbelief. He snatched up Dumont's wrist and then immediately let go of it. "Damn," he said. "The ambulance would have been here in a minute."

29

Palmieri didn't like getting out of the bed in the middle of the night. He seemed to like it even less that Sergeant Mellon had solved one of his homicides. "Jesus," he said, as we watched the attendants load Carl Dumont's body into an ambulance, "I hope they don't make him my partner."

I toed the line for Mellon. I told Palmieri that he had agreed to come after Dumont with me on his own time only because I begged him to provide me with some protection.

Palmieri grunted. He wasn't going to like Mellon more just on my say-so. "They'll probably give the little jerk a medal," he said.

"I wouldn't worry about it, Artie. You've still got the big one left."

"Franklin's killer." Palmieri caught my eye. "You got any bright ideas on that one?"

"Some." I lit a cigarette and shook one out of my pack for him.

Palmieri lit his own and stared at me while he smoked

in silence. "You gonna make me guess?" he said at last.

"If I give the killer over to you, Artie, you've got to see that I get credit."

"I'll see you get credit." He snorted. "I'll see they don't suck the air out of your lungs over at San Quentin if you can prove it wasn't you."

"I'm not so sure that's good enough, Artie. I've put in a lot of hours, a lot of blood and guts on this one, and I'd like to get paid off."

Warily twirling his burning cigarette between his thumb and forefinger, Palmieri said, "How am I supposed to do that?"

"The newspapers, Artie. The television reporters. Anyone who asks. This is going to be the big news and I want my due."

"Is that what you worked out with Mellon? Is that how he happened to be squatting here in the alley at four in the morning with his gun drawn?" Palmieri angrily flipped his butt away. He glared around in the hope of locating Mellon among the technicians still at work. But Mellon had already gone off to Larkspur to try to arrange a hillside search for Helen Dumont's body. "Christ," Palmieri muttered.

It was too dark to tell for sure, but suddenly Palmieri's eyes seemed to brighten.

"I'll tell you what, Hector. If you've got enough stuff to help me nail the Franklin killer down, I'll put in a word for you." He spread his hand toward the markings where Dumont had fallen. "And I'll give you this one, too. In fact, I'll see that you get full credit for it."

"Maybe," I said, "we ought to go someplace and talk."

Palmieri agreed. "I know a great little joint where we can get some breakfast, stays open all night."

"Not Marvella's?"

"Sure," he said. "You'll love it."

Palmieri and I kept each other company until eight o'clock and then we went out to the Temple and demanded to see both Mary Franklin and Thomas Blodgett. Miss Toy, as frenetic as ever, set things up for us while we hung around the office smoking cigarettes.

After half an hour, Miss Toy came back and escorted us up to the door of Mary Franklin's apartment. From there, Peter Riordon took over and ushered us in. I was glad to see Peter, and I told him so. His eyes grew very wide.

Mary Franklin was seated alone on the couch, wearing a black sheath dress and a gray wool sweater pulled about her for warmth. By the looks of her, she hadn't had much more sleep than I. She nodded a curt hello to Palmieri and me. We said "Hello" back and then stood uncomfortably, waiting for her to ask us to be seated. Finally, Palmieri asked her if he could join her on the couch. She looked at him as if he had just challenged her to a bout of Greco-Roman wrestling. Palmieri shrugged and sat down anyway.

I was about to take a seat of my own when there was a knock on the door and Blodgett, looking exceptionally rumpled in his ill-fitting street suit, came slinking into the room. Nobody spoke as Palmieri pointed to the vacant spot between himself and Mary Franklin. Blodgett took the seat as if it were going to collapse to the floor beneath his bottom.

Peter Riordon moved over and stood behind Mary Franklin and I was the only one left standing in the middle of the floor. Blodgett was trying to watch me, but he was disconcerted by the way Palmieri had turned in his seat and placed his arm along the top of the cushions.

"Why are you staring at me, Inspector?" he asked nervously. Palmieri reached down and gently but deliberately tapped him on the knee. He arced one finger toward me.

Blodgett's head swiveled. Then he lurched forward.

"You're not going to believe anything this man says, are you?" He threw his hand in my general direction as though this were the most ridiculous thing he had ever heard. He even faked a laugh. "He just comes here accusing people of everything he can think of."

Palmieri nodded. He looked like he was being very sincere when he did so. But then he very politely said, "Right now, I think he's about to accuse you of murder."

Everyone turned to look at me, but I focused only on Blodgett when I spoke. "I've been to see Henry Willis. He told me about the deal you tried to cut with him, Thomas."

Blodgett was silent.

"You see how it makes you look, don't you?" I said. "Like you were the one who traded Patsy Moore for the pictures, and like you tried to cover up what you did by getting Willis to say he was responsible for taking the girl."

There was no reaction. Not from Blodgett, not from anyone.

"That's why I asked Inspector Palmieri to come along with me today."

Still no one moved.

"He's prepared to arrest you for the murder of Jonathan Franklin."

Blodgett shook his head in one long, slow move. "You've got no proof," he said, but there wasn't much confidence in the way he said it.

Palmieri, by contrast, spoke in an almost convivial manner, as though he knew Blodgett would be delighted to join in his conclusions. "We've got motive, Tom, whether it be outrage at the Reverend's behavior, or just the fact that you stood to take over if the Temple's leader was eliminated. If we can use those pictures to place you on the scene we'll be able to show means. And your subsequent behavior may very well be considered an admission in a court of law."

Palmieri ticked off what he had on his fingers. "Motive, means, admission. I've got more than enough to book you."

I watched Mary Franklin shift her eyes to some meaningless spot on the floor and keep them there. "How about it, Mrs. Franklin?" I said. "Is that what you want?"

The blood drained from her face as fast as if a valve had been opened in her neck. In the paleness that was left behind, Mary Franklin suddenly looked old and withered.

"Thomas," she said after a moment, "is responsible. None of this would have happened if he hadn't talked Ferrell into doing what he did."

"Oh, I agree, Mrs. Franklin," I said. "But if it was Thomas's idea, then it's pretty unlikely that he would have flown off in some self-righteous rage once he saw what the Reverend was up to. I think he arranged the scene, but I think his whole purpose was to bring the Reverend's activities to your attention."

We were talking around him, and Thomas sat like a man on a crowded subway, seemingly oblivious to everything that was happening.

"Maybe," I said, "he thought you'd throw the Reverend out if you caught him cheating on you, I don't know. But it doesn't seem as though anybody had any problem getting the Reverend to participate, so my guess is that this wasn't a one-of-a-kind adventure. I'd say that Thomas knew the Reverend would fall for Ferrell's offer and that he told Riordon, here, exactly where the Reverend would be— knowing full well that Riordon would report everything directly to you."

Blodgett, speaking out of the corner of his mouth, said, "He's fishing, Mary. Don't even answer him."

"Whoever was watching that motel had to have followed me back to the City," I went on. "He had to have seen me come out of my office building with Ferrell, and he had to have followed Ferrell to his hotel. If he hadn't done all that, Mrs. Franklin, there was no way in the world he could have known where Ferrell was staying, because Ferrell had just moved into that hotel that very night.

"That's important, you see, because someone delivered the Reverend's body to that hotel. Someone who was intent on making a little demonstration. It doesn't make sense if that someone was Thomas, Mrs. Franklin. If Thomas wanted to kill the Reverend he didn't have to orchestrate any adulterous affair and then throw the Reverend's body at the feet of the man who helped him arrange it."

Blodgett continued to sit very erect in his seat in the middle of the couch. It was obvious that he was trying to hold himself together, but large tears had formed in the corners of his eyes and there was only so much room there.

"It does make sense, though," I said to Mary Franklin, "if you did it."

Blodgett's hand crept out until it touched Mrs. Franklin's thigh. "They don't know who did anything," he whispered. "And they won't as long as we don't tell them. All they're doing is trying to get us to turn on each other, turn on ourselves. If we don't do that, they've got no case."

Palmieri, leaning forward to get a better look, said, "Tom's mistaken about one thing, Mrs. Franklin. We've got enough circumstantial evidence to make our case against him. You just tell us Hector's wrong and I'm takin' Tom in."

"I'm not afraid, Mary," Blodgett said, moving his hand against her leg, trying to establish some sort of contact with her.

"No," Palmieri said contemptuously, "and I suppose that stuff in your eyes is because you been out in a sandstorm."

Mrs. Franklin turned suddenly and looked at Blodgett,

who was trying desperately to stare down Palmieri. Then she tilted her head back and her own eyes closed, showing lids that were twisted and bulging with veins.

"Who was it, Mary?" Palmieri asked gently, his voice as soft as if he were speaking to a child.

"Don't say anything, Mary," Blodgett pleaded, his body now turned, his hand clutching at her sleeve. "Don't."

A sob escaped from her throat as Blodgett tried to gather her to his shoulder.

"Please, Mary," he begged, "please tell them I did it."

"Oh, you people," she said, her face still pointed to the ceiling, "there's not a single one of you who has any idea what you're doing." And then she brought her face down and looked at each one of us in our turn. "My husband shot himself."

In the stillness that followed I could see the strength seep out of Blodgett. He slumped back against the cushions while Palmieri, casting me one quick, resentful look, pushed himself to his feet and said, "Can you prove that, ma'am?"

"There is," she said, "a note."

"Coroner didn't say anything about suicide."

Using the heel of her hand to blot the areas just below her eyes, Mrs. Franklin said, "He got panicky. He didn't know what Mr. Gronig was going to do with the pictures, or who he was taking them for, but he wanted to destroy any other evidence that could be used against him. . . ."

Palmieri, who was waiting for a response to his statement about the coroner, suddenly realized what she was saying. "Are you telling me that he's the one who set fire to the motel?"

"He was only trying to burn the records. The register books or whatever they're called. He only wanted to burn the office and he never would have done that if he had known she was in there."

Lamely, she added, "Some drunken old biddy who didn't even have enough sense to wake up when the place was burning down around her."

"Is this in the note, Mrs. Franklin?"

She didn't appear to hear the question. She was somewhere else, speaking to someone else. "We found him that next day, Peter and I. We had gone up to the retreat to let him know just what his fooling around could have cost us. Just how close he had come to ruining our whole movement . . . and just how lucky he was that we had gotten the pictures before anybody else did. . . ."

"Was it Franz-Josef you got them from?" I asked, and she looked at me briefly, as though surprised I was still there.

"He came looking for Thomas," she said. "But Peter was waiting for someone to show up and he brought Mr. Moore directly to me. I didn't care what he wanted. I was so grateful that we had gotten to him first, I would have given him anything."

Palmieri, positioning himself to cut off any more questions from me, said, "And then what happened?"

"We got up there and the morning newspaper was opened to the story about the woman dying in the motel. Somehow I knew at that moment . . . I knew even before I saw the note, and I made Peter go look. He found Jonathan in the shower stall, where everything could be washed off." She paused. Her mouth softened. "That was the kind of man my husband was. When he saw what he had done he tried to end things with as little trouble to everybody as possible."

"Mrs. Franklin," Palmieri pressed, "like I said, the coroner didn't mention anything about suicide."

The woman raised her anguish-ridden face to him. "I knew who was responsible," she said, "and I wanted them to pay for it. Peter and I cleaned Jonathan and dressed him.

And then I told Peter to take him right to Ferrell Dumont's doorstep."

Palmieri sighed. The sound he made was a curious one and at first I didn't understand it. He told Mary Franklin that he wanted to see the note and she rose unsteadily to her feet. Almost at once both Riordon and Blodgett were there to support her, and together the three of them moved off across the room.

Palmieri, his teeth set, turned to me and said disgustedly, "Do you believe this?"

"Why not?" I said. "It all makes sense."

"What, are you kidding me?" Palmieri demanded. "Don't you see what she's done? The bitch has a defense now. I wouldn't be surprised if the two of them just doubleteamed us. 'Oh, Mary, say it was me.' 'No, Tommy, I cannot tell a lie. It was him, the guy who's already dead.' I've seen this before, Hector. It's the empty-chair defense. We're gonna have to go to trial to nail her on this one."

I stared at Palmieri in disbelief, my mind filled with strange thoughts, like whether Palmieri was doing this just so he wouldn't have to give me the credit he had promised. But it was nothing so trivial as that. Palmieri was in earnest, and Mary Franklin was in trouble.

Without saying anything more to the big cop, I stepped around him and walked over to where the three Temple members were standing by a cherrywood cabinet. I handed Mrs. Franklin a card, and then I momentarily drew it back and wrote Peg's number just below my office number.

"I think," I said, "you're going to be needing me."

As I attempted to leave the room, Palmieri reached out and grabbed me by the arm. "What's that all about?" he said.

"I've done things in this case for every other reason," I said, "and not much has worked out the way I expected.

Don't you think it's time I did something just because it's right?"

Palmieri reared back, His mouth twisted into a sneer. "Because it's right?" he said incredulously. "Hey, Mr. Private Eye, who do you think you are?"

"I'm Hector Gronig," I said, trying to sound neither too prideful nor too distressed. "And sometimes I'm better at it than others."

"Well, you'll be hearing from me if you try to cross me up," he yelled.

"Good," I said. "I'll tell my wife to have the coffee ready."